C000271659

Tested by Fire

By

David Costa

'Monsters are real, and ghosts are real too.
They live inside us, and sometimes, they win.'
~ Steven King

I dedicate this book to my wife Helena and my granddaughter Erin who, through their love and encouragement, helped me to finish this story.

Chapter One

You never hear the shot that kills you

Costello lay flat in the back of the white Transit van, the tripod holding the Barrett Browning .50 calibre rifle steady. He held the stock against his right cheek and shoulder, the barrel pointing between the slightly open rear doors. As he looked through the scope, the outline of the figure standing beside a car half a mile away crystallised into clarity in the crosshairs. Costello began to take the pressure on the trigger, his aim square on the chest of his target.

Private Stephen Channing 1st Battalion Royal Welsh Fusiliers had been working at the Vehicle Check Point (VCP) since 0800hrs that morning and his four-hour stint was almost up. The VCP was part of a ring of manned check points that encircled the small village of Bessbrook in South Armagh. The job of the patrol was to check the vehicles entering the village which was home to the Bessbrook Mill Army Base, and one of the busiest landing pads in the world with hundreds of military helicopter landings and take-offs carrying troops, police, supplies, and equipment around the outlying bases of South Armagh. The danger of land-mine attacks in the infamous Bandit Country of the South Armagh Provisional IRA had made it almost impossible to travel by vehicle transport. The check points around the

1

village provided a protective shield, preventing vehicles potentially carrying explosives getting close enough to hit the base.

Stephen Channing was happy, the day was bright, and his thoughts were on relaxing in the sun on the grass near the landing pads after lunch.

Costello took the full pressure of the trigger, squeezing through. He felt the cushioned kick in his shoulder as the figure in his sights stood up straight to inspect the licence he'd been handed by the driver of the red car beside him.

The soldier felt as if someone had hit him square in the chest with a sledgehammer, throwing him backwards and knocking him completely off his feet. The pain reverberated through his entire body as the bullet punched through his flak jacket and exited out his back after destroying most of his internal organs. He blacked out before the real pain registered; he was dead when his body hit the ground. What remained of the bullet exploded against a wall behind him, sending shards of masonry in all directions.

The van moved off in the opposite direction, leaving another dead British soldier lying on the ground.

The driver of the red car could only tell the police that the soldier was already flying backwards when he heard the loud bang of the shot. Maybe it was true. You never hear the shot that kills you.

Chapter Two

Monday, 23 September 2019

She checked if she was being watched. Before she became one of their agents, years of being on the run from the British Security Services had left their scars. His voice kept coming back to her. *Trust no one; always expect danger and you'll be all right.*

The man she knew as Joseph had been her RUC Special Branch handler. She'd been his agent inside the top echelons of the Provisional IRA in Northern Ireland. The war was supposed to be over yet now she felt the danger and again, she was turning to the one man she trusted.

She remembered all he'd taught her on the streets of Belfast – London was no different to any big city – she could hear his voice clearly in her head.

Use the shop windows, use the reflection in the glass to see who's behind you. Memorise the clothes people are wearing. If you're in a building, use the lift, professionals won't follow you in because it's hard to avoid eye contact inside. Drop your keys or tie your laces, take a chance to look around you.

She used his teachings as she walked through Victoria close to the main national bus station. Opposite the main entrance to the station was the Red Lion Pub She entered knowing it would be busy and loud, many accents lost in the crowd. She'd been here many years ago with Joseph and he'd shown her how she could walk in the front door on one street and leave by the back door on another, allowing her to confuse anyone who might be following her.

Its main attraction today, however, was the public phone at the back of the bar.

She knew the Belfast number by heart and when the voice answered, she spoke clearly, 'This is Mike, BC15, I need to speak with Joseph at the set location in London. Tell him, Democracy. I'll be at the meeting place at 1 p.m. each day for the next three days.'

She then hung up and walked out of the pub's back door.

Chapter Three

HQ SG9 London City Airport

The brass plaque on the door said 'Business Sales International'. The three-storey flat-roofed building located inside the perimeter fencing of London City Airport was, in fact, the secret headquarters of Secret Intelligence Group Nine. SG9, a section of SIS, the British Secret Intelligence Service, and known as 'the Department.'

The Department had been created not long after the worst terrorist atrocity in the modern world, the 9/11 attacks on the Twin Towers in New York. And when London suffered its own attacks on 7 July 2005, where fifty-two people were killed by four so-called home-grown suicide bombers who exploded their backpacks on the London public transport system during the morning rush hour, since then there had been more attacks in Manchester and London.

The British Prime Minister, in agreement with his Cobra Committee, decided that Britain needed a secret organisation working outside the restrictive parameters of the existing intelligence agencies. Democratic governments around the globe were finding their hands tied by the need for transparency in their methods and the rise in media coverage meant they were scrutinised beyond anything they'd known before.

Prime Minister Peter Brookfield put the unit into the hands of the Head of MI6, Sir Ian Fraser – known to many only as C. He was given the power to recruit the team as he saw fit with the order to report back to the PM only when needed.

The fact that MI5 and MI6, along with other elite intelligence organisations throughout the world, had failed to identify the 9/11 attack meant that western intelligence agencies had to adapt to a new type of war; not only how to gather intelligence, but how to thwart the attacks and, in the case of SG9, retaliate. The CIA and the FBI were to be criticised after 9/11 for the way they kept secrets which, if they had been shared, would have shown an attack was being planned and maybe stopped. The US Government then formed Homeland Security to oversee all the American Intelligence Agencies, filter the information, and ensure those people at the top couldn't work to protect their own little kingdoms in the future. The something else that was needed had been agreed between the Western powers: to share intelligence where they could, identify clear targets, and strike back.

The Department was set up in the two years after the July seventh bombings under the utmost secrecy and on a strictly need-to-know basis.

Back then, Sir Ian and his deputy for Subversive Activity, Jim Broad, personally scoured the files of relevant British covert agencies selecting the operators who would become the core of the Department.

The vetting had been carried out by Broad, a career spy who had gone straight to MI6 from Oxford University where he'd originally met Sir Ian. Fraser had taken a different direction and had worked his way up the army becoming a trusted friend of the PM and eventually heading up MI6 after a service record that saw him as General Officer Commanding British Military Intelligence.

Broad studied the Personal Record File of one of his SG9 operatives. The file was written in a crisp civil service format, telling him a lot but, in the end, very little.

Name, date of birth, and where he'd been born, Belfast. The file described retired Detective Inspector David Reece and his time covering the intelligence training and operational background. RUC Special Branch twenty-three years during the Troubles but what, realistically, was an all-out terrorist war. He'd served through the ceasefires, the peace talks, and the Northern Ireland Peace Agreement gathering – analysing all aspects of intelligence and, when necessary, handling the enemies of peace, even if that resulted in death.

He'd been a successful recruiter of agents and through the agents he had under his control had saved many lives and, on many occasions, prevented terrorists succeeding in their terror campaign. His skills were second to none: specialist firearms, bomb making and disposal, recruitment and training of new agents, surveillance, counter-terrorism techniques, interviewing…Reece was considered one of the best due to his ability to adapt and learn on the spot.

The file also showed that the impact of the dangers he'd come to face daily had taken their toll. Two failed marriages, two estranged sons from the first. Diagnosed with severe stress during a period of heavy drinking, resulting in a period of enforced leave, but somehow, with counselling and follow-up treatment, he'd come through it a changed man, the file said he was hardened to life around him, a loner who kept himself to himself.

The police service had changed since he'd joined and after taking early retirement in 2015, he'd stumbled from one type of personal security job to another, from bodyguard to the rich, to private investigations. This was when in 2017 the file of David Reece, retired Detective Inspector Special Branch RUC George Cross and Police Service of Northern Ireland PSNI had landed on the desk of Jim Broad and after some detailed enquiries, he'd brought the file to the attention of Sir Ian Fraser. Sir Ian respected the skill of his second in command and trusted his judgement, so when he'd read the file, he agreed that Reece should become an agent in the Department.

Now Broad was about to call him in for the most important mission of his career.

Chapter Four

'The ravens are in danger,' Broad said to Fraser before hanging up the secure line between their offices. The code for extreme danger to the British State, borne from the legend that if the ravens that nested in the Tower of London were to disappear, it would be the end of Britain, was not one to be taken lightly, so Sir Ian had immediately left his office overlooking the Thames and was now sitting in Jim Broad's office.

Broad had told Sir Ian to read David Reece's file on his way over so when he'd arrived, he wasn't surprised to see Assistant Chief Constable Tom Wilson PSNI, a six-foot Ulsterman, fit for his sixty years and with a head of silver hair was already there. He acknowledged Fraser's arrival with a welcoming smile. Wilson headed up what used to be the Royal Ulster Constabulary Special Branch, now called the Crime Special Department of the PSNI.

They knew each other well, having worked together in Northern Ireland when Fraser was a Five Operator targeting the same terrorists as Wilson, and both men had a deep respect for the other.

'Well, Tom, I know from our history such a request for an urgent meeting can only be for one of two reasons: something is going to blow up in my face, or the person involved needs my help.'

Fraser sat back in the chair at the top of the conference table and took a long sip of the whisky Broad had handed around.

Broad looked at Wilson. 'When you phoned this morning, you said it involved David Reece, so we pulled his file. What's it all about?'

Chapter Five

Liverpool John Lennon Airport

Every journey begins with a single step, and this journey started in the departure lounge of Liverpool's John Lennon Airport. As usual, the Belfast bound flight was delayed, so he had time to carry out his favourite pastime – people watching. Since 9/11, terrorism was a worldwide sport, and he'd found his talents sought after.

Every nationality seemed to be milling about the departure area. Some he watched for a while, others he would pass over quickly as he worked out in his mind where they'd come from or where they were going. Most of the young people were booking on to flights to hotter climates; their clothes light and cool reflecting that their destination point wasn't within the United Kingdom. Unfortunately, he wasn't bound for a warmer climate.

While watching he began to feel he was also being watched. Every human has this hidden sense from the time we were running with the dinosaurs as a defence mechanism in times of danger. After years of specialist training and living with danger, this gift had been honed to perfection. In the modern world of mobile phones, too many people were losing this special skill. Instead engrossed in the small screens they missed so much in front of them, and unfortunately sometimes because of this the very killers in their midst.

Slowly, he looked around. As he did so, his mind began to break down each section of the room into individual sequences. Within a few seconds he could see the security CCTV camera that typically panned the concourse had stopped and was focussing in his direction. He was sure he was the target of its interest. As he had nothing on him of a sensitive or incriminating nature, he stared back, daring the people observing to show their hand, to show why they were interested. It didn't take long. Two men in suits, both about thirty, walked towards him. Within seconds they were standing each side of him, the one to his right spoke.

'Mr Reece, sorry to bother you. There's an urgent telephone call for you in our office, if you would like to follow us?'

No identification had been offered; he didn't need to see any, recognising the methods they were using from his own training, don't bring attention to yourself unless you need to. His trained eyes landed on the slight filling out of their suits at waistband level; they were armed, so likely Special Branch officers.

The office they took him to was small but big enough for its needs. One of the men handed him the phone and when he said hello, he immediately recognised the voice on the other end.

'Hello, David, I'm glad I caught you. I need you to get down to London asap.' Hearing the voice of Jim Broad made him wary. He reminded Reece of Captain Mainwaring from the TV sitcom *Dad's Army*; part bank manager, part soldier, looking after his kingdom and the people who worked for him. He demanded and received respect. Anyone who had taken the time to research Broad's background would know he'd been there and got the T-shirt.

'What's the matter with my mobile phone?'

'Security, dear boy.'

'I'm on my way. I'll have to get across to Manchester Airport as there'll be a better chance of getting a flight there.'

'Don't worry about that, there's a Puma helicopter on its way to you, should be there in fifteen minutes. It will bring you to the office at London City Airport and I'll meet you here. See you in a couple of hours.'

With that, the line went dead, and he stared at the noiseless handset.

What the hell is going on? he thought.

AS HE SETTLED into a seat behind the pilot and they headed over the English countryside following the contours of the M6 motorway hundreds of feet below, the memory of the last time he'd been in a Puma came flooding back.

He'd been travelling with an army search team over the snow-covered hills of South Armagh in the middle of the night five years before. Although he wore the uniform of a Sergeant in the Royal Ulster Constabulary, he usually worked in civilian clothes as an undercover officer. Later, when walking through the streets of Crossmaglen – a Provisional IRA stronghold – the uniform would give him the anonymity he needed to do his job. As they flew over Camlough

Mountain, it seemed like they were flying upside down as the white, snow-covered land below looked like clouds in the moonlight except for the odd golden light flowing from the windows of the farmhouses dotting the landscape.

The operation involved them landing at the Crossmaglen Army police base then patrolling on foot to a nearby housing estate to raid the home of PIRA commander, Sean Costello, arrest him, and search the house for munitions and documents pointing to his terrorist activities.

The Puma landed on the base square and without shutting down the engines, dropped the raiding party and then accelerated towards the thirty-foot-high security fencing before pulling up into a steep climb away from the base.

The PIRA leader wasn't at home and his family couldn't, or more likely wouldn't, give any information as to his whereabouts. Reece brought back some documents found hidden behind a box in the garage, which provided little intelligence.

The whole time Reece had been in Crossmaglen he was escorted by an eight-man army patrol providing protective cover against any attack. On the way back to the base, an elderly lady passing him whispered under her breath, 'Good morning, Sergeant, take care.'

She kept walking with her head down. Reece hadn't replied; he knew she risked death if seen talking to him. But it had felt good to realise that there were decent people here in a town known for its bitterness and hatred of the security forces.

Although the search hadn't garnered the information they needed, Reece knew Sean Costello had a reputation for death – he'd been linked to at least twenty murders and Reece had interviewed him before.

Sat across the table from him with a fellow Branch Officer in the Gough Barracks holding centre. The other officer had asked Costello what he would do if they met in Costello's local pub: would he buy him a pint? Costello said nothing but reached for a box of matches on the table and taking one out he broke it in half while looking the officer in the eye. The SB man smiled and took out a match from the same box, struck it, and placing the flame in the box, ignited the rest while never once taking his eyes off Costello and said, 'Well, this is what I'll do to you if you ever come across my path.'

It was war, and everyone knew the endgame if caught in the wrong place at the wrong time. Big boy's rules. That was the name of the game.

Unfortunately for Reece, they couldn't make anything stick and Costello had walked free. The biggest regret of his career was that he'd never managed to get Costello off the streets and behind bars.

Unlike the Puma journey on that winter day, this time Reece found himself looking out at green fields and small towns and villages. They landed in a secure corner at the airport where a car waited to take Reece to the SG9 office. As he walked to the car, Reece noticed a shaft of sunlight part the clouds and light up the tarmac in front of him. *The Gods shining down*, he thought, *but bringing good news or bad?* That was the question.

Chapter Six

It was only the second time that Reece had been in this office. The first had been when he'd been invited to join the Department. On that occasion, he'd sat in front of the desk as Broad walked him through his personal file. Sir Ian Fraser had sat quietly watching Reece and only spoke to explain why SG9 had been created, his own connection to it as head of MI6, and how Reece could help by bringing his valuable experience in combating terrorism. Reece didn't need much convincing. He'd been in a rut, with rare skills not needed in Civi Street. His previous life, he thought, had been but a preparation for just such a job. His boys had grown up and left home and there was no one special in his life. Nothing to hold him back. His answer was *where do I sign*.

That was two years ago.

Wilson stood as Reece came around the table.

'Well, Tom, this is a surprise, but a nice one. How are you?'

'Good, Dave. It's been awhile.'

'A few years. It's good to see you.'

Sir Ian interrupted, 'All this is very nice, gentlemen, but we have work to do. Mr Reece, please take a seat. I'll let the ACC explain the urgency and why we had to get you here as soon as possible.'

Reece nodded his recognition of Sir Ian and in turn, Jim Broad, before sitting down next to Broad facing Tom Wilson.

'It's all your fault, Reece.' He smiled. 'If you hadn't been such a good agent handler, we wouldn't be sitting here now.'

Reece returned the smile with a raised eyebrow, showing his confusion.

'OK, Tom, what have I done now?'

'Do you remember an agent: code name Mike?'

'Yes, a damn good agent.'

Reece thought back to the first time he'd seen Mary McAuley.

Just another ordinary day on the surveillance of PIRA targets in and around Newry town twelve miles from the border with the Irish Republic and a few steps from the Bandit Country of South Armagh.

She was coming out of the house of one of his targets. Her long black hair blowing in the slight breeze. She walked with her head up. As she moved, she reminded Reece of a cat stalking its prey: quiet and with concentration in every step.

Reece had decided to follow her, telling the rest of the team on the secure radio network to stick with the original target.

Reece smiled as he remembered his real reason for wanting to follow the woman. She was a lot better looking than the original target.

Looking at the men around the table, Reece sensed the urgency of the meeting.

'What's happened to her? Is she OK?'

Wilson opened the file in front of him and began.

'Over the past few months, our agents, and technical devices in Northern Ireland have been producing information that a dissident

Republican terrorist group, believed to be the Real IRA, is planning something big.'

Technical devices meant bugs…listening devices. They were easy to install in most locations and were deemed the most reliable method of intelligence collection as the information gathered came straight from the horse's mouth.

'The information shows they're in the preliminary stages of planning but to date, we've not been able to ascertain what, but we are confident it's something big.'

Wilson turned another page of the file.

'As I said, it's something big, and the one name that keeps popping up is an old friend of yours, David. Sean Costello?'

Reece's stomach flipped. He looked Wilson in the eye and just smiled.

'All our information points to Costello being back and up to his old tricks.'

Costello had been one of the top ten terrorists in the world during the Troubles. He had a reputation for ruthlessness and was linked to countless murders around South Armagh and South Down. Most of his suspected victims had died in bomb blasts and mortar attacks, but his speciality was to kill his victims from long range shootings using a Barrett Browning.50 sniper rifle.

But with Reece, it was more personal…the never-ending dull pain in his right shoulder a constant reminder of the last time he'd seen Costello. The day had been hot, but as the sun started to go down over Carlingford Lough, the air grew cooler. Carlingford Lough is an inlet of the Irish Sea which parts the Warrenpoint and Rostrevor towns in Northern Ireland from the town of Carlingford in the Irish Republic. The slimmest of intelligence from a technical source had indicated that a retired judge was the target for assassination.

The judge lived in a colonial-style house on a small country hill just outside Rostrevor, overlooking the Lough below. Reece was assigned the job of visiting the judge to tell him of the threat and to discuss upping his security. SB Officer JD had stayed in the car as Reece approached the house. Just before he raised his hand to knock, a small red Ford van drove at speed into the driveway. In the split second that followed the screech of tyres, Reece could see that both the driver and the passenger were wearing black balaclavas. He ran for the cover of his car, shouting at JD to get down. At the same moment, the front passenger jumped out of the van, an AK47 assault rifle in his hands which he aimed at Reece then opened fire.

The rapid-fire struck the police car just as Reece made it to cover with the engine between himself and the gunman. Reece knew the engine block would give him protection and was the safest place for him to be. He took his Smith and Wesson 59 in his hand and blindly fired over the bonnet in the direction the gunman had last stood. The noise of both weapons exploded all around him. Another burst from the AK and a storm of bullets struck the car and Reece felt a thump and searing hot pain in his right shoulder. Falling backwards, he heard the bang, bang, bang from JD's H&K MP5 automatic rifle before the blackness and silence took him.

Ten hours later, Reece woke in the Musgrave Park Military Hospital in Belfast. JD stood smiling by the side of his bed.

'Thought we'd lost you for a minute there, buddy.'

Reece tried a weak smile. The pain in his shoulder now a dull throb. His mouth was dry, and he could just about croak the words, 'What happened?'

'When you yelled to get down, I only had a split second to dive out of the car to my right before the AK opened up. Then you blasted back, giving me time to get to cover and fire towards the van. The driver pulled it round and AK man jumped in and they were gone, but not before I'd hit the back of the van and blew out the windows. They found the van a couple of miles down the road with blood in the footwell of the driver's side. The surgeon was here about an hour ago. He said you're lucky to be alive. The injury was caused by shrapnel, not an actual bullet, if it had been, in such close range, you'd have lost your arm at least. You were in surgery for eight hours. A lot of bullets hit that car, and a lot of shrapnel got you. I've buzzed for someone to come and check on you.' Just then, a young-looking doctor came into the room.

'Good, Mr Reece, I'm glad to see you're awake.' Lifting the clipboard at the end of the bed, he made a few notes on the form.

'I've made a note for some more painkillers, only to be taken when you really need them. You were lucky the round had already shattered before entering your shoulder. It missed all the vital organs, but we couldn't get all the pieces out. What's left are some small fragments and apart from some pain now and then, with a strict physio regime, you should recover full mobility and use of the arm.'

Reece took the doctor's advice and after three months away from work, made as full a recovery as he could.

Occasionally, as the fragments moved, his shoulder would give out a sharp stab of pain just to remind him of that day.

Having later discovered that the gunman was none other than Sean Costello, Reece had laughed at the thought of the surprise Costello must have felt when he found himself on the receiving end of gunfire from two trained Special Branch officers instead of an unarmed old man. His escape wasn't plain sailing as his driver and cousin, Vincent Hughes, took a bullet to the foot.

Sources within PIRA reported that both men hid in the home of a Republican sympathiser for two days, during which a doctor, who supported the cause, fixed up the wound on Hughes' foot. He would be walking with a limp for the rest of his days.

The sympathiser then smuggled the two men across the border into the Republic and the safety of Dundalk town, known by the security forces as 'El Passo' because of the number of on the run terrorists who lived and operated out of there, carrying on their murderous campaigns into the north and further beyond.

The house search in Crossmaglen, several months later, was with the intention of arresting Costello or at the very least, learning information of his movements.

As Reece listened to Wilson, it didn't surprise him that Costello was back in action or that he'd remained involved in the more extreme levels of Republican terrorism. Most sensible people had realised that enough people had died, and some sort of peaceful settlement had to be agreed. Thirty years was long enough. But people like Costello were just psychopathic killers; they didn't want to stop until every living British soul was dead. It wasn't about the Cause for him anymore, he just loved killing.

'This is where you come in, David,' Wilson said. 'Although we're being told that there is a job coming up, we don't have any details. Now, your old agent Mike comes into the picture. Have you had any contact with her recently?'

'No, not since leaving the force, why?'

'She contacted the agent's control number this morning. She gave her code name and number and left a message asking to meet with Joseph. I was coming to London for meetings anyway so I thought I could bring everyone up to date myself.'

Wilson played a recording of the call to the room. The men watched Reece for his reaction.

'Mike. She was my best agent at the top of PIRA. She comes from a long line of Republicans. When I first became aware of her, she lived just outside Newry, but she originally came from the Beechmount area on the Falls Road in West Belfast.'

'How did you recruit her?' asked Sir Ian.

Reece was happy to tell these men the story, but even in a room where secrets were shared daily, there were some things about Mike he wouldn't be sharing with anyone.

Newry, Northern Ireland, 1992

THE FIRST DAY he'd followed her, she'd taken the bus to Belfast and met with Kevin O'Hagan, the PIRA Head of Intelligence, in the Europa Hotel. Realising she had access to those higher up due to her on-the-ground connections, Reece knew she could be vital to providing intelligence for their operations. After a few weeks surveying her, he knew the key to bringing her on-board lay with her husband, Brendan. A drunk and a bully who thought he was higher up the chain of command in the PROVO than he was.

Coming out of a pub one night, Reece watched from his car while Brendan decided to beat her in the street. Not wanting to blow his cover, he had to suffer in silence while the poor excuse of a man pushed her around and taunted her. Reece drew the line through when Brendan took his fists to her. By the time he'd left his car and reached them, Mary was on the floor following two blows to her gut and one to her face, Brendan was about to continue his assault while she was on the ground until Reece grabbed him from behind and swung him around.

About to focus his attack on Reece, Brendan stumbled, but Reece knocked him unconscious before he managed to even form a fist.

Reece offered Mary his hand and helped her to her feet. Assessing her facial injuries, he expected to see fear in her eyes. But she was strong and all he could see was fire. He knew that when she told him to leave, she would be OK.

The next time Reece saw her she was walking in the rain about a mile away from her home. He pulled over and offered her a lift. She recognised him and although it was a short journey, he got the impression from their conversation that she was happy to see him. She was a lonely but smart woman. She tried to apologise for her husband's behaviour, but he knew from how she described his actions that the love, if there had ever been real love, had died, and she could potentially be looking for a way out.

After he'd dropped her off, Reece opened a file on the couple and discovered that although Brendan was a low-level PIRA recruit who had been implicated in moving weapons for Sean Costello and a couple of robberies, he was only alive because of Mary.

She was the one the PIRA wanted. She was unassuming. Looked to all around her like the down-trodden battered wife. But best of all, she was clean.

She'd never been arrested. Never been linked to any crime. Never even had a conversation with a police officer as far as Reece could see.

Using his sources, Reece discovered that she had a Republican background and had only agreed to passing messages on to save Brendan's head being blown off. She was loyal to her family. Regardless of what they did to her.

Reece kept an eye out for her, but it was three weeks before he saw her again. This time she was carrying her shopping and sporting a huge bruise on her face.

He asked if she was all right and she burst into tears. She was in pain. Reece then took a chance and drove to a small lay-by a few miles out of town. He asked her what had happened. She said she couldn't talk about it, especially to a stranger. Reece gave her his cover story – his name was Joseph and he was the regional manager of a hotel chain and he travelled around checking in on their various sites.

No longer strangers, she poured her heart out to him. There was something about him that she trusted, something in his eyes.

He offered to have a word with Brendan for her, but she refused. Said this was just a glitch and she could handle him. Besides, she couldn't leave him. She was a good Catholic girl, after all.

She asked him to take her home and when they pulled over just outside the estate where she lived, he handed her his fake business card and told her to call him anytime. He would be there for her.

About two weeks later she called him and said it would be nice to have that coffee and chat but away from the prying eyes of where she lived.

With cover and backup from a surveillance team, he met her in a café in Banbridge, a town about fifteen miles north of Newry. Expecting her to be battered and bruised and again, he was shocked at the venom in her voice when he joined up with her.

'Joseph, they want to kill you. I know you aren't who you told me you are, you're at the top of their hit list. Their units are hunting for information on you and they will kill you.'

She'd explained that her exposure to the PIRA had turned her romantic ideas about it all to nothing. She was crushed and utterly

25

disgusted with the likes of Sean Costello. Only a few days earlier he'd been bragging about shooting dead a retired security services officer in the street in front of his wife. And another in his home. Both hits had been aided by information she'd personally passed to Costello. But only one of them was ordered from above, so Sean was on risky ground. When she then found out Brendan was the getaway driver, she was physically sick. She'd prayed that the police would lift her so she could unburden herself, but they didn't.

Her last task had been to take pictures of officers O'Hagan wanted rid of to the local PIRA meeting. She'd nearly thrown up again when she saw his face in one of the images and realised he was Special Branch.

Reece had no choice but the tell her the truth and ask her to join him as one of his undercover agents. She was so sickened by recent events that she immediately agreed, waving off his attempts to tell her what risks were involved. She was already at risk and she knew that passing what information she could to Reece was far better for her soul than not doing it.

She took many risks, saving many lives over the years and as a result of the information she provided, they had recovered weapons and explosives and arrested many dangerous people.

She'd played a vital role in the Peace Process and she was one of the best agent's he'd ever know.

SG9, Present

'Is DEMOCRACY a code-word? Why did she use it?' asked Fraser.

'We give it to our agents only to be used in the case of information indicating an imminent attack on the British mainland or against a head of state which means anyone from the Prime Minister or a visiting Head of State to the Queen and senior members of the Royal Family, hence the "the ravens are in danger" call,' Wilson replied.

'Why is she asking for you, Reece? You left Special Branch a few years ago. Does she not have another agent handler now?' Jim asked.

'At the time, she was placing herself in such danger that when she said she would only ever work with me, everyone agreed. It would be like shooting the goose that laid the golden egg if we didn't and she refused to help us – the importance of the information she was feeding us far outweighed the office politics. It was authorised that only after my death would she use a different handler. She knows I've been out for years so whatever she has to say now, after years of silence, it's important.'

'You'll have to meet up with her tomorrow,' said Sir Ian.

'Yes, it's a popular little restaurant near Grosvenor Square. I'll find out what it's all about. I'll report back here at six tomorrow evening?'

'Agreed,' said Sir Ian, before Wilson explained that he was needed back in Northern Ireland but asked to be kept in the loop. It would also be easier for him to learn anything new about Costello that came in if he was in Belfast.

Jim looked at Reece. 'David, I'll have a team for tomorrow—'

'I trust everyone here,' he interrupted, 'but I think until we know more, we keep this between ourselves. I'll wear a wire so you can listen in and record everything, though. Then if you need to act immediately, you can.'

'OK,' said Sir Ian, 'let's go with David's plan and Jim can keep us all updated. I don't fancy having this bugger Costello bumping off the Queen or one of the Royal Family on my watch. He needs to be stopped and that's on you and your team, Jim, do not let me down.'

Chapter Seven

Tuesday, 24 September 2019

Sean Costello watched the crew on the Irish Ferry from the passenger deck as they prepared to bring the ship into the dock at the Holyhead Ferry Port at the tip of Anglesey in Wales. The two-and-a-half-hour morning crossing from Dublin had been bouncy thanks to the strong winds. He'd travelled this route many times and he couldn't remember ever having a smooth crossing. It was as if the gales had made it so rough for a reason: to keep the Irish and British mainland apart.

Unfortunately, the rough sea swell had never been rough enough and he'd spent his adult life fighting to force the British out of his country by other means and see the United Ireland he craved become a reality.

He'd opposed the so-called Peace Process that Gerry Adams and Martin McGuinness had signed up for and regarded them both as traitors. They had betrayed the Cause and Costello knew he couldn't live in Ireland while the British continued to have influence and rule over the north of his country.

He heard the announcement over the speaker system that all vehicle owners should return to the car deck ready for departure. He made his way to his small white Ford van. He'd driven from South Armagh that morning and the registration plates would show it belonged to a deceased farmer near Crossmaglen. He had died from natural causes and the family were willing to let Costello have the van for £200. In a hidden compartment in the back of the van, there was a Sako TRG-21 sniper rifle which he'd zeroed-in between the hills near Camlough and Forkhill.

With the rifle was a 9mm Browning pistol and ammo for both weapons along with 20lbs of Semtex explosive. All with the compliments of Colonel Omar Gaddafi and his terrorist-supporting Libyan regime.

The one good thing since the Peace Process and 9/11 was that the British Security apparatus had turned most of its resources away from Ireland and were now focussing on Islamic terrorism. Costello was aware of the random security checks at airports and docks where, if you were unlucky, you could still get pulled in for questioning and a vehicle search, but he was willing to take his chances.

As he drove off the ramp and followed the line of traffic towards the port exit, he could see the police checking cars and occasionally directing one to a large drive-through building on the left. Costello knew that even if he was pulled in, the search would be a cursory one. He held his breath as he neared the checkpoint and concentrated on the traffic in front to avoid any collision. Two minutes later, he was safely through where he turned left at the port exit and headed towards the A55. He knew this journey east well and soon he would be in the safe house. He chuckled to himself. There was nothing safe about what would be going on in that house.

In fact, his plans were anything but safe for the people of Manchester.

Chapter Eight

He heard them smash down the glass front door to the flat. A few steps into the corridor was the door to his bedroom on the left. It was dark, but he knew where his gun lay on top of the bedside cabinet. He could see the dark outline of the two men filling the doorframe, both pointing handguns towards where he lay. He reached for his own gun, found it, and pointed it at the looming figures. He could get them both if he moved quick enough. He pulled the trigger, nothing happened. Had he forgotten to slash the slide and put a round into the chamber? Had he pushed off the safety catch?

He fumbled with both the slide and safety catch and the magazine fell out, spilling bullets on the floor and the bed. He looked up at the face of the closest figure, which now resembled a laughing skull. The dark gun aimed at him flashed once, then twice, the noise deafening in the small room. Then came the all-consuming darkness…the sense of falling…down…never landing.

He woke in a cold sweat, his heart racing, a sickness in the pit of his stomach. That's how it always was. The nightmares always the same. The feeling of helplessness even though protection was at hand. The dream still came, but the nights between were increasing. Reece turned on the bedside lamp. His Smith and Wesson 59 was still there on the bedside cabinet. He still checked it, as usual, every time he woke from the dream. There was a round in the chamber. The 9 mm rounds filled the magazine, which was tight and secure.

The hotel room looked like many others he'd stayed in. He always carried a small leather bag with a few changes of clothes. His bag small enough to use as cabin luggage, reducing the time he'd spend booking into or leaving airports. As always, when he booked into a hotel, he made sure to pick up a bottle of his favourite Bushmills Irish Whiskey, a bit of home no matter where he went. He loved to tell people that Bushmills in Northern Ireland at 1680 was the oldest licensed distillery in the world. The emphasis is on the word licensed. There were older distilleries, but none licensed at the time and paying tax on their product.

He looked at his Casio G Shock watch. It was four thirty. The night was still dark, but the dawn wouldn't be far off. He crossed the room and poured himself a small glass of Bush. The Pavilion Hotel in Sussex Gardens was one of his favourites when staying in London excellent value for money with close-by transport links through the capital. It was elaborately decorated, and he enjoyed the fact they provided a good breakfast in his room at no extra charge. The hotel was also close to the junction with the Edgeware Road and the area was a great favourite with him.

Despite the short walk from the hotel down the Edgeware Road to Hyde Park Corner and Oxford Street and the shopping centre of London, the immediate area provided a community feeling all of its own with a unique atmosphere. Small fruit and veg shops, old-fashioned barbers, family bakeries, and restaurants. Everything a community should have and everything in walking distance of the front door of the hotel.

After a good start to the day with a continental breakfast and leaving the hotel early, he could take his time using his anti-surveillance to make sure he had no one following him. A few stops at coffee shops along the way would also pass the time. He downed what there was of the glass of Bushmills, climbed back into the king-size bed, closed his eyes, and slept fitfully for a few more hours.

When Reece left the hotel, the morning air was fresh with a slight autumn breeze, the sun shining brightly and reflecting off the glass windows of the buildings as he passed by.

Turning right at the junction with the Edgeware Road he walked at a steady pace in the direction of Hyde Park and Oxford Street a mile away. Reece had tried to avoid the London underground since the July seventh bombings.

The nearest Tube station was where one of the suicide bombers, Mohammad Sidique Khan, had set off his bomb as the train pulled out of the station, killing six people and injuring many more.

He only used the Tube when it rained or if he needed to get across the city quickly. He never used a car in London, traffic congestion and road works made it a nightmare to travel the roads of the city in that mode of transport. It was quicker and more enjoyable to walk getting rid of the kind of stress he would have if driving. Taxi drivers knew the short-cuts and where the roadworks where, so a taxi was OK on those occasions when no other way was possible. For now, he would walk using the tradecraft surveillance skills he was taught on these very streets by MI5 many years ago.

As he walked, he thought about how the training had developed and how it had saved his life on more than one occasion. Because of the continuing terrorist campaign in Northern Ireland during the early eighties, Special Branch officers were sent on training courses in England with the SAS and MI5. Reece had attended a Surveillance and Agent Handling course in London with MI5. The instructors taught all the tradecraft of running agents in a dangerous and hostile environment and the skills of how to watch and avoid being watched through surveillance and anti-surveillance. He'd learnt how to follow someone on foot and in vehicles. The instructors always kept the trainees away from the underground for two main reasons, the difficulty of following someone in the crowded Tube stations, but, more importantly, there was no underground in Northern Ireland so that would have been a waste of valuable course time.

Walking, you could see much more going on around you. Then there were the smells, the noise, and the air that cleared his mind, helping him make better use of the senses God had gifted him.

Today is a good day to walk, Reece thought.

Before leaving the hotel, he'd strapped the holster to his belt, inserting the Smith and Wesson with a fully loaded 9 mm clip. SG9 operators were given permission from the highest level of the Prime Minister's office to carry firearms on operational duties.

The one thing Reece would tell anyone who asked him about his undercover work was that the only person you could really trust was yourself. When he'd returned from the course in London, he'd gone to Newry on one of his rare days off. He'd taken his second wife because she'd badgered him to go to the town's market. The market itself was inside a square walled area with an entrance at each end from the street. While his wife inspected the stalls for a bargain, he put into practice the skills he'd been taught in London. Within a few minutes, he noticed two young men standing at the exit opposite the one he'd used to enter. He saw how they were talking while discreetly trying to look at him without drawing attention to themselves. One spoke to the other, nodded, then, taking one final look towards Reece, turned and left the market. It was that final look that confirmed his suspicions. Reece knew he was about to be set up as a target. The man leaving was the final confirmation that he was on his way to get a gun or a hit team to do the job. The other man stayed to keep an eye on Reece and point him out to the gunmen when they arrived.

Reece didn't hang about to find out for sure. His instinct, backed by the training, told him to get out of there. He quickly found his wife and whispered in her ear that they had to go now. He could see she wasn't happy about having to cut her shopping short, but she knew something was wrong by the way he took her arm and led her back to the car. Soon they were leaving the town far behind.

He'd trusted his instincts, and, on this occasion, he found out later, he was right to do so. Later, agents within PIRA brought in reports that the PIRA unit in Newry came close to killing an off-duty police officer they'd spotted in the town's market. They didn't know his name, but because he'd been spotted entering and leaving the town's police station, his face was known to them.

On his walk through the city he was moving faster than the traffic. On at least three occasions he'd passed the same car stuck at traffic lights on red. He came to the end of Edgeware Road and turned left towards Oxford Street with Hyde Park Corner on his right.

This part of the city was always busy with people moving at different speeds for different reasons. Tourists, workers, shoppers, always the shoppers. This was Oxford Street, this was what it was famous for, people and plenty of them.

When you walked, it had to be with your head up dodging the many people coming your way. Not counting the stupid ones with their heads down looking at screens oblivious to all going on around them, not caring, making others dodge around them to avoid a collision. Reece remembered a senior intelligence spokesman once saying the biggest danger from terrorism was the fact too many people walked about with their heads down looking at screens rather than noticing what was going on in the world around them. This had the effect that the first they knew they were in the middle of a terrorist attack was when the bullets started to hit their body, or the bomb had already exploded. When it was too late to stop the attack.

Reece wanted to get off these pavements as soon as possible. Moving in crowds gave you cover but at the same time gave cover to those who may be following. He crossed the road taking one of the quieter side streets heading in the direction of Grosvenor Square. He picked up a newspaper and found a café with a seat inside at the window.

Reece hated warm milk. It always reminded him of his childhood when his mother would pour hot milk on his morning cereal. He liked good coffee and when ordering in cafés he always made sure to ask for a little cold milk on the side. The waitress brought the coffee. He poured the milk in himself keeping it strong and the way he liked it. He opened the paper and between the stories and the sips of coffee he watched the people pass in the street. He'd not spotted anything that gave him any concern, but he wouldn't drop his guard. He would keep watching, observing. He was working now, and he would continue to take a circuitous route stopping in at least two more cafés before finally arriving at the final point where he would be able to observe from a distance the people moving in and around the restaurant where he would be meeting Mary 'Mike' McAuley.

Chapter Nine

Costello arrived at a service station on the M56 near Chester and made a call to a local number. When the man answered, he said, 'It's Paddy. I've arrived safely and am on my way.'

'Your home is ready. The keys are under the flowerpot by the front door. The fridge is stocked. Make yourself at home and I'll be there about five tonight,' the man replied.

The line went dead. Costello read the text he'd just received giving the address and postcode of the house which he fed into the satnav then drove onto the M56 and headed to Manchester. The street in Irlam was quiet when he pulled into the driveway of the house. He retrieved the keys from under the flowerpot and opened the door to a large garage and drove the van inside. The house and the street were exactly what he'd asked for. There were four large houses, none overlooking another, and the house where Costello was staying was the first on the street. This meant the neighbours wouldn't notice any unusual coming and going. A street where people kept to themselves.

Costello closed the outside door of the garage staying inside with the van. He entered the house by the internal door through the utility room then into the kitchen. He checked out the rest of the house which was fully furnished and of a typical three upstairs bedrooms with a bathroom, with an open-plan living-dining room downstairs.

A small garden to the rear surrounded by a six-foot panel fence completed the picture. Costello estimated that from pulling the van into the drive into the garage and closing the garage door had been no more than a minute. Prying eyes, if there had been any, would have seen little to talk about. Costello brought two items from the van into the house: his holdall and a Browning pistol which he stuck down the waistband of his trousers, pulling the fleece down to conceal it from view. He switched on the kettle, turned the TV on to Sky News, and settled down to wait for the others.

.

Chapter Ten

Reece had walked the full circle around Grosvenor Square passing the old American Embassy twice. He'd walked through the park area of the square and sat on a bench near the statue of President Franklyn Roosevelt where once again he read his newspaper. He'd sampled two more coffees in nearby cafés. All his tradecraft in surveillance confirmed he was alone. At 12.30 he inserted his radio earpiece and spoke, 'Control, this is Alpha One coming online, over.'

The voice in his ear confirmed his message, 'Roger, Alpha One, you're coming in loud and clear.'

Reece replied, 'Roger Control, moving to view primary location. Will keep you updated.'

'Roger, Alpha One.'

Reece made his way to the top of Grosvenor Street just off the square. Corrigan's was one of his favourite restaurants in London, one he'd used many times. He'd first used it the year he'd recruited Mary McAuley.

She'd travelled to London on a shopping and theatre weekend bus trip from Belfast. It gave Reece his opportunity to carry out a long debriefing of information. It also gave him the opportunity to work on her agent tradecraft; the kind she'd need to stay alive. Realistically, to make sure they would both stay alive. He'd taken her to Corrigan's on her second night when she was supposed to go to the theatre.

Mary had turned up with her flowing black hair combed to fall loosely on her shoulders and down her back. She wore a fifties style floral dress. Her brown eyes and dark olive skin gave off a Latin complexion. Reece had forgotten how beautiful she was. He'd tried to be the ultimate professional, but he knew from that night his feelings for Agent Mike would never be the same again. He briefed her on how to contact him using her code name and agent number, BC15, and helped her memorise the special agent phone number. Never to write down anything connecting them both.

Mary took everything on-board quickly, understanding everything Reece explained to her, she was a good listener. Reece had known from the start that she was a smart woman. The more they met and talked, the more he knew the path she'd chosen had been decided after much thought and heart-searching.

The dinner in Corrigans had gone on for some time with two bottles of Chablis, a favourite of his, and one Mary seemed to enjoy as well. She'd given him a sense of what the Republican movements were thinking at that time. What they were discussing and planning with regard to the terrorist campaign and their political movement led by Gerry Adams and Martin McGuinness. The peace talks had been going on in the background with the British Government.

Eventually, the talk of violence and destruction drained from the conversation and she began to open up and speak about her personal life. Her marriage was disintegrating. The drunken abuse from Brendan meant she'd reached the point where she could take it no longer. She wanted to leave but had no money, nowhere to live, and no one she could talk to with any trust. She was opening up to Reece in her own way, a cry for help, without coming straight out and saying so. She was a proud woman. Reece reassured her as best he could. He told her he would always be there for her and he would help her, one step at a time, to leave Brendan and find a new life just for her.

Throughout the night, Reece had to keep reminding himself to be professional. Getting personally involved would be dangerous. But he couldn't help himself. There was something about this woman that broke down his barriers. Her beauty, her vulnerability, her intelligence. All combined to overwhelm his senses. He found himself holding her hand across the table, looking into her dark eyes, and smiling when she smiled. Reece had been through bad relationships, marriage, and divorce, so he could understand her pain although his pain had been psychological. He could see the tears welling in her eyes.

He felt that night that he'd said what she'd hoped to hear. When he walked her to the taxi rank, she was quiet. As they parted, she squeezed his hand and, leaning close to him, she kissed him on his cheek. As she turned towards her taxi, she looked back over her shoulder and said, with a smile, that she'd enjoyed the evening and she'd call him soon.

Reece had told her in the restaurant that if she ever needed to talk to him on a matter that would take time to discuss and if she could make it, Corrigans would be the place to meet. Otherwise, the laneways, lay-bys, and secure safe houses in Northern Ireland would have to do.

Now, as one o'clock approached, he watched her get out of a taxi further down the street and casually check around. Deciding she was clear, she walked up the street towards him and into Corrigans fifty yards   away.

Chapter Eleven

Reece spoke into his mike again. 'Control, target arrived safely and moving to rendezvous, will be in touch.'

'Roger, Alpha One, understood, standing by.' The voice sounded loud in his ear, but he knew that only he would have heard it.

Reece walked the fifty yards to Corrigans, entering at one o'clock on the dot.

The restaurant was busy, but he was able to spot Mary seated near the window, facing the door and before the maître d' could ask him if he needed a table, Reece said, 'I'm OK thanks, my friend's already here.'

Mary smiled as he sat down. 'I've always wanted to come back here ever since my theatre weekend when you wined and dined me.' Reece loved her smile. It seemed to light up the whole world. Her eyes sparkled, her smile meant she cared when she asked, 'How are you, Joseph?'

'I'm well.' Before he could say anything more, the waiter hovered at the table.

'Good afternoon, my name is John, and I'll be your waiter today.' After presenting them with menus, they both ordered the soup of the day and the wild Atlantic salmon in a dill, garlic, and parsley sauce.

'How about some wine, Mary? The one we had the last time?'

'That would be wonderful.'

'We'll have a bottle of Chablis and can you bring some ice water as well please?'

'A very good choice, sir.' The waiter nodded his head and walked back towards the bar at the rear of the restaurant.

'Now,' said Reece. 'Where were we? I've always liked this place. Maybe it's the Irish name that reminds me of home, or maybe it's that the bar reminds me of Robinsons bar opposite the Europa in Belfast. Or, maybe, it's just that it brings back good memories all around.'

'I know what you mean. Maybe that's why I like it too. I sat here yesterday eating alone but somehow it still felt like you were here.'

'I didn't get your message until late yesterday. But, I'm here now; we can talk while we eat.'

Reece noticed that Mary had put in the effort. She'd dressed well for lunch. She wore a navy-blue trouser suit, a white linen blouse, a dark blue scarf hanging loosely around her neck, and a simple set of pearl earrings with matching necklace. Light red lipstick with a dusting of brown eyeshadow enhanced her eyes and olive skin. He was sure a few of the customers and staff had noticed her when she'd come into the restaurant. The waiter brought the wine letting Mary sample a taste before pouring for both and leaving the bottle with the bucket of ice on the table.

Reece tasted the wine. Memories of the last time he'd been here with her. He'd thought that now he'd left Special Branch all those days were behind him, yet here she was again as if there had been no ceasefire, no Peace Process, and the dangers had returned. Despite the wine, his mouth felt dry and he was sure that throbbing pain in his shoulder was stronger than yesterday.

'So, Mary, your message was pretty specific. *Democracy is in danger.* What's up?'

She smiled. 'What, no small talk? Didn't you miss me? How have you been, Mary?'

'Of course, I missed you. I always hoped you were well, and we'd meet again but not under these circumstances. When you hadn't been in touch, I thought you'd left all this behind you. I heard a rumour you'd divorced Brendan.'

'Yes. When he went inside for that armed robbery, I was able to push it through. I sold up and moved back to Belfast. I live there now on the Lisburn Road.'

Reece knew it was because of the information provided by Mike that he'd been able to set up the operation in Newry that caught Brendan McAuley coming out of the town Post Office with a balaclava on his head and a gun and a bag of money in his hand. Reece had promised Mike that they wouldn't shoot Brendan unless he gave them no option; he didn't. When he walked out of the Post Office it seemed to him, his luck had run out when a police patrol had been passing at the same time. The operation had been set up to allow the young getaway driver to escape. This would reinforce the feeling that the appearance of a passing police patrol was just bad luck. As Brendan had carried out the robbery on his own accord, more fool him. There was no inquiry by the PIRA internal investigation team; commonly known as the Nutting Squad. Brendan was given a beating when he was on remand for doing the job without permission and losing a perfectly good pistol.

John, the waiter came again, and took their food order then, leaving with a slight bow, returned to the kitchen.

'I'm sorry I was unable to keep in touch. I've missed our chats, but I've left the force a while now,' Reece said.

'But you still work in the game?'

'Yes, but for a bigger company with a bigger remit.'

'That's good because you're going to need that bigger company with the bigger remit,' she said with a smile that didn't show her teeth.

'Is it anything to do with Sean Costello?'

'Yes, and this time he's mixing business with the Islamic crowd.'

Reece didn't expect that. Republicans and Islamic Jihad usually kept away from each other, both ideologies went about their own terrorism from different points of view.

'In what way?' asked Reece.

'Well, to bring you up to date I must go back some time in my story. What I'm going to tell you, some of which you may already know, starts in Iran and Lebanon some years ago. When Sean Costello joined the Provisional IRA, it was quickly noticed how good a shot he was and how ruthless he could be. At that time, the movement was very closely associated with other terrorist groups such as Black September, Basque Separatists, and the German Baader-Meinhof gang. The top players in these organisations were sent to Arab training camps throughout the Middle East, sponsored by the likes of Gaddafi and Iran. It was at these camps the best the terror groups had to offer went to finishing school; polishing their skills and making them deadly killers. This is where Costello learnt to be an even more efficient killer with all kinds of weapons and explosives. Being that kind of boiling pot for the many terrorist groups of that time, it was inevitable that friendships would be forged across the boundaries of the different ideologies. Friendships that bring me here today. I have to tell you now, one of those forged friendships will be visiting this country soon with a deadly intent.'

Reece hesitated before he took another sip of the cold Chablis.

'I presume Costello is one side of this deadly friendship. Most of what you've already said, especially where Costello is concerned. I know only too well his particular skills.' As Reece spoke, he instinctively felt his right shoulder with his left hand, squeezing the muscle gently.

'Correct, and this is where the other half comes in. Have you ever heard the name Sharon Lyndsey?'

Reece had not only heard of her; he'd been given her file by Jim Broad when he first joined the Department. The White Widow.

Reece had been surprised to see that she'd been born in the town of Banbridge in Northern Ireland in 1983. Reece had been living in the same town at that time while working in the Newry Special Branch office.

The file had told him that Lyndsey's father had been a British soldier and during her early years, she'd moved to England with the family where she'd grown up and converted to Islam. She'd married one of the London July Seven suicide bombers, Germaine Lindsay, and earned the White Widow moniker. She'd claimed not to have known anything about the bomb attacks, or her husband's involvement with extreme Islamic Jihad, and the police had accepted this.

The file went on to say that she'd taken her young family to South Africa and then to Kenya where she became an important cog in the ranks of Al Shabab and al-Qaeda. She was involved in organising the Islamic attacks in the region. She also appeared to be deeply involved in the financing of the terrorist campaigns.

Mary sipped her wine while watching Reece for his reaction.

'Yes, I've heard of her, and from what I've heard she's a nasty piece of work. What's all this about?'

'As I said, it's a bit of a long story. Somewhere along the line, she and Costello crossed paths, most likely in one of the training camps they both attended, God knows, but they met. Now they're working together to attack this country, a spectacular as you might call it.'

'How do you know this?' asked Reece.

'One week ago, I met up with Kevin O'Hagan in Belfast. To say he was angry is an understatement. He told me that working with the Brits and Unionists was always going to be difficult without idiots like the Real IRA and Sean Costello sticking their oar in. He said there was talk that Costello was planning a big job on the British mainland and he would be working with the Islamic Jihad under the control of Sharon Lyndsey. All he knew was that it was going to happen soon and would involve them killing someone of high importance.'

'How does O'Hagan know this?'

'He's been speaking to some guy who used to be PIRA but has now moved over to the Real IRA. This guy doesn't mind attacking Brits but not if it means getting into bed with Islamic nut cases. His words, not mine. The guy went with Costello to an old PIRA weapons hide near the border in South Armagh. There they removed a sniper rifle ammo and some Semtex. Then he went with Costello to the hills near Forkhill and he did lookout while Costello zeroed-in the rifle with a few rounds. All Costello would say was that he would be away the first week of October and that he was working with some old friends from the Middle East. The guy also claimed Costello said something about the White Widow and a high-grade Brit target but nothing clearer than that. He didn't even think it was sanctioned by the Real IRA headquarters but rather Costello operating as a rogue warrior.'

'Do you think you'll be able to find out any more information?'

'Maybe, if I meet with O'Hagan again. But I don't think he knows much more.'

'Well, see what you can do but don't take any unnecessary risks.'

'I'll try but no promises.'

Reece poured them both some more wine. 'It's the twenty-fourth September so we don't have much time before whatever Costello is up to happens. I'll give you a secure access mobile phone number, so you can get me at any time. Where are you staying?'

'I got a good deal at the IBIS beside Wembley Stadium. I'm going to be here two more nights then back to Belfast.'

'Wembley, that's a bit far out?'

'Best I could do at short notice. Anyway, there's a straight run into the city centre from the station just opposite the hotel.'

'If you ever need to get over in the future, I can pick up the expenses and get you a hotel nearer the city centre. Talking about expenses.' Reece took an envelope out of his jacket pocket and handed it to her.

'There's five thousand in there.'

She started to protest as she always did when Reece gave her money. She wanted to think that what she was doing was saving innocent lives and not being a traitor to the cause, her country, or her people. Reece held up his hands and explained as he always did.

'Look, it's for expenses. Plane tickets and hotels don't come cheap. When you're on my time, I pay, not you.'

The fact that he always made it seem that the money came from him personally and not a shadowy organisation seemed to satisfy her sense of morals. She smiled and put the envelope in her handbag.

'If you need more for emergencies, let me know.'

Reece thought back to a male agent he used to run in Newry PIRA who had the complete opposite view when it came to be being paid for his information. He would always tell Reece the same sentence in Gaelic which he would then translate. 'Talk's cheap but drink costs money.'

Agents became agents for many reasons. Some were caught doing bad things and the offer to become an agent, source, informer, whatever you wanted to call it, outweighed many years in jail; their own get out of jail free card.

Reece preferred agent or source. When he'd attended the Agents Handling Course with MI5 in London, he remembered the instructors teaching the reasons someone became an agent. They did it for two main reasons, the first being money. The money to pay the agent could increase depending on the quality and the frequency of the information they provided. If the agent's motivation was money at the start, they would work hard to bring in the kind of information that brought the biggest financial reward. The problem with the agent motivated by money was they could end up taking too many risks and expose themselves to questions from within their own organisation. Being too nosey and asking too many questions could lead to being set up by their own people who would then give them disinformation. They would then sit back to see what the reaction of the security forces would be thus exposing the agent's double cross. The agent would then, after torture end up in a ditch with a bullet in the head. The second problem with the agent motivated by money was that they would start to invent the information just to get more money. A good handler would soon spot this as the agent never seemed to realise there were many other sources reporting in at the same time and when all the information was pulled together like a giant jigsaw, the false information provided by the greedy agent would stand out like a sore thumb.

If an agent was good or bad, if they could produce good or bad intelligence depended, to a large extent, on how good the handler was. The term to babysit was used because, that's what a good agent handler became: a good babysitter. When an agent is first recruited, how long the agent produces good intelligence and how long they stayed alive depends on the understanding built up between the handler and the agent. The handler looked after the agent as a babysitter would a child.

Teaching them to walk before they can run, what to say, dangers to look for, even down to how to spend money. Many agents were lost because they couldn't handle the fact that all of a sudden, they had a large flow of unaccounted cash to spend. A good handler taught the agent well at every aspect of the game as they arose. The handler also needed to study the agent. Know their personal background and habits through and through. What makes them tick? Do they have a drink or drug problem? Are they a gambler? Do they have problems at home? And most important: do they really listen? Can they do this without bringing suspicion on themselves by their actions or what they say? But above all, can they be trusted?

Thinking back on the agents course Reece would laugh to himself when he remembered the room of trainees being asked by the instructor, if they looked at all the instructors on the course were there any of them they would target for recruitment? The whole room including Reece agreed on one of the MI5 Instructor's being ideal material as he drank too much when in company and wanted to be everyone's friend. A few weeks after the course Reece was not too surprised when he saw media reports that the same MI5 officer had been arrested and charged with trying to pass secrets to the Russians.

Reece had always lived by the only trust that really mattered, to trust no one but himself. Mary McAuley came a close second. She also fell into the only remaining type of agent. The one who had been true to their cause but then the cause she aspired to had changed, had died as far as the agent was concerned. In Mary's case, fighting the British, fighting a war against soldiers and police who represented the oppression she'd grown up with, was a war she could put her name to. But when that war resulted in the deaths of more and more innocent men, women, and children, she'd changed. The men and women who had carried out her war had changed from patriotic Irishmen to a bunch of cruel terrorists, like Sean Costello, who killed for the fun of it. The cause was a banner they hid behind.

They didn't bring the Brits to the Peace Table Talks because they were winning, it was more the opposite, the Provisional IRA had been beaten by the Brits mainly by their intelligence organisations. The British had worked on recruiting good agents like Mike and using high tech surveillance methods to bring the terrorist group to its knees. The Republican leadership had, in general, seen this coming. Each year the security forces had taken out more of their top people who were ending up either dead or serving long terms of imprisonment. The dregs that remained were not of the same calibre and therefore even easier for the security forces to pick off. When the talks came about, lowlifes like Sean Costello formed their own killing groups, making Costello a big fish in a small pond. This was the agent bracket Mary McAuley fell into. The agent who, despite still wanting a United Ireland in her heart and was willing to fight the forces of oppression, wasn't willing to kill innocent fellow Irishmen and women to achieve it.

Reece had run many agents in his time and took great pride that his tradecraft training had paid off when it came to teaching his agents how to stay alive. A number of these agents had been lifted for interrogation by the Provisional IRA Nutting Squad. Reece knew of the techniques used by this brutal group to extract confessions of collusion with the security forces from its members. There were no Human Rights or Geneva Convention rules when it came to getting the answers they wanted, so the training from Reece had saved many of his agents from the inevitable hole in the back of the head. They had tortured one lad so badly and taped his so-called confession that he'd been an informer despite the fact he'd never worked for the security forces. The lad had confessed to stop the beatings he was getting and had ended up with two Armalite rounds in the back of his head, before he was dumped in a field in South Armagh. His interrogators sent his taped confession to his parents which only added to the horror and misery they were going through at the death of their son. To add to their trials, they couldn't recognise their own son when his body was brought to the hospital because of the damage done by the Armalite rounds and the brutal beatings he'd received.

Reece understood the world his agents lived in and thought he'd left all that in the past. When he'd left Special Branch, he'd introduced his agents to their new handlers. Everyone except Mary. She'd remained steadfast in her resolve that she'd only work with him and would only stop when one of them was dead.

A long way off, thought Reece. The starter and main course had come and gone, washed down with the cool tasting Chablis, iced water, and a strong coffee. The restaurant had filled and now began to empty again.

'I like this place,' she said as she watched people leaving. 'It always has good memories for me.' Looking at Reece she said, 'You don't know how close I came to asking you up to my room when you walked me back the last time we dined here.'

Reece had thought about that night many times; he knew she was looking for a reaction.

'I've often thought about that night too. After two bottles of wine and being in the company of a beautiful woman, the man in me would have accepted your invitation. But, being the professional and knowing you had travelled over with a party of people from Belfast, the risk of being seen together would have been too great. Now, we have to be professional again, but when this is all over, I would like to see you when we could get to know that other side of our lives outside all this, the personal you. Because, I really do like you, more than like.'

This answer seemed to please her. Her eyes sparkled, and her face broke into a smile. She reached across and took his hand in hers.

'I look forward to that day, but for now, we have work to do.'

With that, she stood and bending down kissed Reece on the cheek. As she left Reece could see that same slow, purposeful cat-like sway that he'd noticed the first day he'd seen her all those years ago in Newry. He also noticed the other men and women in the restaurant watch her as she left, but he knew none of them would have the feelings he was now feeling in the pit of his stomach.

Chapter Twelve

Costello was half asleep when he heard a car pull into the drive parking up at the side of the house and the lights switching off. Underneath the chair cushion on his lap, Costello held the Browning. Slipping the safety catch off with his right thumb he pointed the pistol at the living room door. He could hear the footsteps, the key in the front door, the closing the door, and footsteps towards the living room where he sat in quiet darkness even though it was only five fifteen the light outside had started to disappear. Mohammad entered the room and switched on the light smiling when he saw Costello.

'Ah, Sean, my friend, why do you sit in the dark?' He turned to close the blinds. Costello noted that Mohammad had changed little since the last time they'd met in Beirut. Arabic in looks with a small, well-trimmed beard. Costello knew he was about forty now, but he'd retained his boyhood looks and smile. Now he wore the suit of a well-heeled businessman. Costello flicked the catch back on to safe, put the pistol back in his waistband, and stood to give Mohammad a hug.

'Good to see you too, my friend. How are you?'

'I'm fine, Sean, just fine, and really glad to see you. You have everything you need?'

'Yes, everything, thanks. This place is ideal. What's our plan of action?'

'Tonight, we rest, my friend. We have a delicious meal, maybe a glass of wine. As far as the wine goes, don't tell my fellow Muslims. What they don't know will never hurt them. I am devout but when I'm a soldier not so much. Tomorrow, we go into Manchester for a walkabout, so you get the real lay of the land, so to speak. In the meantime, I have a map of the target area for you to look at after dinner.'

Mohammad went to change out of his work suit into jeans and a roll-neck sweater. Costello thought how the simple change of clothes seemed to change the man himself. He was more relaxed, and the conversation turned to everyday life, the weather, sport, women. He cooked a steak dinner and poured the red wine. Costello got the impression Mohammad had been nervous about today but now that day was here, he was unwinding. It was a feeling Costello had experienced many times before. You knew what you were going to do was dangerous, but life is dangerous, better not to think too much about what lay ahead.

Costello spread the map on the table after Mohammed had cleared the dishes.

It was a basic tourist map but just what Costello had asked for, the kind of map that highlights all the main points of interest for tourists. Mohammed sat back at the table, and pointing to the map he said, 'This is where we need to look at tomorrow.'

'When does she arrive? When do we meet?' Costello asked.

'She'll arrive at Manchester Airport late this evening and will contact us tomorrow for a meet-up. But tonight, we need to get some sleep; we'll be busy over the next few days.'

Costello folded the map, topped up his glass.

'There will be plenty of time to sleep Mohammad. I'll stay here and go over things a few more times in my head. Like you I want this job to go well and when I pull that trigger, I want to see the surprise in the eyes of his bodyguards and his eyes as they go dark. The scope on the rifle is strong enough to do that.'

'Inshallah, my friend, but I am tired so I will see you in the morning.'

'Inshallah, what the fuck is that?' asked Costello.

'God   willing,   my   friend,   God   willing.'

Chapter Thirteen

Control, this is Alpha One. Meeting over, all went well returning to main office, will need to speak to the Chief on return.'

'Roger, Alpha One.'

Reece was surprised to hear Broad's voice answer. It was rare for the Chief himself to answer from the operation room.

Reece hailed a taxi and asked to be taken to the business access drop off at London City Airport.

Reece sat in the back, his thoughts on his lunch with Mike. Now he was thinking of her as the agent and not the woman. For now, he was happy that he had all the information he could get out of her, and he'd locked her words in his memory ready for the cross examination he knew was coming.

Still, he remembered the words. He could see her face, her smile, hear her laugh, remember the colour of her hair, her eyes, the shape of her lips and her body as she moved. He made a promise to himself that no matter what happened he would see her again.

On arrival at SG9, Reece was directed by Broad's secretary to the Ops centre conference briefing room. When he got there, he could see Broad sitting at the large desk used for the spreading of maps and files at the briefings for operations. Sitting beside him was a man Reece only knew from media photographs, Sir Martin Bryant. Bryant stood as Broad made the introductions.

'David, let me introduce the Chairman of the Joint Intelligence Committee, Sir Martin Bryant.' The men shook hands. Reece noted the strong grip.

'Nice to meet you, Mr Reece.'

'You too, sir, and it's David.'

'Sir Martin,' Jim said, 'as you probably know, is the PM's eyes and ears in all matters pertaining to the intelligence community and one of the very few people cleared in knowing who and what SG9 is all about. He is here at the request of the Prime Minister, to hear your briefing from the horse's mouth so to speak and to save time when answering the questions needing clarification. Questions he knows the PM would ask if he were here himself, so you can speak without any worry about security. Now let's get down to business. How did your meeting go? What have you got to tell us?'

Reece knew something of Bryant's background. He was a career civil servant, tall, lean, and fit for his fifty-two years. He was a close friend of the Prime Minister, not just his ear in the intelligence community. He had a reputation for being a straight talker who didn't suffer fools easily. His dark brown hair starting to go grey at the side complimented his square strong jaw line.

Today he wore his regular three-piece blue pinstriped suit with a pocket watch and chain finished off with a blue striped tie with matching pocket hanky.

Reece thought of him as the consummate city banker. He knew that even though he couldn't see his shoes from where he sat, they would be a pair of black shiny Oxford Brogues. Reece also knew that despite the appearance of the city banker, Sir Martin Bryant was a man of steel which many men who crossed his path had found out to their cost. Reece noticed his clear blue eyes were watching him with interest. Watching and listening for what was to come.

'What I've heard has me worried on a number of fronts. Mainly that extreme Irish Republican elements are now working on this operation with extreme Islamic terrorists.'

Reece then told them the details and the fact that whatever the terrorists were cooking up was so big that two opposing ideologies were willing to work together in a common cause to ensure the kind of spectacular success they craved.

It was Sir Martin who spoke first when Reece stopped talking. As Reece spoke, he'd been making notes marking them as bullet points on the yellow writing pad in front of him.

'Point one: It's a spectacular involving two well-known terrorist groups. Point two: It has to be something so big the result would be catastrophic for this country, maybe even the West as a whole. Point three: The first week of October seems to be important to them.'

'Gentlemen, can I remind you the first week of October covers the Conservative Party Conference taking place in Manchester. A Conference attended by the British Prime Minister,' said Bryant.

Looks of understanding fell over the men in the room.

'I'm deeply concerned at the involvement of Sharon Lyndsey, the White Widow. She didn't only earn that name because of the martyrdom of her husband, it's also attributed to the large number of widows she's created through her terrorist actions across the world.'

'Mr Reece, I'll waste no time in briefing the Prime Minister. I'll also put the resources of the police and Intelligence Services at your disposal. As SG9 is a Black Ops organisation, people will be told you're working directly for me and the PM's office and for this work, you and Jim here will always have direct and secure access to me. I'll brief Sir Ian Fraser accordingly.'

Reece was surprised at this. His previous experience of career civil servants was that in cases where decisions of life and death had to be made, they quickly passed responsibility on to someone down the ladder. If things went wrong, they had their scapegoat for the blame. If things went well, they took the plaudits as they would let it be known they'd chosen the person to lead the plan. In Sir Martin, Reece could already see someone he could work with. Someone who was used to taking responsibility and leading from the front, someone, who wouldn't ask from his people something he wasn't prepared to do himself.

'Mr Reece, do you think you'll be able to get any more information from your agent?'

'Yes, she'll get back to me as soon as she has anything, and I can contact her anytime.'

'Good, do you know this Costello personally? Do you know what he looks like and how he operates?'

'The closest I ever got to him was in a shoot-out when I was hit by shrapnel in the shoulder. He was masked then, but I know how he moves under pressure. He won't give up easily, he has nothing to lose and will shoot anyone who gets in his way. He's a vicious bastard who lives to inflict pain and death on others. He uses the United Ireland cause as his excuse to kill. He doesn't have many friends. We now know even his old IRA chums are only too happy to inform on him. To them he's a dinosaur, lost in the past, and they believe he needs to be taken down.'

'We will take him down, Mr Reece, I can assure you of that. The where and when is to be decided. But we'll take him down. I want you to keep in touch with your agent and keep me updated. I also want you to take the SG9 team to Manchester to find Costello and the White Widow and if you find them, kill them both. I don't want these people arrested on our soil to become prison heroes at the expense of the British public, or, to have their so-called human rights dragged through the courts all the way to Strasburg so that unelected judges can make us the laughingstock of the world.

'Did you know that a Mossad analyst once calculated, one terrorist cost as much as a hundred expensively trained men to capture him or her? This is a cost this country can't afford. The decision was made some time ago that SG9 would be our main arm of defence against the people who want to hurt us. We have tried diplomacy, we've tried talking, and financial blackmail and, too many times, we've given in to their demands, yet they still plot to kill us. Have you ever heard of the word Kidon?'

Reece looked at Broad who nodded his head to answer.

'Yes, it's the Israeli unit of Mossad specifically set up to kill its enemies.'

'Correct, Mr Reece. Ehud Barak, a past Prime Minister of Israel, and also a past member of Kidon, once quoted the reason for the existence of such a unit in words I believe could be attributed to our SG9, he said, the intention was to strike terror, to break the will of those who remained alive until there were none of them left.

'Simply put, these people don't want to negotiate with us they just want to kill us, they want to destroy us in whatever way they can. So, we must find them and kill them first. Do you have any problem with that?'

Reece took time to reply. Did this make him a killer, a murderer, an assassin?

'No, I've seen enough of what they do up close. I have no problem with that.'

Reece knew that Sir Martin not only had the ear of the PM but when he spoke and gave directions, it was the Prime Minister who spoke.

'Good, now let's get ahead of this. I'll inform the PM that your team has full control of this operation. Whatever you need, it's yours.'

Standing, Bryant looked both men in the eyes. 'Good luck and good hunting.'

After Bryant left, it was Jim Broad who spoke first.

'Right, well, there you have it, David, a direct order from the top. This is why SG9 was formed. What do you need?'

'A four-man team, sorry, one of which should be a woman. With me as lead, that's three more. Everyone should be good with firearms and surveillance. One should also be a locksmith in case we need quiet access. Where can we run secure comms from?'

'Here, and I'll move a camp bed into my office until this is over. We will need a simple code name for the operation, have you anything in mind?'

'As it seems this is developing into an assassination attempt on the Prime Minister, let's call it Long Shot, it's the same for Costello and us, a real long shot if we're to be successful.'

'All right, I'll let the Gold Commander on the ground for the Conference know you're coming. Five, Six, and GCHQ will all be told to keep their eyes and ears to the ground, especially with the Islamic Jihad input. I'll funnel all incoming information through here and keep you updated. Anything else?'

Reece knew there would be a lot of pressure on SG9 and especially him, so he was going to make damn sure he had everything he needed.

'An SAS CQ assault team on standby in Manchester. I'll brief them personally on what might be needed.'

'You've got it.'

'Can you also have our Special Branch and boarder people go through all passenger and vehicle arrivals into the country from Ireland in the past week? Pass on Costello's latest description and photos, bearing in mind he won't be giving us any full-frontal face displays. You could do the same for Lyndsey through Manchester and Liverpool airports. It's a shot in the dark, but maybe something will turn up. We can assume that Costello won't be on his own, so CCTV around the area of the Conference might look for a six-foot white and fit looking male who may be accompanied by an Asian friend. It's rarer than you might think.'

Broad pulled up the calendar on his laptop.

'OK, let's see, the Conference starts on Sunday twenty-ninth of September, with the main appearance by the PM on Wednesday the second of October, so we don't have much time. The PM will be attending the Conference no matter what. You must remember the legacy set by Margaret Thatcher the morning after the Brighton bomb. She went on stage at the Conference to say the terrorists would never win. Today's Prime Minister will say and do the same. I also remember the words of the Provisional IRA after the bombing, *we only need to be lucky once.'*

Reece stood and reached out his hand. Broad took it and shook it firmly. No more words were necessary, the deal had been made and both men knew what was at stake.

Chapter Fourteen

When Sharon Lyndsey's flight landed at Manchester Airport from Zurich, she'd already travelled from Iran to Tukey to Switzerland under the name Karen Webb. She'd discarded her Islamic dress instead dressing in the dark trouser suit of a Swiss banker with Gucci luggage and handbag to match. She'd dyed her hair blonde and covered her blue eyes with brown contact lenses.

Her documents matched her appearance with a genuine passport provided by an official in the Swiss Civil Service after he'd been blackmailed through a honey trap extra-marital affair with a lady working for the Islamic Jihad.

Once through the airport she took a taxi to the Hilton Hotel in Deansgate and booked in for three days under her assumed name.

Chapter Fifteen

Wednesday, 25 September 2019

It was typical Manchester weather, showers with a little sunshine peering through the clouds now and then. Mohammad had driven them both to Irlam Railway station where they took a train to Deansgate Station Manchester. Costello was now in *operational mode* as he liked to call it. He carried the Browning 9mm in the right-hand pocket of his green Barbour jacket. His hand felt comfortable wrapped around the pistol grip. He constantly observed the other people on the train and again as they walked across the overhead walkway leaving the station and down the steps turning right into Deansgate itself. Costello had been here years before when he'd driven a lorry with nearly one ton of HME from South Armagh, to park it up near the Arndale Centre before activating the timer which triggered one of the largest explosions in Britain since the Second World War.

He was aware he was on the British Security Service's most wanted list but a visit to Tehran and a few cosmetic snips here and there had been enough to change his facial profile, enough to allow him to move about more freely. Only someone who really knew him could spot the man below the new mask.

It was while he was in Tehran that he'd met by accident his old friend Sharon Lyndsey while sipping a cup of strong Arabic coffee outside a café in The Square of the Revolution.

She was wearing the traditional Muslim headscarf and when he called out to her, she stopped and taking a long look said, 'My God, Sean is that you?'

They had hugged and talked non-stop through three cups of coffee. The last time they'd met was in a training camp in the Becca Valley in Lebanon. She was teaching in tradecraft on how to use forged documents to get through security checks and how to set up false covers and bank accounts. Costello had been improving his skills as one of the world's deadliest snipers.

After two more meetings, the plan that brought Costello back to Manchester had been hatched. Lyndsey had hitched her star to a number of Islamic Jihad groups from Hezbollah to Al Shabab but always staying close to the al-Qaeda terrorist campaign. Like Costello, she'd always moved when one group seemed to be going soft on the West. Lyndsey had told Costello she had contacts in England who wanted to attack the British establishment where it would hurt most, its own streets. In particular, there was a small team of three men who she'd helped with false documents and money. These men were now ready to carry out attacks in England but what they needed was a good target and the proper resources to hit it, determination they had in abundance according to Lyndsey. It was then that Costello had floated the idea of a joint operation where he could supply the equipment and they could hit two targets at once. They agreed that Lyndsey would be the finance provider and the point of liaison between the two groups on the ground and Costello would be the leader of the overall operation.

Costello worried that she'd be too well known and might be spotted in England. She'd laughed and told him she'd been there many times helping to radicalise young men to the cause of the Islamic Jihad, then helping them to train and fight in the countries where they were needed.

The three-man team she spoke of were of the highest calibre and commitment. One of them, Waheed, was a cousin of Azhari Husin, who had been al-Qaeda's chief bomb maker. He'd been killed when a house he was in at Batu, Indonesia was assaulted by their Special Forces acting on intelligence received from the Israeli Secret Service, Mossad. He'd been wounded twice but died a martyr to the cause when one of his associates detonated a suicide vest killing them both. Waheed had followed in his cousin's footsteps and was now one of Islamic Jihad's top bomb makers.

The seed of an idea had started to formulate in Costello's mind. He didn't know if he could work with a fanatic who was willing to kill himself to get the job done. To Costello, this was a waste of good talent. Talent like him, who, if with the right organisation and planning, not only gets the job done but gets away to do the same on another day and time. He was prepared to die for his cause, but he would rather live for it.

'Can you get them all to Manchester before October first?' he'd asked her.

'No problem. Two of them are there already; one of them works in an office in the city. The third man is in London, but I can have him there by the first.'

'Good, if we can do what I think we can, we'll bring about the greatest defeat of the British and the West since 9/11 and the day your husband died a martyr in London.'

'If you can do this, I'll help you all I can.'

Now, as Costello left Deansgate Station with Mohammad and walked over the walkway down into Deansgate, then past the front entrance of the Hilton Hotel, he knew what he was looking for and the questions in his head that needed answers.

The hotel staff were standing out in the street on what appeared to be the emergency hotel drill. Many of them in flimsy uniforms offering little protection against the strong, cold wind.

When Costello had told Lyndsey his idea, she'd been sceptical at first but when he went into the details, she'd agreed that with a little planning and the right team, it could be done. Lyndsey had contacted her al-Qaeda masters to brief them. At first, they too were sceptical, especially from the point of view of a Western Terrorist working closely with the Islamic group, but in the end admitted that if the operation was a success, it would be a great victory for both groups. If not a success, they would lose little and could blame Costello for the failure. Lyndsey had told Costello this and what they were thinking. He was still happy to proceed and now, with Mohammad he turned off Deansgate and continued with his recon of Manchester where in just over a week, he hoped to carry out the attack that would put the all-

Ireland question back on the world political stage and the cause of Irish freedom   at   the   forefront   once   again.

Chapter Sixteen

Mohammad left Costello outside the Hilton and crossed the road to the office where he worked. Costello crossed the Great Northern Square into Windmill Street where he walked to the rear entrance of the Midland Hotel. The hotel was one of Manchester's iconic landmarks. Stopping at the rear door he turned to face the square in front of him. Directly facing was the entrance to the Manchester Central Convention Centre Complex. He walked at a normal pace towards the Convention Complex main doors counting the number of paces and seconds it took from the hotel doorway to the steps at the front of the Convention Centre. He noted the line of small trees that dissected his path as he crossed the otherwise open space. He turned and retraced his steps back to the hotel door turning once more to face the open square. This time under the peak of his baseball cap his eyes took in a slow right to left arc. He noted the many CCTV cameras and the tall buildings. Turning once more he walked along the outside of the hotel towards Peter Street emerging with the hotel's main front entrance to his right. He crossed Peter Street into Mount Street towards Manchester Town Hall and Albert Square.

Halfway along Mount Street, he found the café Mohammad had told him about. The Browners Café was quiet, apart from three workmen having a full English breakfast each. Costello took a seat by the window. Outside, the rain had started to fall more heavily. The few people on the street moved to cover from the sudden shower. Costello could see why Mohammad liked the café. Apart from being quiet, the menu was simple and cheap. The people who worked in the café were all Asian and from the familiar way they spoke to each other probably family.

Costello ordered a pot of tea and a full English breakfast with extra toast. Looking outside he could see the rain had started to die down, people started to come out onto the street again but still, few of them. He took out his pocket notebook and made cryptic notes. In between bites of breakfast and hot black tea, his plan started to develop. His mobile phone vibrated in his pocket. The text read:

I'm here, Hilton Hotel, coffee at two.

The   White   Widow   had   arrived.

Chapter Seventeen

The morning after his meeting with Sir Martin Bryant, Reece had thrown his things in his bag, checked out of his hotel, and returned to the Department HQ at London City Airport. When he entered the main briefing room, Jim Broad had already started to brief the three other people present. Reece knew everyone and had worked with them at one time or another. All were in their early to late thirties and each had a long background in the intelligence game.

April Grey, slim with blond hair and blue eyes, smiled as Reece waved a hand of acknowledgement around the table. Grey was ex-military police and someone who knew her way around a surveillance grid. The fair-haired, blue-eyed man sitting next to her was six-foot ex-14 Int and Detachment operator Joe Cousins. Reece had worked with him in Northern Ireland during the Troubles in South Armagh and Belfast, on some of the most dangerous and tricky operations ever carried out against the terrorist elements at that time.

Reece was glad to see him as he knew Cousins was one of the best locksmiths around. If they needed to gain quiet entry to any premises, Joe was the man to do it.

The final agent at the table was the kind of person nobody looked at twice. Steve Harrison could walk into a room and no one would know he was there. He'd come to SG9 via the famous MI5 surveillance team known as the Watchers. Steve had also worked in Northern Ireland backing up the police and military surveillance units when MI5 were assisting Special Branch, usually when installing bugging devices deep into the terrorist heartlands. Although Reece had never worked with Harrison, he'd done his surveillance training under Harrison's watchful eye when he attended the MI5 courses in London. That training had saved Reece's life on more than one occasion.

Broad spoke first. 'David, I know you all know each other, so we can dispense with the introductions. I've given everyone the background as far as we know it. There is a credible threat. We have information that there may be an assassination attempt on the Prime Minister when he attends the Conservative Party Conference in Manchester. Now, David, I'll let you fill in the details as it's your agent who has provided the intelligence.'

'At the moment, we think the Prime Minister is the primary target. His personal security detail and local protection services will still be in place to protect him. Our job isn't to babysit the PM but to identify, find, and eliminate this enemy. We can't remove the Prime Minister from the target zone as it's the Conference in Manchester, where he'll go no matter what. The intelligence we have to go on, although sketchy, gives us enough to take this threat seriously.'

'Do you think we'll be able to get any more information?' asked Harrison.

'My source is heading back to Northern Ireland with that in mind. Our immediate task is to get to Manchester, embed ourselves in the standard security setup, then familiarise ourselves with the possible target area. The operation will be overseen by Mr Broad and run from the control room here. We've been authorised to carry and use firearms. The people we're looking for will be armed and dangerous so, Big Boys' Rules, we take them out before they take us out. So, let's hit the armoury, get what we need...from weapons to surveillance equipment and report back here in one hour.'

'The code name for this operation is *Longshot*,' Broad said. 'Which I think is very appropriate. There's a Puma chopper ready to transport you to a secure location just outside the city. There'll be an SAS team allocated to you so if you need heavy weapons backup, they'll take care of it. Your job is to find these people and if needs be, take them out yourselves. Good luck and good hunting.'

Chapter Eighteen

When Costello left the café, he turned left and walked in the opposite direction with the Midland Hotel behind him. Now he walked into the main square in front of the Town Hall. The rain kept people off the street even though it had now stopped. Costello would have liked to sit at one of the outside tables in front of the cafés and restaurants facing the Town Hall and observe the whole area for a while, but the chairs were still too wet, so he walked on. At the rear of the Town Hall he passed a small group waving coloured flags protesting about something, but he didn't get close enough to find out what in case they were being observed by the local police. He walked alongside the tram lines that dissected St Peter's Square, passing the Manchester Library on his right. He turned at the end of the building and crossing the road, he entered the Midland Hotel through the front revolving doors.

Inside, the large open lobby was busy with customers. The main seated public area had been closed for what appeared to be a conference group having tea and coffee. Costello decided to keep walking through the reception area and down the corridor which led to the rear door out of the building. He stepped outside, stopped, and looked around from left to right. This was the exact route his target would take. He could look straight across at the Manchester

Conference Centre steps and main entrance door. He estimated it would take fifteen seconds to get off his shots, no more than two accurately, as the target would be moving and a line of small trees would protect the target from view for a few seconds during the walk.

Costello kept his head down as once more his eyes, below the line of the peak of his baseball cap, scanned the ground from left to right and back again. He took in the outline of the many tall buildings surrounding the background to the square patch of land with its concrete path and walkways where the target would cross in those few seconds. Two buildings caught his attention. At the rear of the Conference Centre he could see the large outline of the Hilton Hotel towering in the distance; too far away to make it a viable prospect for Costello's needs. To hit his target from one of its high-up windows would be a supreme effort and too far for the accuracy he needed being almost a mile away. At that distance and height, the shot would be too shallow and with possible windage, too much could go wrong. As he looked to his right, a building of what appeared to be apartments with balconies looked more promising.

Costello set off at a casual pace in the direction of this building. As he walked towards it, the possibilities firmed up in his mind. Walking alongside the building down Windmill Street he crossed to the front of the building on Great Northern Square. Looking back the way he'd come, he could just make out the rear door of the Midland about three hundred yards away.

A few more steps took him to the front of the building with a sign that said Great Northern Tower Apartments. Access was via a button keypad and all the apartments numbers were on a metal plate with a button next to them, allowing a visitor to press and speak for access. Costello discreetly took a photo of all this and then the building from a distance across the square. He looked at his watch. He still had an hour to use up before his meeting with Sharon in the Hilton, plenty of time for a little more thinking over a cup of coffee in one of the cafés on Deansgate.

Finding one, and as he usually did, took a seat near the back so he could watch the door and people passing by outside. Ordering a black coffee, he took out his notebook and made a few notes with a crudely drawn sketch showing where he'd walked. He then looked at the tourist map provided by Mohammad. Now he could feel a sense of relaxation come over him; the satisfied calm that always came when he'd completed a profitable recognisance of the ground where he would operate. The next time he'd cover this ground would be with the whole team – each with a different task to complete. Each one of them would have to be sure of the part they would play and where they would be operating.

Chapter Nineteen

When Costello entered the lobby of the Hilton Hotel, he could see the White Widow seated on a settee in the café to his right. The café at the front of the building had large glass windows from the floor to the ceiling looking out onto Deansgate. The windows were slightly tinted to make it difficult to see into the building from the outside but easy to see out from the inside.

Lyndsey was almost alone in the lounge area with only a man and woman sitting in the furthest corner from where she now sat. On seeing Costello, she stood to greet him, kissing him on both cheeks. Costello sat in one of the large armchairs facing her.

'It's good to see you again, Sean, would you like some coffee?'

'Could I have a pot of tea? I've been drinking too much coffee lately.'

She called over the waiter who had been cleaning glasses behind the bar and gave him the order for a pot of tea for two. Costello noticed how the years away in foreign countries had dulled her Irish accent even more than he remembered.

She noticed Costello searching the area with his eyes.

'Don't worry, the people in the corner are American tourists. Their conversation is loud like all American tourists. I can hear them from here, they've been arguing about where to go today and tomorrow. The only security cameras I can see are one directly above them and one over the bar. The cameras are there to spot drug use or for people using their own booze from handbags. We can relax for our little chat.'

'I must say, the change in your hair colour and the contact lenses completely changes your appearance, Sharon.'

'It's a lot easier to change my appearance that way than with plastic surgery.'

'I'm inclined to agree.' He smiled.

The tea came and after pouring, she asked, 'Well, how are things going, is the safe house OK?'

'Yes, it's perfect. I just finished my first look about and everything is looking good to go.'

'So, you think it can be done?'

'The details will need to be worked out. When will the rest of the team be here for a get together?'

'I've instructed everyone to be at the safe house for eight tonight. Is that OK for you?'

'Yes, that's great. Is the finance in place?'

'Yes, all bases are covered, with extra available if you need it. The house has been paid for in advance using false ID. Of course, when we leave it, we leave it clean so no trace back to us. I presume you've brought all the equipment we need?'

'Yes, no problem, we have all we need.'

'Is there anything you need from me in the meantime?'

Costello took out his tourist map, placing it on the coffee table between them. He pointed to the map. 'This building here, it's called

The Great Northern Tower Apartments, is ideal for what we need. Take a walk there yourself, bring Mohammad and work out how we get access to the building and one of the apartments to the rear above the eighth floor. Even if it means renting or buying one. At worse, we may have to take one of the apartments by force. I'll let you work that out, whatever's best. We might even organise a viewing on the day.'

'Sure, no problem. I'll text him now. Hopefully, we'll have some news for tonight's meeting.'

Costello finished the last of his tea. 'Until tonight then. I'll do one more walk about before getting the train back to Irlam.'

As he left, Lyndsey noticed he didn't look back and the two Americans were once more falling out loudly over their tourist plans. If only they knew the plans she'd just been discussing, they might be a little   quieter.

Chapter Twenty

The Prime Minister's Downing Street study wasn't large as studies go. The desk, made of dark stained oak, sat at an angle facing the door with two large winged back leather chairs in front. The room had the dark furnishings of a gentleman's club. The Prime Minister, the Right Honourable Peter Brookfield, sat behind the desk reading a report consisting of two pages of A4 marked Most Secret or Red X as these types of documents were known thanks to the large Red X that covered the front of the buff folder the reports came in.

Sir Martin Bryant sat in one of the large leather chairs quietly watching as Brookfield started reading the second page of A4. Bryant had always liked this room. Its size and lack of windows gave it an air of intimacy, privacy, and most important, secrecy. Bryant always associated his one-to-one meetings with the Prime Minister as confidential at least secret at most. The room different from the sterile rooms of his own office building and its intimacy had greatly helped him build a close bond of trust with the PM which he believed was reciprocated.

Putting the second page on his desk, Brookfield's greyish blue eyes looked back at Bryant.

'How serious are we taking this, Martin?'

The PM always addressed him in personal not formal terms as two friends to each other. Despite this, Bryant, when on business as this meeting was, always addressed the office.

'Very seriously, Prime Minister. I'm assured by the Department head that the agent providing the information is reliable.'

'But this is Islamic Jihad and Republican terrorists working together to kill me.'

'That's the assumption, sir. The high-up target, hints at Manchester being the location for the attack, the same week of the Conservative Party Conference; everything points in that direction. We believe the spectacular result, if achieved, is the bond that's bringing these groups together.'

'Will we be able to firm that up?'

'Hopefully, but as time is short, I've given the go ahead for SG9 to take the lead on this, especially as the agent in question is reporting to the SG9 officer. The operation, code name Long Shot, will run things from the Department's Operation Room at the airport. The officer in question, David Reece, will be leaving with a special team for Manchester today.'

'Has he got everything he needs?'

'I've given Broad the full co-operation of the Anti-Terror Squad in Manchester and a dedicated SAS CBT trained team at his disposal. Reece will pull the whole thing together on the ground when he gets there and report directly to Jim Broad, who will then keep myself and C in the loop.'

'Do you need anything from me?'

'No, not at this stage, Prime Minister. I've given the go ahead for SG9 to use the extreme force it was created for. The best you can do is to go about your normal government business. I'll update your security detail that there is an increased threat, unknown what exactly but to stay on their toes.'

'Well, there's no way we can cancel the Party Conference or even increase the security presence without raising questions from the press.'

'I agree, sir, this is the very reason I've given the Department the lead role on this. It's their intelligence source, their agent, their handler, and the main target, Costello, is known to Reece. Now everything is in hand and moving forward to Manchester.'

'That's good. Keep me updated, I'll be available at all times.'

Sir Martin stood to leave.

'I'm not happy about the Islamic involvement, Prime Minister. It's always unreliable but on this occasion the fact we have an agent reporting on the Republican Costello might just give us the opening we need.'

Brookfield shook Sir Martin's hand.

'Let's hope so, Martin, good luck.'

After Bryant had left the office, Brookfield read over the two pages once more and wondered how he could appear normal to those close to him knowing what the words on the two pages were telling him.

Chapter Twenty-one

Mary McAuley had decided to pay a visit to her old haunting grounds of Newry. She didn't know why but she felt in her blood that some of the answers she was looking for, and that Joseph needed, were to be found there. She'd always trusted her instincts and once again, she was to find that trust was to prove so true.

She'd deliberately taken her time walking around the shopping area in the town centre. She knew that if she was spotted, word would be quickly passed that she was in town. She bought a blouse in Dunnes Stores to ensure she had one of their distinctive green bags. After two hours of walking around and talking to people she knew, old neighbours and friends, she headed to the local Republican Club. When she entered, she noticed it had had a paint job and new chairs and tables. Since the ban stopping smoking in public places had come in, the club smelt of the fresh paint with just a hint of beer. She walked up to the bar knowing the eyes of the few men and women in the room were watching her.

'Well hello, Mary,' said Paddy Maguire from behind the bar. He hadn't changed much except his hair was a little thinner than she remembered, and his beer belly a little larger.

'Jesus, Paddy, are you still here?'

'Club Steward, now if you please. I think the Committee thought that since I've been here since the year dot, I needed a new title to reflect the new paint job. How are you? How have you been? You look great.'

'Not bad. You know me and Brendan got divorced and he's inside?'

'Yeah, he was always a bloody fool. Dint know what a good thing he had. We all knew he knocked you about a lot, sorry about that.'

Sorry it was happening or sorry no one did anything about it, she thought.

But someone did, and it was because of him she was here.

'Well, what will it be, are you staying for a drink, do you know we even have coffee now?'

'Well, that sounds great. I'll have a white coffee please no sugar.'

Maguire pointed to a table in the corner.

'You sit yourself down and I'll bring it over.'

'Why don't you pour yourself one and we can have a catch-up?'

'Sounds like a great idea. Sean can cover the bar.'

Mary sat at the table choosing the chair with her back to the wall and facing the door, another little tip from Joseph. Now she could see anyone coming into the club, friend or foe, and from where she sat, she could also see the half-dozen people sitting in the room plus the two young men playing at the snooker table. She noticed Maguire whisper in the ear of Sean and point in Mary's direction before he arrived at the table placing a tray with two mugs, a milk jug, and a pot of coffee on the table, then he sat down opposite her, but she could see the entrance door over his shoulder.

'Should I be mum? How do you like it?' Maguire asked, but his eyes showed he had another meaning to his question than how she liked her coffee.

She thought she'd play him at his game.

'Strong, with a little milk no sugar, a bit like my men.' She smiled.

This had the desired effect and Maguire's hand trembled slightly as he poured the liquid into the mugs. Mary had always enjoyed the effect her beauty had on men, especially weak men like Maguire. When they were thinking about her, their mouths ran off in all directions trying to impress her. Mary had learnt to ask the right questions and lead them in the direction she wanted, without them realising they were being led. This was when she listened, the trick always being to make them think they were in control of the conversation.

'So, Mary, what brings you back to Newry?'

She'd been expecting the question. She knew the answer could open the whole conversation in the direction she wanted it to go or raise suspicion as to her motives if she got it wrong. She looked over the top of her coffee cup into Maguire's eyes and smiled when she replied which she knew would have the desired effect of knocking him off guard.

'Oh, you know me. Newry has some of the best shops.' She held up the Dunnes bag for effect as she continued, 'I get bored living in the big city sometimes, and I love the drive down here. I take the long way down to Newcastle then through the Mournes to catch up how beautiful it is. Then when I get here, I catch up on my shopping and meet with some old friends as well.'

Now she turned the tables.

'Well, the old town the people and the shops still seem the same. What about you, how have you been?'

She'd deliberately dressed for the occasion in a black button-down blouse with bright flowered pattern skirt, short heeled, red shoes, and just the right amount of make-up; not too much not too little.

It had the desired effect, Maguire started to talk and as he spoke, his answers became more unguarded especially when Mary smiled and on occasion laughed at his attempts to be funny.

'Oh, I'm OK,' he replied. 'I'm still here. The club has a good committee who look after me and listen to my problems and pay me well enough. I'm happy enough.'

'Did you ever marry?'

'Why, are you proposing, Mary?'

'No.' She laughed. 'I've had enough of that lark. Just wondering, I haven't been in here in a while.'

'No. There was one or two who came close but I'm fine and available if you're ever interested,' he said with a wink.

'No, thank you. I've had my fill of men for some time. Brendan saw to that.'

'Ah, sure that's a waste. Is he still inside? Why was he not released with the rest under the Agreement?'

He knew the answer to that question, but she'd play along, anyway. Under the Good Friday Agreement terrorist prisoners were released on licence after two years served no matter what their crime.

'Brendan was an idiot as you know. He did the robbery off his own bat without sanction from the IRA, so his crime was classed as criminal instead of terrorism. He couldn't claim membership of the organisation after disobeying orders.'

'Yes, he always was the idiot, especially with a drink in him.'

Now, Mary thought. Now is the time.

'I know he was an idiot. I was young and immature when I met him and trying to please my mother when I married him. She's old-school Catholic and wanted to see me married in the chapel where she prayed, so the pressure was coming from two fronts Brendan and my mother, and I suppose, in a way, the Catholic religion. The hope of every Catholic mother in those days. Brendan was all right in the beginning as far as husbands go. But then he started to change, and it was only later that I found out why.'

'His involvement with the boys.'

'Yes, if Brendan had one other failing, it was that he was easily led. He got involved with the wrong people who used him, who saw that he was weak and pliable.'

'You mean people like Sean Costello?'

There it was. She knew Maguire was more than just a barman. A good barman doesn't just serve beer…he sees and listens, and he learns to keep what he sees and hears for a day when he might use it for his benefit. This was just what he was doing now, she thought, in the hope of getting closer to Mary.

'Yes, people like Costello. I thought we were supposed to be at peace, that the war was over, but it seems not.'

'Ah, Costello's just a big bully. I've seen his sort many times over. Why, during the whole Peace Process he was in here threatening and blowing his big gob off. "There'll be no peace while I'm around", says he. "No peace until the Brits leave Ireland for good. Anyone who signs up to this peace deal and that includes Adams and McGuinness are traitors and they deserve to be shot".'

Mary didn't interrupt. This was exactly what she wanted Maguire to do, keep shouting his mouth off in the hope she was pleased. She let him continue his flow of words.

'Sure, Costello and a couple of his mates were in here a few times after the Agreement putting a bit of muscle about, letting it be known they'd left the PROVOS and joined this new group, this new gang...the Real IRA. Well, it wasn't long before the word went out from South Armagh telling Costello and his mates to stay away from their places of business, including here. We're just a Republican Club mind. We don't take sides. My customers just want a quiet pint and a bit of peace to drink it.'

'So, where's Costello now?'

'The last I heard, him and a few of his mates were hanging about Dundalk. I did hear that Costello still wants to carry on the war but that he is so afraid of the Brits and the PROVOS that he paid some money to have some plastic surgery done on his face, so no one will recognise him. Did you ever hear such nonsense, the big brute is so ugly it would have cost a fortune, maybe he robbed a few banks?'

Mary laughed again which seemed to please Maguire and helped lift the conversation away from the serious subject it had become.

'Well, I'm just glad people like him are out of my life. I'm like you, Paddy, a bit of peace to do my shopping and a quiet chat with friends over a cup of coffee.'

Maguire took the hint.

'Another cup, Mary?'

'Why not? I have a bit more time to spare, why not?'

It took Mary another hour of general chit chat, smiles, and laughter and finally a promise to return soon before she could escape the Republican Club and what, she had no doubt, the lecherous attempt by Maguire to keep her there. Driving back to Belfast, the thought of Costello changing his appearance kept coming back to her. It was time to get this bastard out of her life once and for all. She would need help to do it. She needed Joseph. She would call him when she reached Belfast.

Chapter Twenty-two

The Manchester rain had reached Irlam when Costello got back. The house was empty and quiet, and he'd gone to his room and lay on the bed, falling asleep almost immediately. When he woke it was dark outside, the noise that brought him out of his slumber was a car engine stopping and car doors closing. He reached for the Browning on the bedside cabinet. He lay in the darkness as he heard the key in the front door and voices, one was Mohammad and the other Lyndsey and one he didn't recognise. Tucking the gun into his belt beneath his T-shirt at his back, he went downstairs to find Lyndsey and two men sitting in the living room.

'Mohammad's in the kitchen putting the kettle on,' said Lyndsey.

He studied the two men sitting on the large couch. They both looked back, one smiling the other frowning.

'Sean, let me introduce you.'

Before she could say more, Mohammad came through from the kitchen with a tray of mugs and a pot of coffee.

'Good, Sean, you're here. Everyone, come and sit at the table, it will be easier.'

Doing as he asked, and with the coffees poured, Lyndsey spoke again.

'As I was saying, Sean, let me introduce you to my friends.' Pointing to the man with the smile she said,

'This is Imtaz, he's from Birmingham and currently studying to be a doctor, Imtaz this is Sean.'

Both nodded acknowledgement to each other. Pointing to the man with the frown she said,

'And, this is Waheed. He lives in London and a true follower as we all are. I told you about his uncle, Azhari Husin, a true martyr, Allah be praised.'

Waheed smiled for the first time showing a gap between otherwise pristine white teeth yet Costello noticed the frown above his eyes seemed to remain.

The colour of their skin was similar to Mohammad, the type specific to Asian men thought Costello, not as dark as an African not as pale as a European's.

They looked like twin brothers apart from the frown, both between twenty-five and thirty years old. Short beards in the style of young Muslim men, both wore jeans with trainers and a casual denim shirt. Similar in every way except Waheed was the more serious or maybe it was just because Imtaz seemed to smile more. It might have been the frown, but, Costello thought, this guy had more history in this game.

'Pleased to meet you,' they said almost in unison.

Costello noticed Imtaz had a slight Birmingham accent.

'Well, where are we now?' Costello asked Lyndsey, 'Can you bring everyone up to date?'

'Sure, only you and Mohammad know our true purpose in meeting here tonight.'

The two new arrivals said nothing just listened, paying attention to every word without any hint of expectation or surprise.

Lyndsey spoke, looking at each in turn.

'Before we start, Mohammad is going to use this device to sweep the room and your phones for bugs.'

She produced a small black electronic device like a mobile phone with two large dials on the front and handed it to Mohammad. She then took her own mobile phone, switched it off, and placed it in the empty fruit basket in the middle of the table.

'Please turn off your phones and put them in the basket.'

Everyone did as she asked, then Costello spoke.

'I thought this was a safe house?'

'It is, Sean, but like you, I've been able to stay one step ahead of the enemy by trusting no one; sometimes not even myself. This way we can all talk freely and in confidence from the start. When we've checked the room, I'll chair the meeting, so we don't get bogged down with too much conversation.'

All nodded their agreement as Mohammad first swept the device over the phones then slowly moved round the room, paying attention to any electrical equipment, before sitting back at the table.

'All clear, we can proceed,' he said.

'Good. Now, as I was saying I don't want to get bogged down in too much discussion of who we are and where we're from, this is not important. Let it be enough to say we're all soldiers in the great war against the infidel the Great Satan, the West.'

'If we're to fight the Great Satan as you say, why is this infidel here, I know you and I trust you. You are the great White Widow. We all know what you've sacrificed for the cause, but we don't know this Irishman?'

It had been Waheed who had spoken. Lyndsey had been expecting the question, it was one that had been asked by her masters in Tehran when she first proposed the whole idea.

'Yes, you might consider Sean the infidel and so he might be, but he is a dangerous one and one who has great skills. Skills he has used to kill our enemies and he has offered them to help us in our cause and in this operation in particular. I've known Sean for many years, and he is a great soldier in the fight against our common enemy: The Great Satan. If I'm willing to trust him and vouch for him, are you willing to follow my instructions to help us succeed in what will be a blow to the West that'll rock them to their foundations?'

Waheed looked Costello in the eyes and smiled, showing the gap in his white teeth.

'I'm happy to accept your word, and I'll work with this man to destroy our common enemy for now.'

'Is it the agreement of us all that we work together to see this done?' she asked.

Around the table each in turn replied, 'Yes.'

When he said yes, Costello looked at Waheed.

I'm going to have to watch my back with you, my little Islamic arse kisser, he thought. When this is over, if you're still alive, I'm going to put a bullet through that pretty little gap in your teeth and maybe one in that frown, right between your eyes.

Waheed could see Costello looking at him and he noticed the strange smile he had on his face.

Lyndsey spoke again, 'This team are going to strike a blow against the infidel that'll go down in history as the greatest ever.'

Costello knew the rhetoric and the inclusion of the word infidel was for the benefit of the two newcomers and not directly aimed at him, even though he knew they would class him as such.

'We're going to kill the chief infidel...the British Prime Minister.'

Imtaz and Waheed looked at each other their eyes widened, their smiles broad...the frown still there. They looked for Lyndsey to continue.

'We're going to do it here in Manchester, at the Conservative Party Conference in five days' time.'

'What, no mortars this time?' asked Waheed. Even he knew the fame of the improvised mortar attacks that had killed so many in Northern Ireland and almost killed the British Prime Minister and his cabinet when the IRA had mortared Downing Street itself from a Transit van parked in Whitehall.

Lyndsey continued, 'Not this time, Waheed. This is not an impossible operation, otherwise I wouldn't have come halfway round the world putting myself at great risk of capture or death. Some months ago, when I met Sean in Tehran, what began as the seed of an idea soon flourished after I'd spoken to Mohammad. He's lived in England for some time and has passed information back to his cousins in the Islamic Jihad and Hezbollah. When I spoke to the commanders in Tehran about a joint operation with Sean, they told me to speak to Mohammad and it fit perfectly with the idea. I'll let Mohammad tell you what he told me, and you'll see why we can do this if we all work together. We each have a particular talent and we are all needed for this to run smoothly. Mohammad, can you tell us where you come into it all?'

'Sharon is correct; I'm originally from Iran and a member of Hezbollah. I've lived in England for eight years, five of them here in Manchester where I went to university before getting a job with a large property agent in Deansgate. From my first days in England I've sent home letters and emails to my people in Iran. If I wanted to send something of a sensitive nature, I would travel to the Iranian Embassy in London where the Cultural Attaché would forward it through secure channels. Sometimes, as on this occasion, the people in Iran would contact me if they had follow-up questions or instructions. Again, this was done through the Attaché and we'd meet in Manchester. This is exactly what happened when Sharon showed an interest in this operation. When I was at university, I joined the Conservative Party as a student. I attended meetings and showed interest but nothing more than making myself known to the local Constituency Chairman. I did this because I wanted to attend the Party Conference for which I had to be cleared through a strict vetting procedure – including police checks, and a reference from my local Chairman confirming who I am.'

'You sound like a spy, brother,' said Imtaz.

'You could say that, what I've been doing would probably fall into that category. I attended the last Conference. As usual, I watched, listened, and reported back. I paid attention to the security surrounding the Conference itself from the outer perimeter of ordinary policing to the inner perimeter of heavily armed police and specialist officers. The whole area is surrounded by high fences and barriers. To gain access, you must wear a Conference identification card which has a barcode that's scanned once on access through the outer barrier gate and a second time when you pass through a large tent fitted with full body and baggage scanners. This is manned by police and Conference security staff, and all this before you pass into the main Conference building.

'The Midland Hotel, where the top government officials, including the PM, and party people stay during the Conference, backs on to the square leading to the Conference Centre. That's where I saw the Prime Minister leave the hotel on the day of his main speech and walk with his bodyguards across the square – information I passed to Tehran two years ago.'

Mohammad stopped speaking, this was as much as he wanted to say at this time, now it was time to hear from others.

Lyndsey turned to Costello.

'Sean, can you tell everyone where you think we are now?'

Costello took his time looking each in the eye in turn before he spoke.

'First, let me say when Sharon and I first began to explore the possibility of such an operation, the one thing we both agreed on was that this would be an operation for serious, professional people, not a bunch of amateurs. That's why you're here. Each one of you has a proven track record of working for your cause, whatever that may be. If we're to be successful, we must work together. As Sharon has already said, even if we have opposite ideas of who the enemy is.' Costello looked at Waheed.

'The information brought by Mohammad has helped bring us here to formulate a plan of attack. We each have a part to play which will become clearer to you over the next few days. We need to be armed. If you're in danger of capture, you'll have to shoot your own way out. We cannot let the enemy know our plan. I've already carried out the observation of the hotel and Conference areas, and I'll do so once more before the security barriers are put in place. I recommend that you all do the same to familiarise yourselves with the area as well.'

Costello opened his tourist map on the table and pointing to it, continued, 'This is a simple tourist map you can buy from any newsagents in the city. The beauty of it is you can pass yourself off as a tourist looking for places of interest. Mohammad, you already know the area well, so you won't need one. Waheed and Imtaz, I want you both to work together and get to know the area well, especially this location just outside the security zone. The final plan is starting to take shape in my head. If the attack is to happen successfully, it will be on Wednesday, 2 October.'

Costello let what he'd said sink in, and then Lyndsey spoke again.

'We must remember we'll all be working on the ground of the enemy. This enemy has one of the biggest and most successful intelligence and security organisations in the world. Our own security must be airtight. Mohammad will sweep the room for bugs every time we meet here. Mohammad, you, Waheed, and Imtaz will stay here until the operation day. When it's over, if we're still alive and safe, we all make our own ways back to our safe locations whether here in England, Iran, or Ireland wherever. Sean, I've booked you a room in the Hilton in the name of Mr Paul Jordan.'

She took an envelope out of her bag and handed it to him.

'There is money and a credit card in Jordan's name. I wanted you to be closer to the target area so that you can observe the day-to-day changes to the conference zone. I managed to get you a room looking in the direction of the Conference Centre. I know it's some distance between the Hilton and the Midland Hotel, but you should be able to view the whole area from the safety of your room. This arrangement will be good for our security with less travelling back and forth between here and Manchester needed. Waheed and Imtaz, you work together for now and carry out your own observations. Sean, no offence to anybody here but a white man walking about with Asian men in Manchester is not usual and could draw unnecessary attention...the kind we don't want. Sean, is your equipment secure?'

'Yes, in a secret compartment in the van in the garage.'

'Good, let's leave it there until nearer the time. Mohammad can drop of us at the Hilton now and collect some Glock pistols from our

Iranian brothers for each of you. We will all be armed for the duration of the operation.'

'I'm OK,' said Costello. 'I have my Browning.' He moved his shirt to let them all see where he'd secreted the weapon when they'd arrived.

'So, Mohammad, it's just you, Waheed, and Imtaz for the Glocks. Like Sean, I have my own weapon.'

She then placed a piece of paper on the table with a set of numbers on it and their names beside them.

'These are your numbers, make sure you save each other's on your phones. Don't worry about security. If you do need to talk to each other on the phone, I'm sure you're wise enough to not be specific.'

When everyone had saved the numbers, Mohammad took the paper to the sink in the kitchen and burnt it.

'Imtaz and Waheed, your only purpose here is to work on this operation. Mohammad will see to whatever you need. Any questions?' she asked.

No one answered.

'OK, we all know our tasks, let's get to work and we can meet back here in two nights' time. Mohammad, can you drop us back in the city? Sean, can you get your bag?'

Both nodded agreements. While Costello went upstairs, Lyndsey took Mohammad to one side and whispered, 'I don't know what it is, but I have a strange feeling about Waheed. I want you to keep a close eye   on   him.'

Chapter Twenty-three

The hop to Manchester in the Puma was uneventful. The noise from the engines made it difficult to hold any sort of conversation. The talk was general with everyone catching up with what each one had been doing and even some chat between April Grey and Joe Cousins on buying property in the Oxford area. Reece was pleased with the team. He knew they were professional enough to know when they could relax and when they needed to be back in the zone.

When they landed at Barton Aerodrome on the outskirts of the city, Reece noticed another Black Puma parked on the grass near to where they touched down. The Aerodrome was just outside Manchester, its two grass runways about five miles from the centre of the city. Reece could see from the banners on the perimeter fencing that it was also the location for private light aircraft and helicopters, and flight training schools.

Now Barton would be their home for the duration of Operation Longshot. They, along with the SAS team allocated to them, would be taking over one of the two large hangers.

When the rotors had stopped, a man approached the team and asked, 'David Reece?'

'I'm Reece.'

'Excellent, I'm Geoff Middleton the Troop Commander. Welcome to Barton. Let me show you where you'll be staying.'

He was around six-foot tall with a shock of blonde hair; he was clean shaven with dark brown eyes. He looked fit with a slight tan and he moved quietly without effort.

'This way everyone.'

As they walked towards one of the large dark green hangers, Reece noticed a lot of people about.

'I know what you're thinking,' said Middleton. 'How secure is this place? My thoughts exactly when we arrived this morning, but apparently, they're used to large numbers of troops and police coming and going in the run up to the Conference, so no questions are asked. The hanger is surrounded by a fence with a secure key padded entrance door. The code is easy to remember: Battle of Hastings – ten sixty-six. My own little joke when I changed the code this morning, I thought what better, after all it was a long shot with the arrow that hit Harold in the eye.'

Smiling, he opened the door and waved everyone through.

Reece was beginning to take to this man. He'd seen this same self-depreciating type of humour before in people who, despite doing a very dangerous job, could still laugh at themselves and the situation they were in. The inside of the hanger was exactly as Reece expected: a large cavernous building with no windows, doors front and rear, split into three large sections by heavy dark sliding doors from floor to ceiling, making three large roomed areas.

'This is your living area.' Geoff pointed to the first sectioned off area. 'The middle section is the general comms area with links for us, the police, and a separate link for your team in London. All the comms links can be combined when needed. The third section at the rear is where me and the boys are bedding down. We had a basic briefing at the head-shed in Hereford this morning so once you've settled in could you come along and bring us up to speed?'

'No problem, see you in fifteen minutes.'

The section allocated to the SG9 team had all the home from home comforts you would associate with a camping trip: basic to say the least, camp beds, blow-up mattresses, a square table with six hard chairs.

No relaxing here, thought Reece.

He threw his bag on the first bed. April took the last knowing the toilet and washroom facilities were going to be the only private place to change. She'd been on many operations before and was used to such places. Reece went to the middle section of the three partitions to find Middleton and the rest of his eight-man team. Two communications officers manned the radio desk and phones. Talking to one of the operators was a senior police officer, the badge on his shirt's epaulets showing he was the Assistant Chief Constable. When he saw Reece, he came over and shook his hand.

'Mr Reece, hello, I'm Graham Lockwood, Gold Commander for the Conference. Whitehall tells me I'm to give you whatever you need but as that's all they've told me. The floor is yours.'

Reece took in Lockwood; he thought he was shorter than most police officers he knew and put him at around forty but with a shock of grey hair that made him look older.

'Pleased to meet you, sir. I presume Whitehall also told you we don't have much time?'

'Yes, they did say the period covered the Conference dates next week.'

Turning to the room, Reece knew the more information he could give everyone the better result the outcome would be. The seated SAS CQB team reminded him of his Special Branch days and briefings such as this. The men in front of him looked fit and alert. They would know that every piece of information would make their job that much easier and the targets that much easier to identify.

Reece brought them up to date with the intelligence he'd received from Mary. 'We don't know the numbers, exactly who they are, or even how they intend to carry out the attack, but we do know the lead terrorist is an Irishman called Sean Costello originally from South Armagh. We have old photos of him which I'll have distributed to you. We have border agencies checking for arrivals and CCTV from Ireland. We will also be checking the CCTV around the area of the Conference. The photo and the information aren't for distribution to the press at this time. Geoff, I'll send the rest of my team to meet with you guys later so that you're all familiar with each other. We will be out on the ground getting to know the area around the Conference and I recommend you do the same but keep it low key. If these people are already in the area, they'll be switched on and on the lookout for anything out of place and could potentially know some of our surveillance techniques.'

'We can make the Conference zone airtight,' said Lockwood.

'I know, but that would do two things: Alert the press and spook the terrorists. That's why the PM has rejected any such overkill in security measures. His own security detail will be aware of a threat increase but nothing more specific than that. Our job is to find these people and stop them before they even get close to him. I'll keep you all updated on any new intelligence we receive, of course. Our communications will be filtered through London and here. Don't underestimate these people. They are determined and more than experienced in what they do, our job is to stop them.'

'Mr Reece,' said Lockwood. 'Please give your team members one of these.'

He handed Reece black armbands with the word *Police* in large white letters written on them.

'They won't protect you from bullets but in a confusing situation they might just save your life.'

'Thank you. May I suggest we meet back here tomorrow at 1800 for any updates? If there're any questions I'll try to answer them?'

No one spoke. Reece knew from experience that the CQB team would spend their time checking equipment, comms, and maps, getting to know the targets and the target area. Questions would come later if they needed to know more.

'Just one more thing, Mr Reece,' said Lockwood. 'All this interagency stuff in such a small area worries me. My central command room is in the city and yours is here. I don't want us all shooting at each other by mistake.'

'As I've already said, Commander, I am in total control of this operation. Everyone will be told what they need to know and if I want people to stay out of our way they stay out of our way. I will, however, let you send one or two officers from your communications team to work here and they can keep you up to date with anything I see fit. The operation code name is Longshot. If that word goes out over your network, everyone should be aware that Special Forces are on the ground and they're to hold fast and wait for my instructions.'

'I'm happy with that. Here, you better have these as well.'

Lockwood handed Reece two key fobs.

'There are two black, unmarked, Range Rovers fully fuelled and ready to go outside for you and your team.'

'Many thanks, sir, now we can get out and about right away.'

'I must warn you, Mr Reece, my men will be especially alert anyway so please ensure that your people don't bring themselves to their attention unnecessarily. Your organisation is unknown to us. London told me not to ask questions, throwing the Official Secrets Act at me, so I'm not asking any questions. I'm just going to assume that you're part of the Security or Secret Service. I'm not happy. I don't like secret soldiers in the middle of my operation, and I told them so. But there it is, I've been told I have to accept it. I only ask that you keep me informed and, in the loop, as much as possible.'

'You don't have to worry about anything that's my job, just do what I tell you and we'll all get along nicely.'

Lockwood looked shocked at being spoken to this way but decided not to make an issue of it turned and left.

Reece knew Lockwood wanted to know who Reece and his people belonged to. Lockwood didn't need to know, nor would he ever know who SG9 and the Department really were. The MI5 cards were for such an occasion; giving Reece and his team the freedom of movement they needed. Anyway, the names on the cards were false though the cards genuine, a gift from MI5 to Jim Broad for use in just such an operation.

'Geoff, are your team familiar with the general area of the operation and how to get there quickly?'

'Yes. From the maps and aerial photographs, but the city roads can be busy at times, so we'll be out in vehicles at different times checking routes and traffic. We have the Puma on standby, so we can rope down if needs be and the Commander has allocated us a room in the Conference building itself where I'll move some of the team when the PM is in the city.'

'Good, I'll have one of my team to come in and establish comms links. Now, we'll get out on the ground ourselves then I'll get back to you later.'

Reece went back to the SG9 team who were now settled into their section of the hanger. They were sitting round the small table where he joined them. After bringing them up to date on his discussion with Lockwood and the SAS team he told them what was next.

'Right, let's get out and see the lay of the land. April, you're with me for now. Joe and Steve, you take the other Range Rover. First stop for me is a decent coffee shop, I need a fix. Joe, can you link all our comms before you go, including through London?'

'Not a problem,' said Joe.

The mobile phone in Reece's pocket came to life. Looking at the screen he saw Mike.

'I have to take this,' he said as he walked outside the hanger putting the phone to his ear. As he pressed the answer button, his heart raced a little.

'Hello!'

'Oh, Joseph, I'm glad I got you.'

'I told you, I'm always free for you.'

'I'm in Belfast and I'm hoping to catch-up with Kevin O'Hagan. I have a few questions I need to ask him. In the meantime, I needed to bring you up to speed with something I've just found out.'

Reece listened as Mary continued to speak, telling him of her trip to Newry and her conversation with Maguire. Reece, like Mary, was concerned about Costello having a face change.

'That's very interesting. Do you think O'Hagan will know more?'

'Possibly, it's worth a try, you never know.'

'OK, but be careful, don't put yourself in any danger.'

'I didn't know you cared.'

'You know I care, Mary, maybe more than you think.'

There was a long silence on the other end of the phone before she spoke again.

'I care about you too, Joseph, maybe more than you think.'

His heart took that wee jump again and his mouth was dry all of a sudden.

'Well, just be careful. Call me back when you catch-up with O'Hagan.'

'I will do, bye.'

Reece stood for a couple of minutes after the click ending the call. His mind was racing through all the times he'd been with Mary McAuley. He knew he was trying to be professional, trying hard to keep her at arm's length, but even without seeing her or hearing her voice he knew she'd found her way into his soul and he didn't want her to leave.

Chapter Twenty-four

Mary McAuley was having similar thoughts. She'd wanted to hear his voice and see his smile, but for now that would have to wait, she had to find Kevin O'Hagan.

It turned out to be easier than she thought. When she called his number, he answered at once and informed her he was in the Belfast City centre shopping. They arranged to meet at the Castle Shopping Arcade in the Starbucks Coffee shop in one hour. This gave her time to get home and change into something a little more casual. Unlike with Paddy Maguire, this would be more business than seduction, so the clothes would reflect that. A dark blue trouser suit with a white blouse and now that the Belfast sky had turned grey, a casual, lightweight, waterproof jacket.

She found O'Hagan already sitting at a table, ordered a latte, and sat facing him.

'What's happening Mary?'

'I've just been down to Newry for a bit of shopping and a catch-up with old friends. What one of them told me confirms what you were thinking. Sean Costello is definitely up to something big.'

'What did you hear?'

Mary told him of her conversation with Maguire and the concern she had over what she'd heard.

'Costello's up to something, I just know it.'

'I agree. It's what we suspected. Our people in South Armagh say he cleared a hide and got in some sniper practice. The talk is that he's up to something big but not on Irish soil as he's completely disappeared.'

'Maybe he knows better, Kevin, and he's lying low.'

'Whatever it is, if I know Costello, he won't stop until somebody stops him. He won't listen to reasoned argument. Either way, he's determined to be a hero, dead or alive.'

'My worry is that he destroys any good work the Peace Process has brought about.'

'One thing I can assure you about, is that the people at the top won't let that happen. Nothing will get in the way of that. Mr Costello is already a dead man. If the Brits or someone else don't get him, we will. Look what happened to Eamon Collins.'

Mary remembered Collins only too well. He was another bastard who deserved what he got. Collins was a British Customs Officer living in Newry during the Troubles. At the same time, he was also operating as a Provisional IRA Intelligence Officer for the area. During his time, he'd set up many off-duty security forces for gun and bomb attacks, assassination but realistically plain murder. They were easy targets shot in front of their friends and families.

This had been one of the reasons she'd decided to help Joseph.

Collins used his cover as a Customs Officer to allow him easy access back and forth across the many border roads. Then, like many others, he came to the notice of Special Branch and was arrested. He broke under interrogation, spilling the beans on not only his own involvement and actions but naming many of his PIRA friends, leading to widespread arrests. Eventually Collins had withdrawn the statements that had made him a super-grass saying they were made under duress. The judge hearing the trial believed him and set him free. Following his release and the collapse of the case against him, all those he'd named also walked free. Collins was ordered by the IRA to leave the country and to go into exile on pain of death for his betrayal and was warned never to return. But Collins was arrogant and believed his past work for the cause would be enough to allow him to return from America where he'd been living. He returned to the family home in Newry after writing a tell-all book and taking part in a TV documentary about his days in the IRA. But he was wrong to think he was safe or would be forgiven. The IRA, especially the PROVOs, he'd worked with in South Armagh didn't want to forgive or forget. One day, while Collins was out jogging near his home, he met with some of his old comrades who gave him a beating before plunging a large knife into his brain. Thus, all traitors of the cause meet their end. Mary knew the risks she took, but she took the risks to save lives unlike Eamon Collins who lived to take lives even innocent ones.

'I remember Collins all right. He deserved everything he got. I just thought you needed to know what I've heard as soon as possible.'

'I know, and thanks for that. If you hear anything else about Costello, give me a call. Now, I must dash. The wife's expecting me to meet her at Primark to help her spend more money. Don't worry too much about Mr Costello, his days are numbered.'

'Sure, Kevin, see you soon.' She smiled.

When O'Hagan had left, she took her time to finish her latte, making up her mind what to do next. She realised that she'd taken the mobile phone out of her bag and had been holding it for some time. Her subconscious mind had already been telling her what her next step would be. Pressing the buttons, she sent a text to Joseph.

Need to meet, can come to you

A message came back almost immediately.

Can you get to Manchester? Can pick you up?

On my way, will phone you when boarding

Next   stop   Manchester   and   Joseph,   she   thought.

Chapter Twenty-five

The Hilton Hotel in Manchester is just like Hilton hotels the world over, clean, efficient, spacious, comfortable rooms, good staff, and pricier than they should be. The one on Deansgate filled the skyline of the city from miles around. Some would say it was ugly and not sympathetic to other architecture in the area like the Town Hall and Library in St Peters Square, but they were far enough away from the hotel not to matter. One of its main features was Cloud 23 the Cocktail Bar on the twenty-third floor with views of the city from the windows on the forty-seventh floor. With an indoor pool and fitness suite, Costello knew this would be the ideal place to relax while preparing for the task ahead.

After booking in, he found that his corner room on the forty second floor gave him the view he'd hoped for. From the window he could see through his binoculars the rear of the Midland Hotel and the top of the Conference Centre. What he could see only confirmed what he'd originally thought on his ground recce. The wind, the distance, and angle would all combine to make a shot from the Hilton almost impossible and therefore too risky if he was to be successful.

Chapter Twenty-six

Manchester was still in one of those autumn moods with bursts of warm sunshine in between the showers of rain. The temperature this time of year still wasn't cold enough for a heavy coat so jeans and a light sweater under her green Barbour jacket covered all the points needed. Deansgate always seemed to have a gale force wind blowing down it but once you entered any of the side streets or squares, this died down and it could be pleasant again. She met Mohammad in a café that looked across the square at The Great Northern Tower Apartments.

The great thing about cities everywhere, she thought, *was that no one pays attention to anyone else anymore.* They are all lost in their own little worlds. They either had their heads down stuck in a screen or in deep conversation with someone else to the total exclusion to everything going on around them. Lyndsey was sure that this must make it very difficult for someone involved in surveillance. To blend in they would have to make themselves invisible to the people they were following. She supposed it could work the other way if she showed she was looking for surveillance following her and not blending in with the crowd making them aware she was being aware. It was a strange and dangerous game that the fox and hounds played out. One she'd played out on two continents coming close to capture occasionally and having to shoot one of the hounds when she was cornered in Mombasa. That was why her shoulder bag felt a little heavier. The .38 pistol added the extra weight but made her feel more secure. For now, she was sure there were no hounds.

'As you can see from here,' said Mohammad over his coffee, 'the security for the apartments starts at the main entrance door with push button access. I've checked the square and there doesn't seem to be any CCTV coverage of the door. I passed by the door earlier and there appears to be a camera inside covering the entrance. I think that's so the people inside can see who has buzzed their apartment allowing them to buzz anyone in.'

'While we've been sitting here, I've seen a few people coming and going,' said Lyndsey. 'How do we get in there when the time comes?'

'I've been thinking about that. I would suggest I knock on a few doors advertising my agency and hopefully I'll get inside one for a look around. I would pay special attention to the apartments where we'd like the operation to go down from.'

'It sounds easy enough but what about your exposure, your face, your business card?'

'Don't worry, my days here are numbered anyway and this operation will be the one to expose all our comrades whether they like it or not. We will shake their foundations so deeply they would find me, so it's home to Tehran and my family.'

'Worst-case scenario, we go in the night before and take over the apartment and wait. All we'd need is two people: Sean and one other.'

'It would have to be me. With my agency credentials, I would be able to give Sean the cover he needs to get in.'

'No, we need you in the Midland and the Conference area, inside the security cordon. You can update Sean when the Prime Minister and his detail are moving towards the target area. There's no photo on your business card so Imtaz can pretend to be you and go in with Sean the night before.'

'What about you and Waheed, what will you be doing?'

'Don't worry I've been thinking about that, let's just say I have a contingency plan which I'll explain when we next meet up. Right now, I'll finish my coffee, have another walk around, and meet Sean for a cocktail. You keep looking for ways to get us in that building. The easier the better, but no matter what we'll be in there and ready.'

Not for the first time was Mohammad impressed by this woman. Her determination, her coolness, her total commitment to the cause and the task at hand. He had no doubt she was ruthless; ruthless enough to kill anyone who got in the way.

Chapter Twenty-seven

Costello sipped his Tom Collins, the gin refreshing. To his surprise, Lyndsey had settled for a fresh orange juice with plenty of ice. From where they sat next to the window, they had a panoramic view of the city at night. The drink added to the whole feeling of calm. Lyndsey had even smiled once or twice, something he couldn't remember seeing from her for a long time. Maybe she was starting to feel more relaxed.

'I'm glad I got here early enough to get the full lie of the land before they sealed it off.'

Lyndsey brought him up to date and what Mohammad would be doing to get them access to the apartments.

'Imtaz is OK, I don't think Waheed likes me,' said Costello.

'Waheed will do as he is told. He has a strong, built-in hatred of the West since his uncle died. He hates everything with the West, but he'll do his job, as we all will. Now that the security is being increased around the Conference, we all need to be more surveillance aware. I have no doubt there'll be the extra vigilance and CCTV coverage.'

'I've already made a note of the CCTV. I know where they're placed and the area they cover, even the cameras in here.'

'I know. Where we'll slip up is if we draw attention to ourselves, so we need to blend in and avoid being seen, that's what the camera operators will be looking for: something different. Ordinary Joe Public will be unaware of our presence until it's too late. They're too lost in their own little insignificant worlds to realise what's going on around them. I've seen it before in Mumbai and Africa.'

Costello smiled understanding, but his eyes showed nothing.

'That's why I'm a country boy at heart. I hate cities and the people in them.'

Looking out the window at the light below, Lyndsey understood what Costello was saying.

'That's why I live in the east. The cities are busy, but the people have time for each other, time to stop and talk, to look around, and to enjoy life. Anyway, one more drink and I'm off to bed what about you?'

'Another   Tom   Collins.'

Chapter Twenty-eight

Thursday, 26 September 2019

Reece and the SG9 team had spent the next morning getting to know the entire Deansgate area.

Reece had been thinking back to his first days of surveillance training with MI5 in London. As a young Special Branch officer, it had been part of the three-week course. On the first day, they'd each been given a copy of the ABC map guidebook to London and told to familiarise themselves with a specific part of the city. Reece had been allocated the Victoria section as this would be where he would be training day to day. Now he was doing the same in Deansgate, Manchester. Where were the bus stops, the taxi ranks, the car parks? Where was the security strong especially at the entrances and exits?

The team had worked first in the Land Rovers, finding their way around the one-way systems, then on foot, all the time getting used to each other's voice in the earpiece each of them wore. Happy with the progress, Reece told the team to return to Barton where they could study the maps, aerial photography, and the only photos they had of Costello and Lyndsey. Reece phoned Jim Broad to bring him up to date. Broad had been in the communications room in London and had been listing in as they'd carried out their reconnaissance of the Manchester streets. Reece told him about the phone call from Mary.

'She's arriving in Manchester shortly. I'll pick her up and drop her off at a hotel, probably in the Piccadilly area as all the hotels around the Conference are fully booked.'

'I hope what she's got will be worthwhile, David.'

'I'm sure whatever she has will be more than we have right now. The more information we can get the better.'

'OK, keep me updated. I have a meeting with Sir Martin Bryant at nine this evening and it will be good to have something to update him with. Call me if you need me or have something new.'

'Will do.'

Reece told the team he was heading to the airport to pick up his agent and he would brief everyone at midnight.

'Meanwhile, you should get some rest; it's going to be a busy couple of days.'

He hated Manchester Airport. Its three terminals were always busy no matter what the time. He'd just parked up in the arrivals area for Terminal One when the text on his phone told him that Mary had arrived, and she'd be out in a few minutes. He'd talked about drop off and pickups at ports and train stations with Mary in the past. He would always be outside observing her coming and going making sure she was alone, that no one was following, or she hadn't bumped into someone she knew on the journey.

The rain had stopped for now and as he stood by the Range Rover, he could see the front door of arrivals and saw Mary coming out pulling a small cabin bag. No one was following her. Since he'd spoken to her on the phone, he'd felt the anticipation of seeing her again, of being close to her, rising in him. Now, when he watched as she crossed to the carpark, his stomach turned, and his mouth was dry.

It had been ever harder for him to concentrate on the job in hand when he could see her face and remember her voice in his thoughts. They hugged as friends would – close but not too close.

'You look tired, Joseph.'

'Tell me about.' He laughed.

On the drive into the city she brought him up to date. The conversations she had with Maguire and O'Hagan was why she was here, why she had to see him, important enough to see him in person. He reassured her she'd been right to come. The change in Costello's appearance and the fact he'd disappeared only helped to confirm he was already here. Not knowing what he looked like now worried him. It was already like trying to find a needle in a haystack, but this would make it almost impossible. He'd booked Mary into the Premier Inn in Piccadilly. It was a typical franchise hotel cheap but cheerful. Reece carried her bag to the room.

'Have you eaten recently?' he asked.

'No, I'm famished.'

'Me too. Let's find somewhere to eat.'

They found a small café near the main Piccadilly Railway Station. The food was basic, and the café didn't serve alcohol, so it was coffee for two to wash down the meal. Reece moved the conversation away from Costello. He could tell from her face the strain she was under.

'When this is all over, I'll show you the sights of Manchester.'

'When this is all over I would rather you showed me the sights of somewhere warmer.' She smiled.

There it was; that smile. His heart gave another little flutter. Once again, when he was with her, he had to force himself to be professional. *Feelings get in the way*, he thought.

She looked beautiful as always, dressed for business, not pleasure, this time, she still looked beautiful.

'Right, we have a busy day tomorrow. Are you up for it?'

'I'm up for it, as you say but what more can I do? I've told you all I know?'

'I've interviewed Costello in the past. We have the most recent picture of him before his face lift. You've met him, you know him personally. Between us, we just might get lucky and see him before he can do any damage. You know the mannerisms that make him who he is. He can change how he looks but he can't change who he is. He can't change his height, how he walks, what he sounds like, how he speaks, his voice, his accent. It's going to be dangerous, Mary, especially if we get close enough to confirm who he is, but I'll be with you every step of the way. Are you OK with that?'

'If he sees me first, I'm dead, at the very best I'm blown.'

'That's worst-case scenario but I intend to get to him first. A dead Costello doesn't talk. But I need your help. I need you with me on this.'

'It's nice to be needed.'

There was that wicked smile again but this time there was moisture in her eyes.

He reached over the table taking her hands in his as much to reassure her as to feel the warmth of her skin, to be close to her. She squeezed lightly back.

'OK, I'll do it but only for you, Joseph.'

It was his turn to smile.

'I'll walk you back. You get a good night's sleep, and I'll pick you up in the morning.'

'What, no night-cap?'

'Well, maybe just the one, I'm driving.'

When he left her at the hotel, he hugged her, holding her closer and for longer than normal. She responded by pulling her arms around his shoulders. It was then he knew he couldn't wait or hold back any longer. When his lips met hers, he could feel a surge of electricity flowing between them both. When they separated both were breathing heavily.

'I'm sorry, that wasn't very professional of me, but I've wanted to do that for a very long time.'

'Don't be sorry, Joseph, I've wanted you to kiss me, to hold me. What do we do now?'

His professional head kicked in, overruling his heart once more.

'I promised you when this was over, I wanted to see more of you. I want that more than ever, but for now, I need to keep my head for the job in hand. Can you understand, can you wait?'

'I don't have much of a choice. I'll wait, but not forever. See you tomorrow then,' she said as the lift doors closed and took her to her room.

Not for the first time did he admire the strength in this woman. When she'd gone, he realised he was still breathing heavily, his pulse racing.

I'll see you tomorrow and for longer to come, he thought.

Reece liked driving through cities at night. Less traffic, more time to think. Peoples' laughter as they moved between the restaurants, pubs, clubs, theatres, and parties. A city at night has a breathing, living sound all of its own.

His thoughts were still of Mary, her face, her brown eyes, and dark hair, her smile. His thoughts were interrupted by the in-car phone system.

'Hello?'

'Hello, David, can you talk?' It was Jim Broad.

'Yes, I'm using the hands-free. Just dropped Mike off. I'm on my own.'

'We have some news which might be helpful. The ports' people have been checking back over their CCTV and records as we requested, and they may have something. A couple of days ago a small white van with one male on-board landed at Holyhead port from Dublin. The van went through without a close stop check but a few things have been highlighted. The registration shows it came from Crossmaglen, but a quick check with the local police shows the real van originally came from a farm belonging to a recently dead farmer. There're some grainy images of the driver. The height and build fit Costello's description but the driver's wearing a baseball cap, so we can't be sure. The interesting bit is that CCTV was able to follow the van's movements from Wales through to the M56 then the M6 and then leaving the motorway at Warrington.'

'That is interesting. If he was heading straight to Manchester, he would have stayed on the fifty-six.'

'I've sent you the CCTV and informed the police to be on the lookout for the van. It might just be the break we're looking for. Anything new from Mike?'

'No, but I'm going to keep her here. She knows Costello better than any of us and that might just give us the last piece of information we need to complete the jigsaw of what's happening.'

'OK, if I get anything more, I'll be in touch, you do likewise.'

'Will do.'

This was going to be another long night looking at CCTV recordings before getting to bed. Reece knew all the activity of the day would make it difficult for his brain to switch off and for the sleep to come.

Chapter Twenty-nine

Mohammad had wasted no time; he'd carried out more research into the apartment block and noticed on the *Right Move* website that there were two for sale and a few for rent. Apartment C13-1 and apartment C6-3 both in the region of £300,000 or £1,000 per month for the rental properties. The history of sales in the building showed that they had two or three coming up for sale on a yearly basis, so this was a lucky break. He spent more time digging further and identified two of the rental apartments, fully furnished for immediate occupancy. He phoned Lyndsey and arranged for her and Costello to meet with him at the apartments later that morning. Then he phoned the agent for the properties and arranged viewings for eleven at the two for sale and two of the rentals which seemed to fit Costello's requirements.

Costello was in the lounge drinking his coffee when Lyndsey sat down beside him.

She told him about her call with Mohammad.

'We can go together as the Webbs and you can have a good look around and see what you think.'

'Sounds like a plan.'

'We'll have a better idea where we stand, and we can bring everyone up to date tonight.'

They met Mohammad outside the apartments at eleven on the dot.

'I just have to buzz the one that's for sale and the agent will let us in.'

'Introduce us as Mr and Mrs Webb, I'll do the rest of the talking,' said Lyndsey. 'Then I'll keep the agent occupied while you two look around.'

'Fine by me,' said Mohammad.

He buzzed a number on the metal keypad for apartment C-13 which was on the first floor.

'I'll buzz you in and you can take the lift to the first floor where I'll meet you,' said a man's voice.

The door opened with a loud click. When they came out of the lift they were met by a young man. Costello thought he was just out of school.

'Hello, I'm Jake, welcome.' He shook everyone's hand.

'Good morning, Jake,' said Mohammad. 'I made the appointment with your office for Mr and Mrs Webb, my clients.'

'Nice to meet you. Let me show you the first apartment which is up for sale.' He spoke as he led the way to the door.

'As I told your office, my clients would like to see both the properties for sale and to rent with a future option to buy,' Mohammad said.

Mohammad knew the commission for Jake would be larger if he sold a property rather than rent one, but the fact they would rent one with a future option to buy would perk him up. The prospect of a rental becoming a sale as opposed to a straight rental improved his commission prospects even more.

'There are eight apartments on each floor four facing front onto the square and four facing the rear of the building. All the apartments are of similar design with two bedrooms except for the top floor which has four penthouse apartments.'

Jake opened the door of number 13 and led the way, still talking as he walked.

'This apartment as you can see looks out to the rear. All apartments have a balcony. This one because it's for sale is, as you can see completely empty of furniture although all the main electric goods, cooker, fridge, washing machine are installed all included in the price.'

'Really, we're more interested in a fully furnished let for now,' said Lyndsey.

'No problem, we have two on the twelfth floor. I'll take you there now.'

Lyndsey looked at Sean, she didn't need to speak. She could see for herself the first-floor balcony gave no view of the target area.

'Great, Jake, let's have a look at them.'

It took another half hour and the inspection of the second rental on the twelfth floor, apartment C-12 for to Costello to nod to Lyndsey that this was the one. Jake had walked her round the fully furnished apartments she'd questioned him for long periods in one bedroom giving Costello the time he needed to check the view from the rear windows and balcony. He took a few discreet photos on his mobile of the main living area and from the glass doors onto the balcony using the zoom on the camera phone he could clearly see the rear door of the Midland.

The monthly rent was £1000 with a deposit of £3000 Jake told Lyndsey.

'I'm happy with that and I think this apartment is perfect. We might need a second viewing if that's all right, but it would be soon if we do.'

'Yes, that's no problem but a property like this is highly sought after so first come first served, as they say.'

'No problem. Mohammad will be in touch with you later today. How quickly can we get the keys?'

Jakes eyes lit up at her answer.

'There's just a little paperwork and once the deposit has been paid, you can have the keys right away.'

'I think it's just what we're looking for. We'll be in touch this afternoon.'

After leaving Jake and the apartment they sat once more in the café looking back towards the building. Looking at the photos on his camera it was Costello who spoke first.

'It's good. I can get a clear shot from there, at least two good ones if needed. Can you cover the paperwork? They might ask for references and credit checks.'

'The credit check I can cover. References might take a little longer and it will take them longer to check than we need but they can be provided. Cash jumps many fences, my friend. At the very least we can ask for another viewing on Wednesday morning do the job and get away. We will meet tonight to go over things and tie up details. In the meantime, I'll go with Mohammad to Jake's office and complete the forms to get things moving. A cash up front offer should get us the keys.'

'While you're doing that, I'll take one more walk from this side to the front door of the building then back to the hotel. The NCP down the street will be ideal to park the van up when we're in the apartment.'

'Until later then. Mohammad can pick us up outside the hotel about seven. I'll see you in the lounge about six thirty.'

Chapter Thirty

Friday, 27 September 2019

Reece hadn't slept well. The pain in his shoulder and the dreams woke him during the night. When he'd returned to the bunker it was late, but the team were still up. They'd been watching the CCTV sent from London tracing the van along the motorways from Holyhead to Warrington. Jim Broad had also contacted the GARDA in Ireland asking for any identification of the driver. The same request had been made of the Irish Ferries shipping line that transported the van across the Irish Sea. Reece had watched the short clips showing a man, tall and lean with the black New York baseball cap, and asked the SAS team to watch too so they had every piece of information he did. He'd also told them about the supposed cosmetic surgery.

The only photos the GARDA and Tom Wilson had of Costello had also arrived. They were of the old Costello; the one Reece knew so well from across the table in the interview room. But if he'd changed his face, as Mary had reported, they wouldn't be much use.

'Concentrate on the eyes people. It's the hardest thing to change,' he told the team. 'The CCTV also gives an idea of how he moves. He walks with a slight stoop, head down looking at the ground and keeping his face hidden from the camera.'

When Reece went to bed the team were still in the communications section going through everything they had.

Now awake, he'd taken two paracetamols for the shoulder pain and given an hour, they'd do the trick for a while. After breakfast he assembled the team.

'Today I want you to check the railway stations, bus stops, and tram routes through the city but especially near the Conference Centre. With a focus on the route in from Warrington. Walk the area again and again and get to know every nook and cranny. I'll pick Mike up and do the same, then let's all meet up for a bite of lunch. There's a Weatherspoon's beside the Town Hall; we can meet there. It will be noisy, but nobody really pays attention to anyone else, so we should be OK to talk. When you're out, don't forget never let your guard down. They're out there too. I know you won't, but I have to say it, anyway.'

'You look tired, David,' said April, saying what they were all thinking.

Reece laughed. 'I always look this way when I'm busy need a long shower and a strong coffee and that's next on my list. Let's get out there, people, and find these bastards. We don't have much time to work with so let's make it count.'

After an almost cold shower and then a large, strong coffee, Reece could feel his body recharging. Standing outside the hanger in the clear morning air, he could see the hustle and bustle of activity around the small airport. He could smell the aviation fuel and see a few of the SAS troopers jogging around the perimeter of the runways keeping up their fitness levels. Mechanics, aircrew, people all mixed together with their own worlds keeping them occupied. Parked up at the end of the runways were three small, single-engine aircraft in the corner of the field close to the farthest hanger. Next to them, a dark Puma helicopter, the one the SAS would use if needs be.

Reece went back inside for one last check with the comms team and found the troop commander with his men around the table going over the CCTV, photos, and maps. Going over the information they have he knew that's what makes them the best at what they do. The training, the shoot-outs, the flash bangs all leading to the dead opponents and successful compilation of the operations they're involved in, plan then plan again. The training, the preparation the skill all combined to ensure the best possible result.

'Have you got everything you need?' asked Reece.

'Yes thanks, as they say PPP...Piss Poor Planning is what fucks up the operation so get the plan right and we will get the job right.'

'Let all your people know that we'll be out on the ground. We need to keep our comms open and linked.'

'Will do. See you later.'

The coffee and the shower had done the trick and the paracetamol had finally kicked in, Reece felt better; refreshed, and ready for the rest of the day. Time to pick up Mary; the thought making him feel even better.

The traffic was light on the drive into Manchester which helped him make good time. He parked up and found Mary waiting in the hotel foyer.

Her dark hair hung loosely around her shoulders. Her clothing showed she was ready for a working day with denim jeans with dark blue trainers a tight-fitting jumper with a light blue short jacket.

'Good morning. Did you sleep well?' he asked.

'Yes, thank you, what about you?'

'Not bad,' he lied. There was no sense in worrying her or telling her he'd spent most of the night between bad dreams and dreams and thoughts about her, with a little shoulder pain put in for good measure.

'Are you ready for a long day?'

'Lead on, McDuff,' she replied.

'I thought we could start with a drive round the centre. Have you had breakfast?'

'Yes, I'm OK thanks.'

'Right, let's go; we can stop for a coffee later. On the way I can bring you up to date on what where we are now. Then I want you to meet the rest of the team later when they grab a bite of lunch, if that's all right by you?'

'No problem. Do they know who I am?'

'They know you're my agent and your code name. The only questions they're likely to ask will be about this operation, nothing else.'

'OK,   let's   go.'

Chapter Thirty-one

The rest of the SG9 team had been out driving around the target area for about an hour. Now they picked up their target they were following on foot. Their unsuspecting quarry a young white male didn't know he was being followed; his every move noted. It was an easy way for surveillance operators to keep sharp and check their communications. Pick a target then follow them for at least one hour without raising the suspicion of the person being followed.

They followed the young man from Deansgate train station into St Peters Square. He'd spent time in some shops moving around the area with a surety that confirmed he knew this part of Manchester. The team took turns, always one in front of the target, one behind, and one keeping level on the opposite side of the street. The comms were working perfectly, and the team eventually joined up with the target when he sat unaware off them in the reference area of the Manchester Central Library.

April Grey sat down two desks to the right of the young man. Joe Cousins browsed the reference books on shelves in front of him while Steve Harrison sat near the exit doors reading today's newspaper copies. April moved close enough to see that the young man was browsing the Internet page for Ernest Hemingway and his life.

A scholar, maybe a budding writer, she thought.

'OK, guys, nearly time to get to Weatherspoon's,' said Harrison over the airwaves. 'Let's go. I think we can call this a successful morning.'

'Roger,' came the responses.

Reece drove through central Manchester and around the area of Deansgate at least four times, all the time watching the traffic, the people, the streets, and the buildings as they passed by. Up close, Mary noticed the change in him from the casual Joseph, who always, to her at least, appeared relaxed and calm, to the Joseph she now saw, concentrated, focused, quiet, intense.

'Are you OK, Joseph?'

'Yes, why do you ask?'

'You seem so distant, as if you're somewhere else.'

'Don't worry about me. I was just thinking if we don't stop these people, I could be responsible for the death of the Prime Minister.'

'Don't be silly. You're doing everything you can to stop them. That's all you can do; no more, no less.'

He smiled. 'Have you been to Manchester before?'

'I came once on a shopping trip to the Trafford Centre when it first opened, a long time ago. We stayed one night, then back to Belfast, not much time for sightseeing. What about you? Do you know Manchester well?'

'Not really, since I arrived, I've driven and walked around this section especially and studied maps and aerial photographs, but I'm getting a feel for the place. I would prefer Belfast or London, even though there seems to be fewer people than London and not as many foreigners, so hopefully Costello will stand out. His favourite landscape would be the countryside, empty roads, hills small towns, and villages like the place he comes from…more room to move about.'

There he goes again, she thought. Back to the work, the Joseph who can't relax, back on the job. Maybe one day she'll see him with his guard down, see the real Joseph underneath, the real man, or maybe he could never change.

'Right, let's find a parking space, then meet with the rest of the team. I'll introduce you as Mike. They already know you're my agent so don't worry about people knowing who you are, who you are doesn't matter to them. Your security is safe. They're here to do a job and you're part of the team that'll help them get that job done.'

'Nice to be wanted.'

'Don't worry, I'll look after you. You'll be with me most of the time, it's just good that they get to know you and you them. Knowing each other in the flesh so to speak makes things easier when we are out there doing the job. Anyway, I'm starving. I need a bite to eat, how about you?'

'I'm famished.'

Reece parked just of the Town Hall Square in one of the side streets and put a few coins in the parking meter displaying the ticket on the inside of the windscreen. They found the rest of the SG9 team in the Weatherspoon's restaurant already waiting at a table near the back with two spare chairs for Reece and his agent. This was the Joseph she wanted to know, was getting to know, to see him working with his team, the secret Reece. The one she thought cared, the one she wanted, more than he knew. As they entered the restaurant, she'd noticed the way he looked around without moving his head.

Would there ever be a time when the professional side would relax, just switch off, she thought as he placed his hand in the small of her back and guided her to the table where the rest of his friends were sitting. Reece introduced her as Mike and going around the table, introduced the rest of the team, first names only; no need to complicate things.

'Well, how has your day gone?' Reece asked no one in particular.

'We've had a good morning getting to know the place better,' said Joe. 'We took a dummy target from the station to the library. Good run, good comms. We're ready for any surveillance foot or mobile in this area.'

'Great, before we go on, have you all ordered, we're starving.'

'Yes, our drinks food on the way, you need to order at the bar. Our table number is 44,' said Cousins.

'What would you like?' Reece asked Mary.

'Whatever your having.'

Reece went to order at the bar. Mary noticed the people around the table looking at her. She smiled and looked back.

'Welcome, Mike, it's nice to meet you at last,' said April.

'It's nice to meet you all too,' said Mary.

'Well, I can tell you from everyone here we very much appreciate what you're doing for us and Joseph,' Grey replied.

Reece returned and sat beside Mary, placing a glass of wine in front of her and a large diet Coke with ice for himself on his beer mat.

'Now we're all acquainted, I want to bring everyone up to date. We're still catching up on the CCTV and ANPR from the port in Holyhead to the Manchester area. The PSNI are also checking out the van but all the family will say is that it belonged to their dead father and they sold it to an unknown male for a few hundred quid. The police are trying to put pressure on them because it's against the law not to inform the DVLA who you sell a vehicle to, but the family don't seem too worried about not doing things by the book. The Prime Minister will deliver his main speech on Wednesday afternoon and he's staying in the Midland for the duration.'

The food arrived for the other three SG9 operators. Reece waited until the waiter had left before he spoke again.

'I'll work with Mike and you three should work together and I want us all to be in contact at all times. For the rest of the day we should keep going over the ground, getting to know every inch of the ground.'

Reece continued to speak as they ate, 'We can only speculate to the who and when, but we have no ideas on the how. Answer that and we can end this and go home to our own beds.'

He knew he was speaking to professionals, no sense in teaching them how to suck eggs when they already knew the game and what was needed.

'Mike has joined us at great risk, but I've asked her to come to Manchester for two reasons. One, so we could all meet as a team and get to know each other. Two, she knows Costello personally. Even though he may have changed his appearance, she knows how he moves how he walks, how he stands, how he dresses. The habits of a lifetime that are hard to change. It might mean Mike having to get close enough to put herself in danger. That's where we come in. If she does point out Costello, we need to be ready, we need to be there. Not only to protect Mike and the Prime Minister but to make sure Costello and his friends don't get away. Mike knows the dangers and she is willing to take the risk. Is everyone happy with this?'

'That's what we're here for,' said Harrison. 'I hope the boss, the PM, and everyone else realises the risk we're all running. If we could get a little more information that would help.'

'Don't worry, Steve, that's what we're working on. Everyone knows the risks. There are no guarantees, but the PM has decided he won't hide from terrorism. It's our job to do our best, that's all we can do. Mike and I'll go for a walk after lunch and walk off some of these fish and chips. I want you all to go back to the hanger for eight tonight for any update.'

'Great. We will do a couple more runs around and we can all catch up later,' said Harrison.

Reece stood. 'Well, Mike, do you fancy a walk?'

'Yes, that sound great.'

Leaving Weatherspoon's, Reece walked in the direction across the front of the Town Hall Square. For a change it wasn't raining, and the wind was slight, with the sun breaking through white clouds.

People were moving through the city, but it's not as busy as London, he thought.

'We can walk the whole block, so you'll have a better feel for the place in case you're on your own at any time. What did you think of the team?'

'Scary and quiet, but I think strong too.'

'Scary?' He laughed. 'I think they would love to hear that. If I met them cold like that for the first time, I would probably have to agree with you. The one thing to remember is they're the best at what they do. They cover each other's back, and now they'll cover yours.'

They continued to walk down Deansgate and as they passed the front of the Hilton, Costello watched them from the café lounge through the tinted windows. The man was familiar to him, he was sure he'd seen him somewhere before. The woman he defiantly knew.

'So, Mary McAuley, what brings you here and who's this man you're with? I know him, but from where?'

He left the hotel and crossed the street to follow them; keeping at least one hundred yards behind. He watched them cross the road at the bottom of Deansgate and go into the railway station. He decided not to follow them further. Having travelled through the station himself he knew it was small with nowhere to hide, it was too open an area where he risked being seen. They might be getting a train or tram, they might even come back out, so he couldn't hang around, he needed to get back to the hotel to call Lyndsey and put in an important call to Ireland.

Reece felt that sixth sense he'd felt many times before. He knew they were being watched and he'd studied the glass panel on the station wall and using its reflection he could see a man turn and go back the way they'd just come. He couldn't see him clearly, and he could be jumping to conclusions, but Reece felt certain. The man had been following them, watching them, and he was wearing a dark baseball cap. By the time they were through the entrance and Reece could risk a look over his shoulder, the man was gone.

'What is it?' Mary asked.

'I'm not sure. Stay here.' Reece ran back down the station steps and across the road in the direction he'd seen the unknown man but there was no sign of him. He returned to where Mary was waiting and watching.

'Nothing, and something, I don't know for sure but let's get back to the car.'

Reece took Mary a different route to the one they'd used, passing the Bridgewater Hall, and following the tram lines back to the Library Square. As they walked, he spoke to the team.

'Alpha One to Alpha Team, I'm leaving Deansgate Station heading back to the car near the Library Square. An unknown male with a dark baseball cap was behind us for a while on Deansgate but did a U-turn, and might still be in that area, can you check, over?'

'Roger, I'll take a look,' replied Grey.

'Just being careful. It might be nothing but felt a little strange.'

They walked the rest of the way back to the car in silence. Reece drove out of the city centre to the Lowry Centre in Salford. He used the time driving to check for followers. He was sure there were none. At the Lowry, they found a quiet corner in a café. Mary could see his eyes checking the faces of the shoppers outside.

'Are you OK?' she asked.

'Yes, I'm just being careful.'

'Who do you think that was?'

'I don't know. I'm not even one hundred per cent sure he was following us, but I'm not taking any chances. It's slim, very slim but I'm going to get the team to continue to concentrate in the Deansgate area. We can find ourselves on the CCTV too. It will show if anyone was following us. Hopefully then we will have a clearer picture. And, if it was Costello, then he had to have picked us up somewhere near there as we walked through. And he still just might be in the area. But don't worry, I checked on the way here, no one is following us, we can relax…for   now.'

Chapter Thirty-two

Costello went straight back to the Hilton having phoned Lyndsey on the way and asking her to come meet him.

'You sure it was this Mary McAuley?'

'Definitely.'

'And this man. You know him too?'

'I've seen him before. I'm not sure where but I'm sure I know him. It will come to me.'

'Could he be one of us?'

'Maybe. But I don't think so. The feeling I got when I saw him was danger, something from my past.'

'Do you think they saw you?'

'No, that's why I didn't follow them into the station or get too close. I came straight back here. But I checked, no one followed me.'

'We need to find out what McAuley is doing here. Can your people at home find out? Who knows, she might be here with a boyfriend for a dirty weekend or just shopping, but it's the kind of coincidence I don't like.'

Costello didn't like it either. The unknown man still bugged him.

'Yes, it will take a few hours, but I should be able to find out.'

'In the meantime, stay in your room until I call you or you get a reply from Ireland.'

'I need to switch off for a while, anyway. I find when I do that and relax my memory chip it reboots the computer in my head it will check in and bring up who this guy is.'

He left her and returned to his room. Using his mobile phone, he dialled the number of a trusted contact in South Armagh. The familiar voice on the other end asked the caller to leave a message.

'Hi, mate, it's me call me back as soon as you can.'

Costello   lay   on   the   bed   and   closed   his   eyes.

Chapter Thirty-three

Reece dropped Mary back at her hotel.

'I'll catch-up with you later. Do you fancy going out for a meal tonight?'

'That would be lovely. Do I need to dress up or are we slumming it?'

'Somewhere in between would be nice. Pick you up around eight.'

'See you then.' She kissed him on the cheek as they parted.

Once again, he felt the butterflies in his stomach take flight.

'Alpha One to Alpha Team, where are you now?'

It was Cousins who answered.

'We're still around Deansgate, over.'

'Roger that. Can we all meet in the café in the Town Hall in twenty, over?'

'Roger,' the team replied one by one.

Reece found another parking space near the Town Hall. Keeping the change for these parking meters was costing him a small fortune. He made a point to include the cost in his expenses sheet. Unlike James Bond, real secret agents had to account for every penny they spent, that meant receipts and forms in triplicate.

The inside of the Manchester Town Hall brought an old-world atmosphere with the building housing and excellent café and the council offices together. Reece had visited the café in the past and always enjoyed its relaxing atmosphere; the open space inside made it cool and welcoming.

The team were already there at a corner table. He briefed them again on the man he'd seen.

'What I didn't say in front of Mike was that I'm sure it was Costello. Mike didn't see him, and I can't put my finger on it but it's my gut telling me it was him. The comms people have got back to me with the CCTV coverage which they uploaded to my mobile. Mike has seen it but the quality's not great so she couldn't be sure.'

Reece showed the grainy coverage of Deansgate and they could see Reece and Mary walking towards the station and a tall man wearing a baseball cap who appeared to be keeping pace with them from the footpath on the opposite side of the street. Although they could estimate the man's height there was no clear shot of his face even when he turned and walked back towards the camera before disappearing out of shot.

'Many times, during surveillance, you get that gut feeling as you call it, that sixth sense. It paid not to ignore it and nine times out of ten I was right to listen to it. So, what now?' said Harrison.

'Well, I think we can assume that it was Costello and he spotted me and Mike. We hadn't been walking long so he must have been somewhere in this area.'

Reece placed his map on the table.

'This is the route we walked after we left you in Weatherspoon's. I don't think he was following us too long or I would have spotted him earlier. So, if he wasn't dropped off by a car, we need to start paying attention to the main Deansgate area. The cafés, restaurants, bars, and hotels. If he has been travelling in and out of the city, if not by car then public transport the trains and buses then we need to get Lockwood's people to step up their CCTV coverage in the area. They might even have him following me today although they should already be doing that, anyway. I'll give him my timeline for walking down Deansgate earlier see what they come up with. We might get lucky and see where he went after bugging out from following me.'

'The Hilton Hotel is smack bang in the middle of where you were walking, we should certainly check it out,' said Cousins.

Reece had been studying the map,

'Good idea, we need to take a look, but we should always work in the belief they're here. We need to be careful at all times, keep your eyes open, and everyone keep in touch.'

'David, if you're right, and I think you are, why did he stop following you when you went into the station?' asked April Grey.

'You've got to remember that essentially, Costello is a coward. All his kills are with the built-in caveat that he can catch his target by surprise, and he can get away afterwards. For him to follow me into the station would be to follow me into an area he was unsure off with a confrontation scenario he didn't know. He would have assumed I was armed, maybe Mike too. He would also have been worried that we might be meeting other armed colleagues in the station. Too many unnecessary risks. He will now be more aware of our presence, so he'll be taking more precautions, even more alert, we must be the same.'

'Do you think he knows who you are?' asked April.

'He just might remember me from our days of bumping into each other between shoot-outs and question sessions. He would know Mike, she worked with the top tier of the Provisional movement and lived in Newry during the Troubles, so he would know her for sure. I'll be meeting up with her later. Let's do a little more digging in the Deansgate area and see what we come up with.'

'As he has spotted you, he must be spooked. I think you should operate in the area using the Range Rover, the tinted windows will give you the advantage should you need it. I can check the Hilton,' April said.

'Good idea let's do that, but everyone keep in touch. Anything at all let me know. I'll bring London up to date and get the boss to speak to Lockwood and I'll have a look at the CCTV myself. Let's not forget people if you do spot this guy, we have to put him down no second chances no calling on him to surrender because he won't.'

Chapter Thirty-four

When the phone blinked into life, Costello's first thought was that it was Ireland calling back, but instead it was a text from Lyndsey.

I will pay the bill. Booking out now. M picking us up in twenty.

Costello packed, making sure to wipe down as many surfaces as possible, so no fingerprints were left. Then he went down to meet her in the lobby, Mohammad was waiting in the car outside.

The drive to Irlam took another thirty minutes but in total silence as they all looked for the suspected security presence, but there was none. Inside the Irlam house, and after Mohammad had done another sweep, they sat around the table. Imtaz and Waheed were still in Manchester.

'Why did you follow them, Sean, why did you expose yourself?' asked Lyndsey.

'I'm sure they didn't see me. I recognised Mary McAuley and I'm sure the man she was with worked for the security forces in Northern Ireland, I can't remember in what capacity, but it will come to me. I'm still waiting on my contact in Ireland getting back to me then hopefully, I'll know more.'

'Well, we always knew there were risks, but by your actions you could have put us all at risk. I just hope you're right and they didn't see you, but we can't take chances. The fact that they were in Deansgate could be expected. McAuley can be taken care of later. If we're successful, you can have the pleasure of that, Sean. Still, it's good that you did spot them before they spotted us. If they're that close, then it could only be a matter of time before they check the hotel and even with our cover, we're at risk. I'll book us into a hotel further out from the city for the next few days. Mohammad, where are we with the apartment?'

'I have good news. I called with the estate agents like you said. The forms were fairly straight forward and after I showed young Jake the three-grand cash for the deposit, I can pick the keys up on Tuesday afternoon.'

'Were my passport and credit ID OK?'

'Yes, everything went smoothly. I have all your documents in the car.'

'That's great. We know the area. We now have the apartment to work from we keep to our schedule. A final meeting here tomorrow night then you pick up the keys on Tuesday, and we make our final moves into position on Tuesday night. Mohammad, I have one more job for you. Can you have a look around for a van similar to Sean's?'

'Yes, do you want me to steal it if I find one?'

'No. Make a note of the plates then get copies made. Bring them here and change them onto Sean's van in the garage. We'll be using the van to move to the apartment, so we need to be as secure there as possible.'

'Sure, no problem, I'll do that right away.'

'Good, let's have a coffee then you can drop me off at one of the hotels near the airport.'

Fifteen minutes after Lyndsey and Costello had left the Hilton, April Grey had approached the reception desk.

Chapter Thirty-five

Grey spoke to the receptionist, then to the day manager, and last to the concierge. It always amazed her the reaction of people when she presented her MI5 Identity Card. People seemed to be relaxed and expectant when presented with a Police Identity Card.

Probably because of the glut of police TV programmes, she thought. But when shown a card from the security services, first there was a look of surprise, then a double take to be sure what they were seeing. Then a look of fear. To the everyday citizen this was a whole new world, completely outside their comfort zone, stepping into the unknown, this was serious. This meant they were only too pleased to help. A man fitting the description of the one in the photo she showed them had just booked out. It was the concierge who had been the most observant and gave Grey the information she needed to call Reece.

'April. What is it?'

'Can you talk?'

'Yes, I'm on my own.'

'I've just been speaking to the staff at the Hilton. It looks like our friend was staying here but left in a hurry about twenty minutes ago.'

'How can they be sure it was him?'

'I showed them the photo we have, and they weren't sure, but when I mentioned the baseball cap, they all agreed that the man fitting our guy's description never seemed to take his off and had just booked out. And here's the clincher, David, he may have been with a woman also staying here. They had different rooms on different floors, but they met in the Sky Cocktail Bar. It was the woman who booked and paid for both rooms using a credit card in the name of Karen Webb. If it is Costello, and I think it is, he was booked in under the name Paul Jordan? I've asked for the CCTV for the last few days. The day manager was a bit reluctant to let us have that but when I explained the arrest powers for terrorism under the Official Secrets Act, he phoned his boss and was more forthcoming.'

'Did you get any more about them when they left, a taxi, and if it was a taxi did the doorman hear where they were going? A forwarding address maybe?'

Grey laughed. 'We should be so lucky. The concierge is ex-army and the most observant of them all. He saw the man and woman leave together. Both were picked up by an Asian man in a black BMW which could be private hire as he opened the doors for them and put the bags in the boot before driving off in the direction of the station.'

'Can you get descriptions of all three, as well as the CCTV?'

'Sorted, I'll bring them back to the hanger for our briefing.'

'Good, call everyone and we can go over it later. I'll let Lockwood know after we've our debrief.'

'David, by the look of things they left in a hurry and not long after you spotted your tail. From what I've found out I think they're aware of you and most likely Mike, so you need to be twice as careful and so should she.'

'Agreed. I'll call with her and bring her to the hanger. I'm fucking angry that we were made, angry that he spotted us and angrier that I didn't spot him earlier, and now we are going to have to keep her much closer to the action. See you back at the hanger.'

Chapter Thirty-six

'Hello.' At last, John Jo Murphy had called back.

'John Jo, it's Sean here I need you to do something for me, it's important.'

'Ah sure, Sean, no problem seeing it's yourself. What do you need?'

'Do you remember Mary McAuley?'

'The lovely Mary from Newry; the one that was married to Brendan?'

'Yes, that's her. Now, she's moved back to Belfast to be closer to her mother I believe, I think the mother still lives in the Beechmount area off the Falls Road, but she lives somewhere else in the city, I don't know where. I need you to call with the mother and find out where she is now. Can you do that for me?'

'Sure, Sean, I'll try to find out how soon do you need to know?'

'As soon as you can. Tell the mother you're an old friend up from Newry for the day and you want to catch-up with her daughter.'

'Leave it with me and I'll get back to you when I know anything,'

'Good man.'

Lyndsey had been listening to Costello's side of the conversation. Since they'd left the hotel and returned to Irlam, she'd been reassessing the plan. Imtaz and Waheed had taken the train to the city to look around the centre, now they joined her, Costello, and Mohammad around the table. After Costello had finished his call, Mohammad made another technical sweep of the room.

'Our plans have had to change. We always knew security around the Conference was going to be tight but the fact that we've seen some people from Sean's past seems to indicate they know about the Irish connection to our operation,' Lyndsey said.

'I knew we were wrong to trust this infidel,' said Waheed.

'You and I are going to have a serious falling out, my friend,' replied Costello looking Waheed in the eye.

'That's enough,' Lyndsey cut in. 'Sean is not your enemy, Waheed. He is here, like everyone else, to strike a blow at the real enemy, the real infidel. On Tuesday night we move to the apartment and complete our attack on Wednesday morning. Mohammad, did you manage to get new plates for the van?'

'Yes, they're in the boot of my car. I can change them now.'

'Good, I've been thinking. Sean and I'll stay in the Radisson Hotel at the airport. Sean, you can park the van in one of the carparks near Terminal Three, then meet up with me at the Radisson. I'll book a twin room in the name of Mary Scott as they might be looking for Karen Webb already. Small hotels outside the city are unlikely to ask for identification so we should be all right as we will stay there until Tuesday. Waheed and Imtaz will stay here until Wednesday and move to the target area early that morning. Mohammad, you can drop me off at the hotel and meet up with me and Sean at the apartment block at 6 p.m. on Tuesday. Sean and I will stay in the apartment until the operation is over. Mohammad, you'll be in the Midland Hotel to give us the signal that the target is on the move, this will give Sean the few seconds he'll need. Sean, your van will be swallowed up in the airport carpark; it couldn't be in a safer spot. On Tuesday, we can move from the hotel to the NCP near the apartment and leave it there for the duration of the operation. Do you have some sort of carry case for the rifle that won't stand out?'

'Of course. The rifle has been broken down to fit into a small sports bag. I can assemble it quickly and it's already zeroed to my own specifications.'

'Good,' she replied. 'Now you can bring in the Semtex for Waheed and Imtaz to get to work on their side of the operation.'

Chapter Thirty-seven

Before picking up Mary, Reece had called Broad and brought him up to speed. Reece let Broad know of his concerns of interference by Lockwood. Because the operation was on British soil Reece felt the dangers posed by what he knew was normally a very proficient Police and Security service.

'I think I'll have to come up there if just to keep the likes of this Lockwood in check. He's been complaining to his Chief Constable, who's beginning to feel the pressure from him.'

'What's he doing?'

'He's asking for his ass to be covered in writing from the Prime Minister's office. How we want this to end is supposed to be Top Secret and I can see this idiot mouthing off to the press.'

'Idiot is the right word for him. He doesn't have a clue who we are or who he's dealing with here. He's a desk jockey jobsworth and to tell you the truth, I don't need his interference now that we're getting closer to Costello and his crew. We'll need police boots on the ground eventually, but until then, I want Lockwood to help without question when I ask them.'

'I'll be up there tonight. The Chief Constable and Mr Lockwood will be told where they stand. In the meantime, let him know in no uncertain terms that you're in charge and he will do as he's told. They can be replaced if needs be. See you later.'

'Let me know when you get here.'

Reece felt a little better knowing Broad had his back.

He waited in reception for Mary. When she came out of the lift her smile cheered up his day as always.

'What's up?' she asked.

Reece filled her in as they walked to the Range Rover.

'Hilton Hotel eh, a bit more upmarket from Newry.'

'Yes, but where is he now? We're going to check over the CCTV at our base location. That's why I want you there to have a look yourself. I also think it would be safer, being close to the team instead of out there on your own.'

'Where you lead, Joseph, I'll follow.'

There it was again, he thought, that smile that reached her eyes. Those dark brown eyes that seemed to see into his soul…his thoughts.

'Don't worry about booking out just yet, you might be here a little longer than I expected.'

'Again, I'm at your disposal. I'm not expected anywhere else, so let's go.'

As Reece drove to Barton, he watched her as she looked out at the passing shops, restaurants, streets, and cars.

'What are you thinking?' he asked.

'Thinking, now that's a question I don't hear every day. Not many people, especially the men, in my life are interested in what I'm thinking.'

'Well, I don't know about the other men in your life, but I'm interested, right now I'm interested.'

'I'm thinking, what am I doing here and what brought me to this place and time? Then I answer my own questions. I remember when I met you, I didn't know who you were at first, but I knew I wanted to get to know you. I wanted to get closer to you. Now I'm sitting beside you, driving through Manchester at night and I'm thinking despite everything, I'm exactly where I want to be. What about you? What are you thinking?'

'To be honest, I'm trying hard to keep my mind on the job at hand but you're making it very difficult for me.'

'I don't mean to.'

'I mean difficult in a nice way. It's the kind of difficult I could live with every day.'

'I'm sorry, I don't understand. I'm not sure what you mean?'

He pulled the Range Rover into the carpark of a pub just outside Barton.

'Why are you stopping? I thought we were going to your base?'

'I need a drink and so do you.'

The bar was surprisingly busy, maybe because it was serving food as well, but they were able to find a table all to themselves. A whisky and soda for him and a glass of pinot grigio for her.

'The only Irish they have is Jameson's, my favourite is Bushmills built these English bars never seem to stock it or rarely if ever. Did you know that Bushmills Whiskey comes from Bushmills in County Antrim in Northern Ireland?'

'Yes, I'm not a whisky drinker but I've heard of Bushmills.'

'Jameson's will do, but it's not Bushmills. Jameson's I would use for making hot whiskies. Bushmills I can drink straight on its own it's that smooth, did you know Bushmills is the oldest licensed distillery in the world 1608? The word licensed being the operative word. There were many other distilleries in places making the stuff before Bushmill's, but they weren't licensed or paying the tax man. I went to the Bushmills distillery once. Do you know what's written above the door?'

'No.'

'Here we turn water into gold.'

'The way you talk about it you might convert me.' She laughed.

'That's why I thought we should have this drink. Not just to give you a lesson on whiskey but, despite me needing one right now I just wanted some free down time with you on my own. You know nothing about me. We should get to know each other, who we really are.'

'Are you sure you really want to know the real me? You might not like what you hear?'

'That goes both ways. I know where you were born, where you were brought up, where you live now. I know your age, where you went to school, and that you were married to Brendan. The *you* I don't know is the one that made you who *you are*…the real you. What's your favourite book? Your favourite movie? What makes you cry? What are you afraid of? These are all the things that people in a normal relationship know about each other.'

'What's a normal relationship? I don't think I've ever had one. I was brought up by a strict Catholic mum and dad. My dad died when I was fourteen. I was at a convent school run by nuns who were even stricter than my parents. When I left school at sixteen, I was vulnerable and easily swayed. Brendan came along; the slightly older man of the world or so I thought. Someone who wanted to take care of me. Then, well, you know that part of the story and how that ended up, and here I am. What about you, what brings you to here and now?'

He was sipping his whisky. It might just be Jameson's, but he wanted to take his time. He'd listened to her with interest in the way she was opening up beginning to relax. This was what he wanted. The whole thing with Costello would make anyone nervous and he was no exception.

'Well, believe it or not, I come from a large Catholic family myself. I was born in Larne which was then a predominately Protestant town. My father was a bit like Brendan; a bully when he had a drink in him. My mother who was a lot smaller kicked him out when she found out that not only was he having an affair with another woman, but he'd gotten her pregnant as well. I had a lot of Protestant friends and in those days, religion was never a problem. In the estate where I lived the Catholic Chapel and the Protestant Church were the two buildings at the entrance gates to the local cemetery. On Sunday mornings both opposite congregations would finish their service at the same time and then everyone would stand between the two buildings chatting and laughing. Those were the good times when neighbours were neighbours before they started killing each other.'

'They're not all bad, Joseph, I have to believe that, you should too.'

'I know, you're right, I still have a few friends from those days but in my working life I've seen too much violence, too much hatred to know better. I fell out with the Catholic Church when the Priest at Mass started to spout off in his sermon one Sunday morning about fallen women. After my father had been kicked out, he moved to England with his new woman. My mother had originally been devastated. I was the eldest, only ten at the time and suddenly, I was the man of the house. After a while, my mother met and fell for another man, a Protestant. That day, in the Chapel, the Priest seemed to be looking straight at me, my brother, and sister. He was talking loudly about fallen women, jezebels as he called them. I knew he was speaking about my mother because everyone turned to look at us. I took the hands of my brother and sister and walked out. I told my mother what had happened when I went home and told her what happened. I also told her I would never go inside a Catholic Church again, and what's more, I would have nothing more to do with that religion.'

'My God, that was a big thing for a small child to deal with back then. You never went back?'

'Just once when I attended the funeral of a Catholic police officer who was shot dead by the IRA. I was reluctant to go inside the church. I waited outside thinking I would be able to sit at the back when the church had filled up, but my plan backfired. When I went in the only seats left were at the front beside the flag-draped coffin, and I was ushered to one of those seats. My anger for the Catholic Church was reinforced when the Priest said in his sermon, "If anyone knows anything about this terrible crime, they should tell the police."

'I nearly laughed out loud. I wanted to shout, you fucking hypocrite, if the gunman came into your confessional tonight and told you what they'd done, you would absolve them of their sin and give them six Hail Marys and three Our Fathers and let them go on their way to kill more policemen and you would tell no one.'

Mary could feel the anger in his words and feel the pain he was feeling. She decided to change the conversation.

'Where's your mother now? Is she still in Larne?'

'Yes, in a way. She's buried there.'

'Oh, I'm sorry, Joseph.'

'No reason to be sorry, everyone dies. If you smoked as much as she did then that time comes sooner than it should. She smoked all her life and the cancer sticks caught up with her in the end. It wasn't until she was gone that I really realised how hard life had been on her, yet she'd raised seven children practically on her own.'

'Seven? Christ that would be a struggle. Did you ever marry and have kids?'

'Yes, married twice and lived to regret it or should I say survived. I've two grown-up boys from the first marriage, one living in America and the other in the North of England, we don't talk.'

'What happened, or don't you want to talk about it?'

'Like all marriages the start was OK then come the children, both of us working to bring in the money to keep the roof over our heads. Then comes the drifting apart like passing ships in the night. We didn't know each other anymore. Then I found out she was having an affair with the husband of one of her friends. I challenged them both, but they denied it to my face. Then came the rows the arguments long into the night. I remembered how as a child I used to lay awake listening to my parents arguing, the loud voices the horrible words. It was then I decided I didn't want them to go through what I had as a child. One night after another long argument into the early hours I asked her what she'd do if the boys were grown up and left home. She didn't hesitate. I'd leave you was all she said. I told her I thought the same and there was no sense in keeping the marriage together for the sake of the children if there was no love anymore. We both agreed to see the solicitors the following day and that was it, really. The hardest thing was me leaving the family home leaving the two boys behind. I remember the first rented house I moved to after leaving the thing I noticed most was the silence without the boys running around. But she was the first-class bitch I'd been arguing with. She got the house. She squeezed me for every penny she could get always using the boys against me, telling them I didn't love them and trying to dictate when I could see them. It was a constant battel. After two years the divorce came through and guess what?'

'She took up with the other guy.'

'Not only that. He left his wife and kids, moved in with my ex, and married her.'

'How did that make you feel?'

'Strangely relieved. I'd been vindicated. It wasn't all my fault after all. She was the cheating bitch I said all along, but now she'd made her bed, she could lie in it. I concentrated on my work and any spare time I had was dedicated to the boys. I would have them three night a week, when work allowed, and during school holidays. But it was never enough and eventually, I guess they held things against me; blamed me for all their problems. As they got older, got married, had children of their own…we just didn't seem to talk anymore, we just got on with our own lives I suppose. They listened to the poison their mother liked to spout about me. It angered her that I could survive on my own, and when the boys finished school and the money she was bleeding from me stopped, she hated me even more.'

'Families can hurt you more than enemies sometimes. I'm an only child so I was lucky, and Brendan and I never had children, thank God. Can you just imagine what he would have been like as a father? No, that side of my life worked out OK for me.'

Reece could see a sadness in her eyes as she spoke of something close to her heart. *She would have made a good mother*, he thought.

'But what about us, Joseph? Where do we stand?' She didn't ask about the second wife and divorce and he was happy with that, another story for another time.

It was the question that had been keeping him awake at night but now it needed an answer, a decision for both.

'You know I said that while we're working on this Costello thing I needed to be as professional as possible and afterwards we could talk about our feelings for each other. Yes, Mary, that's right…I have feelings for you.'

173

She was quiet, letting him talk, she smiled. This gave him the courage to continue.

'I think I should be honest. I've had feelings for you since the first day I saw you in Newry then followed you to Belfast.'

'I'm glad you followed me.'

'This job can get in the way of relationships, you don't have to tell me, I know. But this time I won't let it. The Costellos of this world will have to wait. For this hour at least.'

He took her hand. He could feel the warmth of her soft skin as she squeezed his fingers. She watched him expectant but not knowing what. Then still holding her hand he said, 'Let's go.'

They left the bar still holding hands walking back to the Range Rover. She didn't feel awkward, everything with Joseph felt natural, meant to be, and if she was honest with herself, exciting. As they reached the Range Rover, she could see their reflection in its window. The street lights lit up the car park. Then without warning, he stopped and turning to face her she felt his arm around her waist while he held her face gently with his other hand. He pulled her closer towards him, then he kissed her. She felt the warmth of his lips on hers and she responded, kissing him back, and putting her arms around his shoulders. She'd never felt this way. She wanted him here and now. They kissed for what seemed like hours, then he just held her. Standing there with their bodies close enough to feel every curve and muscle without using their hands.

'I want you, Joseph, I want you.'

He felt a surge of strange energy go through him. This woman had broken through his barriers. There would always be secrets, things he couldn't tell her, things she didn't need to know.

'I want you too, Mary, so much,' he said through a dry mouth.

'But, for now we'll have to wait. Our feelings for each other will have to remain between us. I'm worried about the danger this mission can bring. That's why I don't want you exposed any more than you should be.'

'I'm a big girl, Joseph. I can look after myself.'

'I know you can, that's one of the things I love about you.'

'There's something else, Joseph. I love you.'

There they were. The three words that change everything. He knew they would come. The feelings he felt were more than just feelings, they were life itself.

'I love you too, Mary, and that's why I don't want you in danger.'

'Bollocks. You want me all to yourself.'

He started laughing as he felt all the tension and anxiety inside him evaporate as he held her tighter in his arms.

'This is how I want it to be, Mary, always close together and it will be. First let's get this job out of the way, nothing to interfere in our lives.'

'OK, agreed. But I'm waiting no longer than that. I want to be with you, to lie with you, to make love together.'

'This will all be over Wednesday one way or the other, then we can be together. It might mean you giving up Ireland.'

'For you, Joseph I'll give up the world.'

'That's always been my nightmares. Either someone is coming to kill me, and I can't get my gun to work or I'm too late getting there to stop someone dying. Sometimes I wonder is the world worth it.'

'It has to be, Joseph, or we all go down the pit with it.'

Chapter Thirty-eight

When they got back to the hanger Jim Broad had arrived in another Puma and he came bearing gifts. Some good, some not so good.

'Good to see you, Joseph. How are things?'

'Well, first we need to dispense with cover names, it will save any confusion as we go on.'

Turning to the woman standing beside him he said,

'Boss, this is Mary McAuley. It's thanks to her information we're all here. I think as names go; I'll stick to boss for you.'

Broad shook Mary's hand.

'Mary, I'm so glad to meet you at last, David has told me so much about you.'

'It's good to meet you and nice to know that Joseph is David.' She smiled. 'Although I think I prefer Joseph…it suits him better.'

'I'm sorry about that, Mary, another part of the job I'm afraid,' said Reece.

'Well, David, can you take Mary to the canteen and fix her up with a coffee then come back and see me as we need a chat?'

'No problem, see you in five.'

Reece left Mary in the canteen. She said nothing, other than, with a wicked smile on her face, 'I'll see you soon, Joseph.'

When Reece returned to the hanger, Broad and the rest of the SG9 team were watching the large TV screen on the wall. The hotel's black and white CCTV showed a man with a baseball cap leaving the Hilton with woman wearing a headscarf and sunglasses. A man wearing a dark hoodie with the hood up was waiting for them in a dark BMW and after putting their bags into the boot, he drove them away towards Deansgate Station. It could have been a private taxi or someone there to pick them up, the fact the driver appeared to be protecting his identity and was identified as a young Asian man, made the deliberate pick up a distinct possibility.

'We've looked at these pictures a number of times. The hotel staff confirmed that this was the man with the New York baseball cap who never seemed to take it off, and this,' April said as she pointed to the woman on the screen, 'they confirmed as the woman who paid both their bills. She used a credit card in the name Karen Webb. He was registered as Kevin Jones. The car is a black BMW registered to Hertz Car Hire here in Manchester, paid for by a man who fits the description of the driver but who used a credit card in the name of Kevin Jones. The address and driving licence he gave are fakes. He's hired the car until next Thursday, the day after the Conference ends.'

'Do we have any more on the car after it left the Hilton?' asked Reece.

'They were picked up heading out of the city near Salford before we lost them. They didn't use the motorways but disappeared in the side roads.'

'This is good,' Broad said. 'We have them running scared and being scared they'll make more mistakes. They might even call the whole thing off, but I doubt it. These are dedicated terrorists who will do everything in their power to get the job done, so we can assume they're still on schedule.

'We need to make sure Lockwood understands where we are. I'll bring the Gold Commander up to date and they can continue to keep an eye out with their CCTV coverage and patrols. I'll be telling him if they are spotted, they're not to be approached but that intel will be immediately passed to us and to your team, David. The SAS can view the footage we have too and make any preparations they need, but the police and SAS will only move on my say so.'

Reece was pleased that Broad was now taking control as it would leave the SG9 team out on the ground where they would be more effective.

'As for Mike,' said Reece 'We've brought her fully on-board now there's a chance she was spotted so we're doing away with code names. It's Mary and David from now on. Boss, if you could arrange for a third vehicle for our use that would be helpful?'

'No problem, I'll arrange it when I have my little chat with Mr Lockwood. But now the bad news, people. I was contacted an hour ago by Tom Wilson from the PSNI. As you know, they've been working on their own operations against the dissident Republicans in Ireland, especially the ones in the north, and they've confirmed it's him and he's here. Costello knows we're here and most likely looking for him. That's why they were spooked and got out of the Hilton. With the BMW on the radar, we might just get lucky again so keep on your toes. Get out there and get the bastards. Realistically, David, now that Costello knows about Mary, we should keep her out of things; she's blown. But I'll leave that up to you.'

'We will keep her on board for the time being she also knows Costello and he will be easier for her to spot him than us. She can look at the CCTV, but I know she will only confirm its Costello.'

After Broad left, the team waited for Reece's instructions.

'I really can't say more than the boss. The next mistake they make will be their last. They have been spooked but I think they'll continue with their plan as it's too late in the day to change it now.

'Tomorrow's Saturday, let's go over everything we know tonight: CCTV, maps, the buildings around the Conference area, then get a good night's sleep because God knows when we'll get another one.'

Chapter Thirty-nine

Saturday, 28 September 2019

Just after midnight, Costello and the team sat around the table in the Irlam safe house. The plates on the van had been changed and they now watched Waheed expertly handle two small blocks of Semtex. He wore blue surgical gloves and from his rucksack he'd produced two sandwich-sized Tupperware boxes with small holes drilled in one end.

He handled and caressed the explosives as he would handle and caress the butt or stock of a gun he'd seen for the first time, thought Costello.

Waheed then removed two detonators from his bag. They were wired to a timer that looked like a buttonless mobile phone. Placing halve the Semtex in one of the boxes, he pushed the detonator through the hole and pressed it into the block of explosives. He placed the Semtex inside the Tupperware, accompanied by a bundle of five-inch nails secured together with Sellotape, closed the lid, and stuck the timer on the outside. Everyone held their breath as he repeated the process with the second Tupperware box.

When he'd finished, he produced two real mobile phones.

'The devices are now ready,' he said. 'These mobile phones – the trigger devices – will initiate the explosive. When they are switched on, they'll send a signal to here.' He pointed to the timing device linked to the detonator. 'Just switch it on, enter the code – which is 1,2,3,4 – and bang…off they go!'

'How close do you have to be for the signal to connect?' asked Lyndsey.

'The signal will bounce off the normal phone masts in the area, so anywhere up to one mile away.'

'I'm impressed, Waheed,' said Costello. 'I've seen and used explosives in Northern Ireland but usually with a line of sight on the target. This way you don't have to.'

'There will be large crowds at Piccadilly and around the Conference itself. Mohammad said there will be many left-wing agitators demonstrating there all week. Imtaz and I will place the devices near both locations, retreat to the safe zone, and then detonate for maximum effect. We are both prepared to die for Allah, and to take as many infidels with us as possible. If we are cornered, we just need to press the send button on the phone twice quickly.'

'Mohammad, you'll go on Wednesday morning,' said Lyndsey, 'and then stay with Sean until the mission is complete, I'll be waiting for your call. Sean, you'll leave the rifle behind. I'll be in the van in the NCP car park and I'll pick you both up when the job's done. In the initial confusion, we should be able to get back here and lie low until things cool down. Mohammad, make sure the kitchen is well stocked with food. After you've dropped me at the hotel, I want you to take the BMW outside the city and burn it.'

'Burn it?' said Mohammad.

'Yes, I'm sure the Hilton CCTV has you picking us up today and they'll be looking for the car by now. We aren't far from the airport, so you should be safe to drop me off then dispose of it. Waheed and Imtaz, you stay here until Wednesday morning and then take the train into Piccadilly. From the information Mohammed's given us about the conference and the PM's speech, we can expect him to walk out the rear door of the Midland between eleven and eleven thirty on Wednesday morning. Sean will be set up in the apartment ready and everyone needs to be in position for that time. It will be down to Sean to shoot the Prime Minister with the sniper rifle. Mohammad will send us all the text ONE DOWN confirming that Sean has completed his mission, that's when you tap in the code on the mobile phones then press the send button. The explosions and following confusion should give us the cover we need to escape the area. If you feel you can't get back, try to return to your own city and home.'

'I'll gladly offer my life for Allah, all praise to his name,' said Waheed.

'Me too,' said Imtaz.

Costello thought Imtaz looked a little more frightened at the thought of being a living sacrifice.

'If we kill the British Prime Minister and hundreds of people, we'll need all the angels on our side to get away, that's for sure,' said Costello.

Costello felt the buzz from his mobile phone in his pocket. Mohammad had already done his usual security scan, so he answered when he saw the number.

183

'John Jo, how are you?'

'Oh yes, hi, Sean, it's me, OK. Got a bit of information for you. Sorry it took so long. It took me a bit of time to track down Mary's mum. People are still very suspicious when someone starts asking questions. She lives in the Beechmount area on her own.'

'What have you got for me, John Jo?'

'Well, I told them that an old friend of Mary's had died and as I was up in the city for the day, I thought I'd call with her and tell her if she didn't already know. She told me Mary lives on the Lisburn Road, she didn't have the number, but Mary'd phoned her a few days ago to say she'd be away for a while and would call her when she got back. Does that make sense to you?'

'Yes, that would add up.'

'She believed my story, so she gave me Mary's number. I'll text it to you now.'

'That's great, John Jo, I owe you one. If you hear anymore, give me a bell.'

'Will do, bye for now.'

The phone went dead and almost immediately, the text with Mary McAuley's number appeared on the screen.

Chapter Forty

When he parked the van at the airport, Costello thought that even he would have a problem finding it again in what looked like the biggest car park in the world. He made a special note of what lane and section the van was in in case he needed to find it in the dark in a hurry. He was thankful that all being well, he'd be coming back to find it in daylight.

He walked to the Radisson Hotel about a mile from where he'd parked up. A good distance for security purposes. He could check for surveillance and the van was far enough from the hotel it wasn't obvious where he was if the security forces found it. Had he flown out of the country, they would wonder, and if not, it'd be like finding a needle in a haystack.

Rain was falling, so he pulled his coat closed, slipping the Browning pistol into his right-hand pocket…the cold steel comforting in his grip. It reassured him knowing this was the final stages of the operation. He was happier now that the action was close. He felt more in control…this was his world now.

Lyndsey was sitting in the foyer of the hotel when he entered. They kissed each other on the cheek then he sat opposite her.

'No problems getting here then, you're parked up OK?'

'No problems. No one following, and you were right, safely lost in a car park for the night.'

I know someone who won't sleep tonight, he thought. Before he'd left Irlam, he couldn't resist calling the number John Jo had sent him. When the woman answered, he recognised her Newry accent.

'Hello, Mary. Surprised to hear from me?'

He could hear her breathing, the hesitation in her voice as she spoke.

'Who is this?'

'I think you know, Mary. I just called to let you know I saw you and your friend today. It took me a while to figure out where I'd seen him before, your Special Branch friend.'

'Who are you? I don't know what you're talking about?'

'Don't worry, you'll be seeing me soon, you and your friend.'

The call had only lasted seconds not long enough to get a trace but just long enough to give her and her friend a message.

'I could do with a bite…I will order a plate of sandwiches for the room What floor are we on?'

'The third, room 302.'

'I'll have a quick wash then a bit of kip.'

TEN MILES AWAY, in a field near Warrington, Mohammad had parked the BMW. He knew that a short distance away was the small train station of Glazebrook where he could catch a train in fifteen minutes that would take him to Irlam.

Plenty of time to do what he needed to and get to the station. He was sure no one had seen him turn into the field and the darkness would give him the cover he needed. Taking out the tea towel he'd brought from the Irlam safe house, he opened the petrol cap and stuffed the towel in as far as he could, then, using the lighter brought for the job, lit the piece of towel hanging outside. Making sure it was well alight, he turned and walked towards the road and, turning left, he walked the short distance to the station. Halfway there, he heard the loud explosion and saw the sky light up in the darkness as the car turned into a fireball.

Chapter Forty-one

The Prime Minister had arrived in Manchester and was now in a meeting with senior ministers at his suite in the Midland Hotel when Jim Broad called to update him on progress.

He'd parked his car some distance away and had used the walk to take time the time to think, putting together in his mind what he would say to the PM. It was early evening and though the conference delegates had, in the main, left the main Conference building for the day, there was still a large group of demonstrators in the area. The crowd were a mixture of all sorts. Some with placards showing their grievances and some more organised the rent a mob the kind that were always complaining about something and looking for trouble instead of getting of their backsides and doing something to change the problem. Then there was the usual Union and left-wing protesters and agitators with placards from Save our NHS to Tory Scum, Ban Foxhunting all accompanied by the usual chants of 'Tories Out', 'Tory Scum', 'Down with the capitalist system'. It was all meant to intimidate the delegates who had to pass them to get into the Conference area.

Broad liked to think that he would fight for was the free speech these demonstrators represented, even if he didn't like how they used it. The thing that angered him most was that the puppet masters behind the demonstrators who organised the rent a mob would show up when the crowd was at its biggest, spout a few words for the benefit of the cameras, then having heated up the crowd once more, would disappear to the warmth of their limo and the expensive hotel being paid for with Union or taxpayers money.

Broad knew some of the history of the hotel that had been used by kings, queens, presidents, and now prime ministers. The prime ministers mostly staying when attending the Conservative Party Annual Conference which Manchester had shared every two years with Birmingham. The two main political parties in Britain had moved their conferences into the big cities away from the old costal resorts due to the fact the numbers attending had grown, now more hotel space was needed.

Broad had no problem getting through security and was now sitting outside the suite of rooms being used by the Prime Minister. He wasn't alone. There was a secretary behind a desk and standing at the door to the rooms was one of the PM's Personal Protection team standing quietly but alert.

'You may go in now, sir,' said the secretary.

When Broad entered the suite, Peter Brookfield came and shook his hand.

'Jim, welcome, thank you for coming. Please, take a seat.'

Broad sat in one of the large winged leather chairs that made up a three-piece set surrounding a large glass coffee table which had two empty coffee cups and a buff folder with TOP SECRET across the top of the file and the words Operation Longshot in smaller letters below. Brookfield sat in the other armchair. Sitting on the large sofa were Sir

Hugh Fraser and Sir Martin Bryant. After everyone said hello it was Bryant who spoke.

'Well, Mr Broad, where are we now, can you bring us up to date?'

His question indicated two things to Broad. He'd used the word 'we' which he could take to mean we're all in this together. But he'd started with a more formal, Mister, which Broad took as we're together in this but if the shit hits the fan, you're on your own.

Broad spent the next twenty minutes bringing them up to date.

'So, despite all the resources we have, we're not much closer to getting these people? You say we are, but how close?' Bryant asked.

There was that 'we' again, thought Broad, and he was sure Sir Hugh had picked up on it too when he smiled and winked at him.

'I do think we're close. We have them moving out of the Hilton in a hurry and obviously spooked. They exposed themselves and we can now confirm that the Real IRA and Islamic Jihad are working together. Most likely, led by Costello and Lyndsey. From the CCTV we have a full description of the driver of the BMW and its registration details. Thanks to the PSNI we've confirmation of Costello phoning Ireland, the conversation recorded, and the number of the burner phone he's using. CCHQ are monitoring it with the hope of pinning down his location.'

'Is there anything else you need?' asked Brookfield.

'Not now, Prime Minister. Can I ask, have you briefed your own protection detail or changed any of your plans?'

'Yes and no. We have increased my Personal Protection by two and my plans for the Conference remain the same, on schedule.'

190

'The Prime Minister will be attending some Party events in the city tonight then back here to work on his speech and more meetings with ministers. We don't want the Press alerted by drastic changes to his security or itinerary,' said Bryant.

'Thank you, Martin,' said Hugh Fraser, 'I think we can let Jim get on with the job in hand. We must remember his team aren't policemen but a specialist unit with a specialist task as set out by the Prime Minister and the Intelligence Committee. Their job is to find the terrorists and deal with them.'

'Yes, thank you, Jim, for all that you and your team are doing, please keep me updated,' said the Prime Minister.

'Come and let me buy you a cup of coffee, Jim,' said Sir Hugh putting his arm around Jim's shoulder and guiding him to the door.

'Yes, good night, Mr Broad, and thank you,' said Bryant.

'Good night, sir,' said Broad before he left.

There it was again, the politician's language of formality. You're not one of us, you're on your own. At least Broad knew who his real friends were and who he could trust the kind of friend who would follow him through the door of danger. The politicians he'd come into contact with always looked for a scapegoat if things went wrong.

When they got to the hotel lobby, they found a seat in the corner of the crowded room still full of delegates talking in full flow.

Instead of the coffee he'd suggested, Sir Hugh ordered two large malt whiskies and a jug of water. Now, as he looked over his glass at Broad, he smiled again.

'I needed this, Jim. Any longer in that room with that jumped up one-trick pony, Bryant, and I would have shot him myself.'

Broad laughed. He knew Hugh Fraser hated the grey suit mob, as they called ministers and their lackeys, as much as he did. Bryant, because he had the Prime Minister's ear, could be a tough-talking mandarin one of the boys when he wanted to, but talk was cheap – action on the ground sorts the real men from the boys. Bryant was the kind of civil servant who had perfected the art of smiling to your face while stabbing you in the back. He would have been comfortable in the company of the gang that surrounded Julius Caesar on the steps of the Senate all those years ago. The locations might be different, but the tactics were the same.

'But, Jim, I want you know that no matter what we think of Bryant, he's smart and because he has the ear of the PM, we need to think like a politician. We work in the background of life not in the full glare of the British and world news cycle. The first people know about us is when something has happened, usually when people are dead.'

More people were filling the spaces in the bar. The Conference and its fringe events were closing down for the day. The sound of voices filled the air and the two men found they could speak without being overheard.

'I know what you mean, Hugh. But the politicians might change but as far as we're concerned, their politics doesn't. Look at what they're now doing in Northern Ireland pandering to the Republicans and then getting the PSNI to hound old soldiers in their seventies trying to prosecute them for killings they were involved in during the

Troubles when serving Queen and Country. The politicians did the same after Iraq; allowing ambulance chasing lawyers to lead spurious, made-up investigations on the behalf the terrorists we were fighting. That's what I fear now for SG9. Our people put their head on the block at the behest of these same politicians who are only too pleased to point the finger of blame when the shit hits the fan.'

Hugh took a long sip of his malt then leaned a little closer towards Jim.

'I know, and I agree with what you're saying. All our lives we've had to deal with these pen pushers. I've always stood by my people. I would never ask them to do something I wouldn't do myself. I don't want you and the team to have any worries. If push comes to shove, I have enough information on the skeletons in their cupboards to bring down the lot of them. In the meantime, let's get on with the job. I know your team have been briefed and trained to take these bastards out. But, if there is a chance to take Lyndsey alive, the information she has on the Islamic network would be more useful without a bullet in it.'

Broad understood what his boss was saying. It would give him the ace up his sleeve he needed to continue playing his game with the politicians.

'We will do our best. Now, can we get out of here and get some food, I'm starving, somewhere a little quieter?'

'There's a little club I just happen to be a member of not too far from   here.'

Chapter Forty-two

The call to the Warrington Police Station from a disturbed resident said there had been an explosion near Glazebrook the small village on the edge of the Warrington Police Divisional Boundary with Greater Manchester Police. Detective Chief Inspector Kevin Connor, Cheshire Constabulary was old school, you always keep your senior boss up to date, and there was no one more senior than his Chief Constable so he was the first call.

'Kevin, I'll contact the Gold Commander and Chief Constable in Manchester to let them know what's happened. In the meantime, you can keep me up to date and I'll get their Gold Commander to speak with you,' said the Chief Constable.

'I look forward to hearing from him.'

'Call me at any time you need to, Kevin.'

'Will do, sir.'

The call came from the Gold Commander at 10 p.m. 'Usual commands keep me informed.' Lockwood came across to Connor as snappy and demanding.

'We need all the information we can extract from this scene, Chief Inspector, and we need it as soon as possible.'

When the phone went dead, Connor could only smile to himself as he thought, *You will get it when I have it and not before.*

His mobile phone buzzed on the desk, he didn't recognise the number or the voice when he answered it.

'Hello?'

'Hello, Chief Inspector Connor?'

'Yes, speaking, who is this?'

'My name is David Reece and I'm leading a team working on the people who burnt the car on your patch. I would like to visit the scene and maybe meet you there for a chat.'

'Are you police, Mr Reece?'

'No, I work for the Secret Intelligence Service and as I say, we're after the people who burnt out that car. I'm not far away, I can be there in twenty minutes.'

'Well, we have floodlights and officers at the scene and you're welcome to visit it and I'll meet you there, but I don't think you'll get much from it.'

'I would still like to have a look for myself.'

'That should be OK, wait for me if you're there first, how will I recognise you?'

'I'll be in a black Range Rover. I'll stay in the vehicle until you knock on the window.'

Reece had been called to the comms room by April to be told they'd found the black BMW burnt out. The comms team had been monitoring the police networks, and it was just as well because they'd received nothing from Lockwood. Although just what Reece had expected, he was furious.

Reece found Mary still sitting in the canteen with a cold coffee.

'Sorry, but something's come up. Do you mind waiting here a little longer or if you want, I'll get someone to drop you back at the hotel?' After Mary had told him about the phone call from Costello and the confirmation of what they already knew. Baseball Cap man was Costello and he knew Mary was working with the security forces, Reece was taking no chances with Mary's safety.

'No problem, I'm happy enough here. You take care.'

REECE COULD SEE the blue and white tape sealing off the approach to the car which was lit up with the bull lights making it look like a beached whale in the dark. He parked the car on the main road and waited for Connor.

He sat in silence watching the traffic go by and the police vehicles park up then leave after a while taking the evidence with them.

After ten minutes, a blue Renault Megane parked just short of the entrance and a large man in a grey overcoat got on and spoke to the officer at the field entrance. The man then turned to walk towards the Range Rover., Reece stepped out to meet the man halfway.

'DCI Connor?'

'Yes, Mr Reece, I don't wish to be formal but have you any identification?'

Reece produced his SIS Identity Wallet.

Connor was in his late fifties around six feet tall with receding grey hair and light blue eyes. He looked fit and spoke with a north-west accent but with a hint of Irish.

'Good to meet you. Now, how can I help?'

'To put it simply, sir, this car has been used by what we believe to be a terrorist cell operating in the north-west. We're on their tail and the car is just one more piece in the jigsaw to helping us catch them. We think they're in the final stages of a terrorist attack, so the quicker we can get the forensic information from this car the better.'

'Well, it would appear that when the car exploded after the petrol tank was lit the damage was mainly to the rear of the vehicle. These BMWs have a strong chassis, so I'm told. So, despite their best efforts to destroy any evidence, the front of the car is still intact, even the built-in satnav. Our technicians are working on it as we speak, and I hope to have the results within the hour. Hopefully we'll know where the car has been for the last few days.'

'You'll know the car was hired from a local Hertz dealer, we've already looked for the tracker they sometimes fit, but this one didn't have one – just so your guys don't waste their time looking for it. We need the info off that satnav.'

'I see that you've been working with Graham Lockwood the Manchester Gold Commander for the Conservative Conference, has this anything to do with that?'

'Yes, but I would appreciate you giving me a heads up on anything you get as time is of the essence.'

'Are you ex police by any chance?'

'Yes, RUC twenty years.'

'I thought so. My parents were from Northern Ireland. I have a lot of time for you guys. You held the line when some would jump ship.'

'I thought I could hear a bit of Irish accent.'

'Listen, between you and me, I know Lockwood and he's an ass of a paperclip pusher and I know he always wants to be the big boy claiming all the glory to himself. So, anything I get you'll be the first to know.'

'I know from experience how things can get bogged down in little kingdom battles at senior level. No pressure, but whatever you get I get before anyone else including your Chief Constable and I need it in a hurry. Nothing stops it or gets in the way. If you have any problems let me know. You have my number. If we can find out where the car has been, then we have a chance of catching up with these guys.'

Connor smiled his understanding. 'You have my word. I'll be in touch later.'

Connor went back to the tape line and spoke to one of the SOCOs dressed in a white full body forensic suit. Reece returned to the Range Rover and started the engine. Using the radio, he spoke with Jim Broad.

'Just had a good chat with DCI Connor at the scene. I believe he knows where I'm coming from and that he's now working for me…we should get the information from the car soon. He doesn't like some of the top brass in Manchester that's for sure and he's going to work with us cutting out the red tape that slows things up. I would think that by the time I get back to the hanger, information will start to come through.'

Reece spoke as he drove. 'Have the SAS ready for a briefing when I get back.'

WHEN HE GOT back to the hanger, despite the time of night, everything was movement. Reece found the team and the SAS in the comms section of the hanger, checking their equipment.

'Great, you're all here,' said Reece who noted Jim Broad sitting quietly in the corner, the sign of a good commander. When all the training had been done, the recces complete, and the target known, a good commander would brief his troops with everything he knew then sit back and let them do their job.

'I met the DCI from Warrington who is in charge of the burnt-out car and he'll be in touch soon giving us all he can. The good news is his forensic technicians just might be able to give us a location for these people from the inbuilt satnav which survived the fire almost intact. Our people could do it but considering they already had people there who could pull the information why delay further. It's going to be a long night people so make sure you have everything you need.'

Mary was watching from a chair at the entrance. Seeing Reece in full flow like this impressed her. This was the side of him that had been hidden, the professional side he'd talked about, and now, when she saw it in action and up close, she felt a little scared, and for the first time, she was aware of the real danger ahead.

'Where do you want us?' It was the SAS troop boss Kevin who asked the first question.

'Realistically, until we know a location to start from, we all stay here, conserve our energy until we have something to get our teeth into. But let's get everything ready for when we get the information.

Everybody go through your equipment: your comms, your vehicles…everything needs to be right.'

Reece knew he didn't need to teach these people how to suck eggs but years of doing these things right had kept him alive and if people were going to die today, he wanted it to be the bad guys.

'Any questions?'

No one spoke.

'Good, I'll be back in a minute.'

Reece nodded for Mary and Broad to follow him. He walked them to the canteen and ordered three coffees. When he sat down with the hot drinks in front of them, he looked at Mary.

'Mary, you may have a very important part to play in this and there might be some danger. Are you still happy to continue and help us? I would rather keep you out of things, but we need to stop this fucker and to do that we need to spin all our cards.'

Mary took a few seconds before she answered.

'After the phone call, there's one thing I know, if we don't get him, he won't stop until he gets me so don't worry, Joseph, I mean, David. I still can't get used to David I still like Joseph and I might just call you that now and again.'

'I have no problem whatever you call me. Boss, can you provide a couple of cars for us to use? Range Rovers are comfortable but not practical when it comes to mobile surveillance as they stand out. By the look of things, we'll be involved in more vehicle surveillance than foot for now and we might have to move quickly in a built-up area.'

'No problem. We have access to the police vehicle pound in Manchester, I'll get you what you need, might take an hour or so.'

'By the time they arrive we should have something from DCI Connor for us to get our teeth into.'

'OK, let me make the call.'

When Broad left, Reece looked at Mary. She seemed to be calm, no signs of stress or pressure. This lady always impressed him but now, more than ever, he felt the deep feelings that were emerging every time he was alone with her.

'When we move, Mary, I want you to stick with me. I need you to be in a position to identify Costello if we see him. I know he may have changed his appearance and maybe wearing a disguise, you know the little things that make Costello, Costello. But I don't want you to take any risks...nothing that would put you in danger.'

'As I told you just now, Costello will kill me if he finds me. I have no choice; I need to find him first and you're my best hope of doing that. I'm in it to the end, Joseph. Yes, I prefer Joseph. I've known you longer as Joseph, so until this is over, and we have more time to ourselves, Joseph it is.'

'Well, there's not much more time, Costello and his gang have to come out of their hole soon and we need to be ready to cut their heads off when they do. Let's go back and see how the team are getting on. It's our job to wait until they make a mistake...then kill them.'

Chapter Forty-three

Costello unpacked the few clothes he had from his bag and placed them in the wardrobe and drawers. The final item he removed was about ten inches long and in its leather sheath. He withdrew the Muela Pro Throwing Knife and felt the cold, solid steel as he balanced it in the palm of his right hand. He always thought of the knife as his get out of jail card to be used as a last resort if he needed to. When he first got it, he'd practiced for hours throwing it at a tree in South Armagh until he could pull it from the sheath secured in his boot, throw the knife spinning through the air, and hit the target dead centre in a split second.

He'd sharpened the Blade producing razor-sharp sides. He'd taken the knife to a farm in Monagahan one night. He picked the farm for two reasons. The first was that the owner was old and slightly deaf, and the second it was a pig farm. He'd approached the sty quietly and stepping in, he picked out one of the larger pigs and approached it from behind. Pigs are like humans in many ways, they hear well and sense movement so the whole exercise made it all the more real for what he wanted to do. In one quick movement he stepped astride the pig pulling its head back and, just as it started scream, Sean cut its throat from ear to ear with the throwing knife. The blood spattered across the pen and the pig, now silent, collapsed its whole-body weight going limp. He knew the experience would be similar if preformed on a human being.

He felt the balance once more before placing the knife back in the sheath and secured it the boot on his right ankle.

He heard the door opening and Lyndsey came into the room.

'Have you picked which bed you're sleeping in?' she asked.

'The one furthest from the door…it gives me more time to react if we have unwelcome visitors.'

'Mohammad got in touch. He's burnt the car and was able to return safely to Irlam.'

'Good. Will he stay there until we move?'

'No. He has to pick up the keys of the apartment before he meets up with you. Before that, he'll attend the Conference to see if there's been an increase on security and report back. Tonight, we relax, tomorrow we work.'

Chapter Forty-four

Mohammad had left Irlam Station and found the pizza shop was still open. He ordered two ten-inch pizza's one with four cheeses and one with mixed meats but no bacon. When he got to the safe house it was quiet, but he found Imtaz and Waheed watching the TV in the living room the sound down low, barely audible.

'Hi, guys, food's up.'

Both men smiled; Waheed showing the gap between his front teeth a smile but not a smile. He could see they'd been watching the news showing that day's report from the Conference a government minister talking to the camera.

Getting plates from the kitchen, they all sat at the dining table.

'No bacon I hope, brother,' Waheed said.

'No bacon,' said Mohammad with a smile. Waheed wouldn't last long living in the west, he thought. There are times in war when you had to make sacrifices and Allah would understand.

'Where have you been?' asked Imtaz.

'Getting rid of the car. It's burnt, job done.'

They ate in silence, each in his own thoughts.

'What now is there any change to the plans?' Imtaz asked.

'No, we stay on track.'

'Can I ask a question, Waheed?' asked Imtaz. 'I've never seen what a bomb can do in a crowd, do you have any idea of a safe distance when I leave it?'

Waheed gave that wide gapped toothed smile this time it looked genuine thought Mohammad, like he was going to enjoy the answer.

'Of course, my brother, I can answer from personal experience. I was working with the Jihad and Taliban in Afghanistan and we attacked a market of the enemy. I placed a rucksack bomb exactly like the ones we'll place in Manchester. I set it under a table in the centre of the market and went and stood about one hundred yards away, behind a wall, and pressed the phone button. When it exploded, many of our enemies died and many more were badly wounded.'

'Was it the Semtex and the nails that did the damage the most?' asked Imtaz.

'Not Semtex. This time I used captured Russian plastic explosives, but it's the same. The bomb had nails just like the ones I've used but you have to remember, when it goes off in a crowded place the blast tears bodies apart. The nails tear through the skin, breaking the bones underneath. Pieces of the broken bones fly like shrapnel, creating more damage to the bodies of people nearby. You can never believe unless you see it yourself, pieces of men, women, and children, still burning…the smell of charred flesh and hair. Sometimes, those closest to the blast disappear altogether, leaving nothing but a bloodstain where they stood.'

'It sounds like a scene from hell. How do you live with the memories, how do you sleep?' asked Imtaz.

Looking from one to the other, Waheed let out a long slow breath.

'You must always remember, my brothers, we're always at war. If these people support the Great Satan and refuse to acknowledge the one true God that is Allah, then they're the enemy and they must die, all of them, every one of them. Are you ready to carry the fight to the enemy for our God for Allah?'

There was silence for a few seconds as Mohammed and Imtaz thought about the question.

'That is why we're here,' said Mohammad. 'We know what needs to be done. We've already taken the risk that's needed, and we'll complete the task ahead with Allah's help.'

Mohammad then pulled his Glock from his coat pocket and laid it on the table. Imtaz and Waheed followed suit and placed their guns on the table too. The gesture was felt by all three. This was a battle they were determined to win, a fight to the death.

'Let us pray to Allah, let him give us strength, courage, and the wisdom we'll need,' said Imtaz.

All three knelt on the living room carpet and side by side, they fell forward, touching their heads and hands to the floor in a silent prayer to Allah.

Chapter Forty-five

When the call came in from DCI Connor and it was Broad who took it. Reece and everyone else in the comms room watched for any reaction but Broad gave nothing away. After he put down the phone, he turned to face the room and the expectant faces.

'It's good news. DCI Connor has just informed me that his boffins have been able to decipher the BMW satnav. The car has been all over Manchester but has been paying particular attention to a small area in Irlam near here. It parked up on at least three different occasions in the last few days. The DCI is sending us the location as we speak. I've asked him to keep his own people back and he informed me that as Irlam is the Greater Manchester Police jurisdiction, it won't be a problem. For now, this is a surveillance only operation to identify what and who we're up against.'

Broad then turned to Geoff Middleton the SAS commander.

'Geoff, I want you and your men mobile not too far in the background in case we need you quickly.'

The SAS officer nodded his understanding. 'Don't worry we'll be ready.'.

'David, the extra cars you wanted have just arrived...two BMWs outside. They are fully fitted with armoured windows which I hope you won't need, and the up-to-date comms you will need.'

'The information from the Cheshire police is just coming through, sir,' said one of the two men monitoring the communications.

'Can you bring it up on the big screen and print off a few copies?'

'No problem, on the screen now.'

He pressed a few of the computer keys in front of him and a split picture appeared on the large screen at the end of the room.

Half of the picture was typescript detailing the movements of the burnt-out car the other half was a street map of Irlam with a red X showing where the car had been parked.

'Fuck they're only a few miles from us,' said Reece.

He then spoke to the SG9 team who were already pulling together what they would need, again checking their comms and weapons.

'I want us to work in two-man teams using the BMWs. April, you go with Steve and I'll go with Joe, that way we have good coverage. Mary, you'll come with us, if we spot someone who fits Costello's description then your eyes on the matter will be a great help. I know you have Glocks, but I want each car to have some heavy fire power, should we need it, so each car carries a H&K MP5. We're all trained with them and I'm sure our SAS friends can lend us two with two, thirty-round mags for each.'

'Do you think that'll be enough?' asked Cousins with a smile.

'Well, as my old firearms trainer used to say, if you can't hit the target with everything you have in the magazine then you may as well throw the damn gun at them,' replied Reece.

'Let's go over the ground we need to cover,' said Reece as he walked closer to the screen on the wall to inspect the streets in Irlam.

'Comms. Can you blow up this picture of the map please and can you link it into the satnavs of our BMWs?'

'Yes, no problem to both,' came the reply.

'The car seemed to be parked here in Kings Road there's four other streets off it three avenues and one small close. By the look of things there's around one hundred houses so we take it slowly we don't want to spook them if they're there.'

'It will be tough to spot anything in the dark,' April said.

'I know,' answered Reece. 'We will do a foot and drive round of the area to get to know it. If they're in there, they'll most likely be in bed at this time of the morning. We also need to do a trawl of the CCTV of the Irlam train station which isn't far from this area so it's a good bet they've been using the train in and out of Manchester. Boss, can you chase that up for us?'

'Will do. Do you need anything else?'

'Not for now. I think we should get out there and see what we have. As Irlam's not far away if there is anything you need us to come back and see we can do so quickly, and while you're at it get them to check the CCTV between Glazebrook Station and Irlam for shortly after the time the car was discovered.'

Turning to the comms and the SG9 team Reece spoke slowly and quietly making sure they heard every word.

'We will need everyone to be on their toes tonight, guys. I'll be Alpha One. Joe, you're Alpha Two. April, Alpha Three. And, Steve, Alpha Four. Boss, you and the comms team here will be Alpha Control. We will all have the built-in radios in the cars plus our own body radios.

I'll also borrow body armour from the troops. Make sure you all have your arm bands that were provided by the police just in case we need to move about in a hostile environment. Everybody happy?'

Everyone nodded their agreement.

'Right, I'm off to have a chat with our SAS friends to borrow a few items. Mary, stay here, I'll be back shortly.'

Reece found the SAS team already tooled up and ready to go.

'Geoff, I need two MP5s and four mags of thirty, plus a couple of flak jackets. Can you help me please?'

'No problem. Mickey, can you get these for David?' he asked of the nearest trooper, who left the room to return a few minutes later with the requested items.

'If you need to use them, I don't want it coming back on me so as long as you involve us in the fun, I'm saying nothing,' Middleton said with a grin.

'Don't worry, if we need to use them,.you'll be the first one, I call.'

Reece then briefed the troops on what the SG9 team would be doing and their call signs.

'We'll keep things simple. I'll be Tango One and the rest of the team will use the Tango callsign followed by a number so that you know it's us. Can you get your boss to get the local police to put the area out-of-bounds so that we don't have any snoopy wooden top straying where they shouldn't be?'

'Good idea, Geoff, Northern Ireland Rules, eh?'

'Big boy's rules always worked for me.'

When he'd worked in undercover operations in Northern Ireland during the Troubles, they always put the area they were operating in out of bounds to local forces to prevent them spooking the targets or getting involved in a Blue on Blue where the security personnel could end up firing on each other by accident. Undercover people would refer to it as part of the Big Boys Rules when involved in operations that were likely to result in a shoot-out with the terrorists.

'David?'

It was Joe Cousins.

'The Cheshire Police are quicker than we thought. DCI Connor has just sent through the CCTV from Glazebrook Station, it's not great but there is only one person on the platform just after the car was set on fire. I think it's our hooded Asian.'

Reece and Geoff followed Cousins back to the comms section where the grainy black and white images were already on the big screen, they were in black and white and again the suspect had his hood up. There was no way they could identify him but this time he had a sports holdall with the Nike logo on the side.

'The bag gives us something else to look out for,' April said.

'Can we track where he went?' asked Reece.

'He got on a train for Manchester but got off at Irlam, then the cameras lost him when he turned right out of the station towards the streets where we know the car was parked up,' Broad replied.

'So, he goes back to the nest tonight. No one picks him up that we've picked up,' said Reece. 'We need to get out there and try to find out exactly where he went. OK, everyone, let's do this.'

This was the part Reece liked best; when they had something to go on, everyone knew the task ahead, and they could get out there and do something positive. Now the jigsaw was coming together Reece felt the same adrenalin he'd felt when extreme danger was around the corner in Northern Ireland during the troubles. The feeling you get when a car swerves towards you. You know the danger but the knowledge that in a short period of time you could be killed or seriously injured can spur you into the action that will make the difference over life and death.

Chapter Forty-six

'This is Alpha One, comms check?' said Reece. His team responded.

'Alpha Two, clear.'

'Alpha Three, clear.'

'Alpha Four, clear.'

'Alpha Control, all clear signals.'

'Tango One, clear and on the edge of town, over.'

'OK, everyone, loud and clear,' Reece said. 'I'm going to take a drive around the Kings Road area. Alpha Two, park up on the main road through Irlam, Tango One, hold position.'

Two voices replied, 'Roger that.'

Mary was in the back of the BMW being driven by Reece. Sitting beside him, Joe Cousins had a clipboard with a notepad, watching every movement in the streets as they passed.

Mary soon worked out that Cousins was writing down the registration numbers of cars in the street and on driveways, passing them onto Alpha Control for a search of ownership. Every car registration they checked out came back to the house address they were parked outside.

The centre of Irlam appeared to be one long main street about a mile long with shops, bars, and take away food stores A typical English high street thought Reece, a bit run down with a mixture of old and new buildings.

As Reece had turned into the Kings Road, the narrow street had two more streets running to the left two dead ends with a further street running to the right another dead end. Kings Road itself was also a dead end all the streets surrounded by the fencing of an industrial estate.

The first street on the left was Henley Avenue which was the smallest of the three streets branching of Kings Road having about ten houses in all a dead end with a turning space at the bottom. Although it was dark, the street lighting was good so Reece drove in slowly then, after driving through each of two other streets once and, making sure Cousins had all the registrations he needed, he drove to the top of Kings Road and turned left onto the main street stopping a few hundred yards from the Kings Road.

'Alpha One to Alpha Three, come in, over.'

'Alpha Three send, over.'

'We had a drive around Kings Road and the streets off it. As you would expect at this time of the morning it's all quiet, nothing moving, and only one or two with interior lights on. I'm thinking that although the satnav shows Kings Road, if they're in a house here then it could be any of about one hundred. The good thing is that if they're in there, they're going to have to come out of the top of the Kings Road. If we cover the road, we should get them coming out. We decide what to do next depending on what we see,' Reece said.

'Roger that. We've taken a drive down the full length of the main street and it's all quiet. We're on the Manchester side of the street away from Kings Road. On the other side of the Railway Bridge, can you see it from your side?'

Reece could see the bridge over the main street in the rear-view mirror.

'Yes, I see it.'

'Just as you drive under the bridge there's a side road up to the Irlam train station. We took a drive up to look and I must say the station looks in better nick than most of the buildings on the main road. It looks Victorian and has two lines going between Manchester and Liverpool. There's a tunnel walkway that goes under the lines for access to the two platforms then on down to the main road coming out at the traffic lights beside the overhead bridge. It would be ideal for anyone using the trains in and out of Manchester and staying near the Kings Road.'

Reece was having the same thoughts his memory went quickly back to his foot surveillance training with an MI5 officer who was one of the famous 'watchers' team who followed the Russian spies during the Cold War. This day one of the other instructors had been following Reece and his instructor when they'd gone down a walkway under the main road outside Madame Tussaud's in London. As they went down the subway steps and turned the corner to go down further the instructor in front of Reece just managed to avoid stepping on a Tramp sitting at the top of the steps with a large glass sitting on the step beside him. Stepping over the glass he told Reece to listen as they walked along the long tunnel. He knew that as there was a number of exits from the tunnel the instructor following would be following close behind concentrating on where they were and what exit they were taking. Suddenly there was a loud crash and smashing of glass with a burst of profanities. They had both looked around able to identify their following watcher as he picked himself up off the ground.

There was more than one way to get caught out when following someone and that was the point being made by his instructor.

'OK, we need eyes on the end of Kings Road to cover foot and vehicle surveillance. We will take another run around the Kings Road and make sure we have all the vehicle registrations, then we can all meet up in the station carpark for a quick chat.'

'Roger that,' said Grey.

Reece drove around the streets once more slowly this time to try to identify the driveways without vehicles on them. This was easy as only Henley Avenue had driveways and garages and only two houses had no vehicle the first number two on the left as you entered and one at the end of the street number ten, both could have a car in the garage.

Mary had been sitting quietly in the back but now she spoke.

'If you find them in one of these houses, what then, Joseph?'

'Then we decide what to do. That's what I want to chat to everyone about.'

He drove to the Irlam Station carpark where the second BMW was parked in a corner that avoided the span of the security cameras covering the station.

Everyone stood by the cars, the rain had subsided for a change.

'I'm happy where we are,' said Reece.

'We now know the basic lay of the land and I have to believe they're somewhere in the Kings Road area. The problem is, we don't know exactly where, or if they're together, or how many of them there are. We could call in a big squad of police and soldiers, seal off the area, and wait for them to show their hand, but there may be people we're not aware off, and again they might not even be there. We would be showing our hand what they don't know right now works in our favour. They don't know we're here. Now's the time to be patient and wait them out wait for them to make their move. It's three in the morning. I'm going to drop Mary off at the hotel, then Joe and I'll get back to the hanger for a little shut-eye. April and Steve, you park up on the main road with a view of the entrance to Kings Road anything coming out, especially on foot, make a note of it. If it looks like anyone we're interested in, follow them. Joe and I'll be back at 7 a.m. to let you get back for some rest. We know the target for these guys will most likely be Wednesday, so we still have time, let's use it. Any questions?'

'What if we think there's a danger to the public?' asked Harrison.

'We have a green light. We're here for one reason and one reason only: to find these bastards and take them out of the picture. If that means permanently, then so be it. This area has been put out of bounds to local police so if they need to come in here for any reason, they'll let us know for clearance purposes. That's the reason we don't carry handcuffs, that's not our job. The one thing we don't need is a Blue on Blue situation when they might run into us doing our job.'

When he dropped off Mary, he could see the tiredness in her eyes. He kissed her on the cheek and watched her walk slowly into the hotel, she'd turned to wave goodbye, but Reece was already gone. When he got back to the hanger the comms team were doing the same getting some rest leaving only one at the desk to cover the team out on the ground. All was quiet, so Reece and Harrison headed to the team section of the hanger. But as usual when he was in the middle of an operation, Reece found sleep hard to come by the different scenarios would constantly swirl around his head the questions he needed to ask the answers he needed but didn't know yet.

Chapter Forty-seven

TUESDAY, 1 OCTOBER 2019

The dawn light had started to come through the bedroom window where Mohammad was sleeping at the front of the house. Stretching, he got out of bed and looked out through the net curtains to the street below. It was 5.30 a.m. and the street, like the rest of the house, was quiet. There was a slight drizzle of rain with hardly any wind and the sky was a miserable grey hinting at more rain to come. After he'd showered and dressed, he went down to the kitchen and made himself scrambled egg and toast. Sitting at the table he checked his phone, no messages. He sent a text to Lyndsey.

Up and ready heading into town about eight.

A reply came back almost immediately:

See you later.

He switched on the TV, keeping the sound down, to get the early morning news from Sky. Alongside worldwide events, it dedicated lots of airtime to the Conference. They were speculating on what would be in the Prime Minister's speech on Wednesday. As he watched, he could hear footsteps above him; someone was awake. A short while later, Waheed came into the room.

'Good morning, brother, did you sleep well?' he asked Waheed.

'Yes, soundly thank you. I'm going to make a coffee; do you want one?'

'Yes, that would be great white no sugar.'

When he returned with the coffee, they watched the Sky reporters speaking to people attending the Conference yesterday. It was too early to speak to any of today's delegates as the doors wouldn't be open until around 8 a.m.

'Are you nervous, brother?' asked Waheed.

'Not really. I've already sent a text to Sharon and she is also awake. Today we move toward to the completion of our plan. On Wednesday we'll make the world shake with our Jihad. We just have to believe in Allah, and all will be well.'

'I agree, brother, my heart is set now that the end is near. When are you leaving?'

'I'll set off early to get there for eight.'

'I still don't trust that infidel. His agenda is not ours; his God is not ours.'

'He has his own agenda if he is successful and it suits Allah's purpose, then it will be in Allah's name that the word will go around the world. The false God he worships will be of nothing compared to Allah.'

They could hear Imtaz as he started to move about upstairs. Waheed looked at the ceiling. 'When he comes down, I think we should pray to Allah together,' he said.

APRIL GREY HAD slept a little before the radio mike in her ear sounded the voice of David Reece waking her from her slumber.

'This is Alpha One, we'll be taking over the watch. Alpha Three, we'll be parking up close to you about 07.30, anything to report.'

'No,' said Grey. 'The world here is starting to awake. The road has been getting busy, it's coming up to rush hour. But nothing significant from Kings Road.'

'Roger that, we'll be with you shortly then you both get back and get some shut-eye for a few hours.'

Twenty minutes later, Reece and Cousins pulled into the parking space behind Grey and Harrison. When Harrison pulled away, Reece moved his BMW into the space they'd vacated as it provided a better view of the entrance to Kings Road and two of the streets adjoining it.

Turning off the engine, they watched the traffic and the pedestrians moving about, starting their working day. The registration numbers taken down by Cousins earlier had shown all the cars belonged to residents who had lived in the streets around Kings Road for many years. But that didn't mean they were all clear.

One of them could be a long-time sleeper but the names had also been checked for criminal and terrorist links and apart from some with minor traffic violations nothing flashed up to show there was reason to investigate further. In the first few minutes they'd been there two cars had come out of Kings Road the occupants elderly grey haired and white skinned. After two hours it was beginning to look like a long day. It was as Reece was looking down Kings Road, he saw a man come out of Henley Avenue and turning right, he walked towards the top of Kings Road. Reece fired up the wiper blades to clear the slight rain sitting on the windshield. Yes, the man was definitely Asian, with a slight beard and glasses, he walked with his head down he was wearing a suit with a shirt and tie but what was more interesting was that he was also wearing a jacket over the suit with a hood pulled up over his head. Not only to protect him from the rain, Reece thought but also to protect his identification. Now Cousins could see the man. Both held their breath, straining their eyes to make sure, afraid to speak in case the figure disappeared.

'I think we have a hot one,' said Reece. 'He's not carrying any bags and he looks like he's going to a business meeting.'

Reece grabbed his Barbour jacket from the back seat and slipped his gun into the pocket.

'Alpha One, to control. I think we have our Asian hoodie. He came out of Henley Avenue, so we need to pay more attention to the residents there. There could be more of them in there, maybe even Costello and Lyndsey. I'll follow our friend on foot, I'm sorry, but get Alpha Three and Four back here as soon as possible, no sleep for anyone today.'

'Roger, Control, Alpha Two will stay and cover until backup gets here.'

'Roger, Alpha One.'

'Are you OK with all that, Joe?' Reece asked.

'No problem, David. Anything more comes out before help gets here, what do you want me to do?'

'Do what you can to check it out, anything moving try to stay with it; the street won't be going anywhere.'

'Roger that. Will do.'

Reece left the vehicle and started walking at the same pace as the target who was now about fifty yards ahead on the opposite side of the main road. Reece was watching for signs that the target was conducting anti-surveillance techniques, but he didn't appear to be. He was keeping a steady pace towards the junction at the railway bridge overpass. Reece pulled a tweed flat cap out of his pocket, it wasn't much, but the cap was also good protection when following someone as it would make it difficult for the target to see the concentration on the face of someone in a crowd.

As Reece expected, the man stopped at the main junction and waited for the traffic lights to turn green before he crossed the road to the side Reece was on before turning right once more towards the railway footway underpass to the station. Reece held back until he was sure the man had entered the underpass.

'Alpha One to Control, Tourist One now heading to the Irlam Railway station I will stay with him.'

'Roger, Alpha One.'

Reece took the turning into the underpass following the path under the railway line above and walked up the stairs on to the platform. The station was very busy with a large band of early workers on the platforms on both sides of the tracks. Looking around slowly, Reece took in the faces and spotted Tourist One buying a ticket at the machine then walking to the front of the crowd to wait for the next train.

Reece took his time and slowly moved to the same machine and purchased a ticket that would cover his travel for the rest of the day, then he moved behind the target. The man was about five-foot ten, with a lean build and smart appearance. His clothes looked like they'd been purchased from Marks and Spencer and he wore smart black shoes. The shoes were important and made Reece smile. They were not the kind of shoes for walking long distances, more for working in an office environment. To Reece this meant unless Tourist One was stupid he wasn't going to be walking far today, and that was OK by Reece.

When the train arrived, the loudspeaker announced that it was the nine fifty to Manchester Piccadilly, calling at Manchester Deansgate. Tourist One boarded the middle of the three carriages by the forward doors, Reece boarded the same carriage at the rear doors. The carriage was packed, and it was standing room only, the passengers from Irlam filling the aisle almost to capacity. Reece could easily observe Tourist One for the journey. He faced forward throughout the trip, speaking to no one and Reece could see him move towards the exit doors when the train started to slow on its approach to Deansgate.

When the carriage stopped, and the passengers alighted from the train, Reece followed Tourist One over the walkway and down the steps then a sharp left street level. Reece followed him at the same pace from fifty yards behind.

'Alpha One to Control. Tourist One took the train from Irlam and we got off at Deansgate. We're on foot heading towards the city centre.'

'Roger, Alpha One. The rest of the team now in Irlam maintaining observation.'

Where are you going, pretty boy? thought Reece. He walked with his right hand in his pocket feeling the grip of the Smith and Wesson helping to reassure him. There were fewer people on the street and Reece made a point of not gaining on his target and walking to his left rear as most people in Britain are right handed, they'll look over their right shoulder when turning around to see if anyone is behind them, this would leave Reece in the targets blind side. If the target did turn to his left, Reece would definitely know he was looking for followers, Tourist One was making no effort to turn. Reece assessed that Tourist One was sure of where he was walking to, and that he wasn't carrying anything of concern, his steps continued in a set direction with the walk of a man who had no cares no fears.

'Tourist One now walking past the Bridgewater Hall following the tram tracks towards the Midland following the security barriers on the outside of the Conference Centre.'

'Roger, Alpha One.'

'Bloody hell he's just turned towards the main security entrance to the Conference, wait out.'

Broad stared at the speakers in the comms section of the hanger trying to imagine what Reece was seeing and reporting, the rest of the room was silent.

'Alpha Control, you're not going to fucking believe this but Tourist One just produced a Conference Pass and went through the security checks into the Conference Hall itself. I closed the distance between us; if he'd made a wrong move, he's one of the bloody delegates. I'm heading to the security suite within the building to see if I can get him on CCTV, will phone you when I get there.'

'Roger, Alpha One, I await your call,' said Jim Broad.

Chapter Forty-eight

Costello had been up and had breakfast an hour before Lyndsey had appeared in the dining room.

'I must have been tired; I didn't hear you get up.'

'If you didn't hear me snore, then you must have been dead to the world,' he replied with a grin.

When she left for the hot buffet table, Costello called a waitress over and asked for a pot of coffee for two. The coffee arrived just as Lyndsey sat down with her bacon and eggs. Costello poured two cups of coffee.

'Any word from the boys?' he asked.

'I spoke with Mohammad before I came down, he was just leaving to catch the train into Manchester. He'll be in touch later when he's had a look around the Conference area. I suggest we wait for Mohammad's call have lunch and maybe head in later.'

'Sounds like a plan. We can't do anything anyway until he gets the keys for the apartment on tonight.'

'Yes, a slight change of plan there. I have to be with Mohammad this evening at the estate agents with my passport to sign for the keys at five. The agents are on the main Deansgate street, so you can drop me off at the NCP and I'll let you know when we're inside the apartment.'

'Good idea, I don't want to be hanging about anywhere.'

'We can send Mohammad out for something to eat when we're in there otherwise we're just making it a longer stay than we need to.'

Now that they were close to the finish, and there was nothing more they could do, the hours would drag out, they knew this from experience.

'I can never think of food in the future when I'm eating, it's the same if I go to the supermarket on a full stomach,' said Costello.

'After tomorrow we can have a banquet wherever you want.'

'On a yacht on some beautiful ocean.'

'Sounds wonderful, it's something I've never done.'

'Let's make that a date then. Job done tomorrow then yacht in the Mediterranean for dinner. I'm off to get a paper and do some of that relaxing you talk about. See you later.'

Chapter Forty-nine

After he'd shown his identification to one of the security men, Reece was escorted to the security suite on the first floor of the Conference Centre. The Centre itself was full of delegates and the noise of a thousand voices in conversation was deafening. The security suite held around ten people who were either talking on phones or radios or watching monitors. Sitting at the back was Graham Lockwood, Gold Commander, who stood to greet Reece.

'Mr Reece, for what do we owe the pleasure?'

Reece sensed the question was in no way a pleasant greeting.

'Good to meet you again, sir,' he lied. 'We've been following a suspect this morning and it would appear he is one of your conference delegates.'

A look of panic came over Lockwood's face.

'You mean they're here, in here now?'

'It would appear he is on his own and completely clean, not carrying anything of danger to us but we can't take any chances.'

'Can you be sure? Where is he now? What are you going to do?'

There it was again, thought Reece, what are you going to do, the old swift two-step making sure he knew that if anything went wrong, it would be Reece to blame.

'That's why I want to use your screens to monitor him while he's here and try to get his details from when he scanned his Conference card at the security tent.'

Lockwood knew Reece was in charge and he was only too happy to hand over control in this particular instance.

'Everyone,' shouted Lockwood attracting all the eyes in the room to look his way. 'This is Mr Reece I want you to give him whatever assistance he asks of you, this is important. Mr Reece, you have the room.'

Reece could see the questions on the officers' faces as they looked from Lockwood to him.

'At this stage, I need someone who can use the screens to cover the whole Conference area from the main hall itself to the side shows and cafés, so which screen is best and who can do this for me?'

A young-looking constable put up his hand.

'I have good coverage, sir.'

'What's your name?' asked Reece as he pulled up a chair and sat down beside the constable.

'Jones, sir.'

'OK, Jones, first off I'm not a Sir call me David. Second, show me what you can see.'

It only took Reece five minutes to spot Tourist One sitting on his own in the café area.

'That's him, Jones, keep your eye on him while I make a phone call.'

'Yes, sir, sorry, David.'

Lockwood had been watching over Reece's shoulder.

'Are you not going to grab him?'

'No, not yet. He's only a part of the plan. We need to see if he'll lead us to the rest. Where he is now is no risk to us, after all he's just gone through your security. He uses a false name of Kevin Jones. I checked with your people at the front security tent when I followed him through, and they confirm it's the name he's used to attend as a delegate. A quick check through my people shows the address he's given exists, but it's a dead letter drop; he doesn't live there. Mr Lockwood, as you can now see, these people are very professional and there has been a lot of thought put into their planning. We're close and this Kevin Jones, who I'm sure is no relation to our Constable Jones here, will help us bring the lot of them down.'

'I hope for all our sakes you're right, Mr Reece.'

'So do I, so do I. Now, if you don't mind, I need to speak to my people and let them know where our friend Kevin Jones is right now.'

Reece then phoned Jim Broad describing what had happened and where he now was.

'What do we do now, David?'

'We need to keep Tourist One under tight surveillance. We can't afford to lose sight of him. Send April here to work with me. Get her to pick up Mary we might need her insight to help us identify people we don't know if Costello is the only Irish connection here. Keep Cousins and Harrison in Irlam for now while you find out what house Tourist One came out of this morning. If we find that, then we can move in closer and work out if we use the troop to hit it or wait and follow whoever leaves it.'

'We might have some good news on the house. We discovered number two Henley Avenue is the only house in the street that's rented – the rest are long-term ownership.'

'That's great. Get the boys to walk past a few times to see if they can spot any occupants, but not to get close until after dark, by that time, with the Conference more or less closing up around five, we should find Tourist One on the move again.'

Reece went back to the screens and Constable Jones.

'Anything to report, Jonesy?'

'No. He's just sitting there drinking and appears to be watching the world go by.'

'Is he watching anything in particular?'

'No, that's just it, just watching.'

'Keep watching but change cameras regularly; he might be watching us watching him. I haven't had a bite for some time, so I think I'll go down and see what they have to offer. If he moves, follow him and phone me.'

Reece wrote down his number and headed for the ground floor. It was easy to find the café and to mingle with the large crowd. He entered the open café behind Tourist One, who was still sitting at the table and reading a newspaper scanning the crowds. Reece ordered a coffee and a ham sandwich before sitting down six tables behind Tourist One. As he ate, he watched his target. Dressed like many here, a navy pin striped suit and shiny black shoes. His hair was short and neatly trimmed, a short-trimmed beard, and a round face with square thick framed black glasses.

He looked calm and relaxed, but Reece knew he was at work here, on a mission of his own. Watching the world go by was just a part of his reason for being here and Reece now knew he was assessing the security surrounding the Conference.

Good, he thought, you're in my playing area now.

As he watched, Tourist One folded his paper and leaving it on the table, he got up and started walking towards the main Hall. Reece took another bite from his sandwich then left half of it on his plate. His phone buzzed. It was Jones to tell him his target was on the move.

'Yes, thanks, Jonesy. Stay with him I'm not far behind. Can you print up some close-up photos of him from what you've been seeing?'

'I already have, David, they're here waiting for you and I have just sent one to your phone.'

'Good man.'

Reece followed Tourist One into the main hall staying about five rows behind him. On the main stage, the Conference Chairman was holding a three-way discussion on education with two company directors. This was followed with a speech by the Education Secretary.

Tourist One clapped at the appropriate places but he continued to move his head around making it obvious to Reece that he was also looking for CCTV and security but also checking for anyone watching him.

Near the end of the education speech, Tourist One left his seat and began to make his way back into the main area. Reece remained a safe distance away and watched as he circulated the stalls and displays, taking some of the freebies, one a bag to carry his goodies in before going back to the café and resuming his position with a pot of tea and a different newspaper.

Grey text him to say she'd arrived, so instead of resuming his position in the café, Reece went back to monitor Tourist One from the safety of the security room.

On entering the security suite Reece felt his spirits lift when he saw Mary sitting at the back of the room. Smiling he went and sat beside her.

'Well, how are you today?'

'I'm fine, Joseph, all the better for seeing you. Are you OK, you look tired?'

'I haven't had much sleep in the last twenty-four hours, but, it's always the same when you get to the end game in these things, and we're definitely nearing the end. I hope you've had a good night's sleep because it might be a long day.'

'Slept like a baby, with some nice dreams involving you.'

April, who had been watching the screen from behind Jonesy, joined them.

'He's still enjoying his paper. Here are the stills, they're good,' she said handing over the pictures.

They were very good, thought Reece. Almost as good as a passport photo showing Tourist One's face looking directly at the security camera.

'Get these emailed to the hanger, the troop, and the rest of the team. We can hang on to these.'

'David,' called Jonesy from across the room.

Reece went over to look at the screen to see what Jonesy wanted.

'He's on the move again, heading towards the front door.'

'Keep on him. Can you access into the CCTV outside the Conference in the general area around it?'

'Yes, no problem.'

'Good. Keep on him wherever he goes and record it if you can. If you see him make contact with anyone, record it or get a picture of them. If you need me call me.'

'Will do.'

Turning, Reece spoke loud making sure everyone heard him.

'As ACC Lockwood knows we are involved in a very important operation here which is protected under the articles of the Official Secrets Act, which means, as I'm sure you know, that what we've been doing here is of the utmost secrecy and is to be kept within these four walls.'

Reece could see Lockwood smile at the praise of his name, even though Reece had now specifically dropped him into the same well they were all swimming in.

'OK, let's go.'

Grey and Mary followed Reece down the stairs and towards the exit to find Tourist One. He wasn't hard to find; he was slow and deliberate…the pace of a man taking everything in as he walked. He'd turned left out of the main entrance and left the secure zone through the revolving gate onto the outside street.

Speaking into his body mike, Reece brought the hanger and the rest of the team up to date with what was happening.

'Tourist One on the move, now in the streets outside the conference zone, we'll stay with him.'

'Roger, Alpha One,' Broad replied.

'Let's break up,' said Reece as they walked. 'I'll cover him from the rear. April, you try to get ahead of him and cover from the front. Mary, you stay with me; a couple walking together is less conspicuous. April, where did you park the car?'

'On the other side of the Town Hall.'

'It doesn't look like he has a car, but we need to be ready just in case he gets one or is picked up. He's heading in the direction you've parked so we should be OK for the minute and Jonesy is keeping a watch on him too.'

April crossed the street and increased her step to get ahead of Tourist One. Reece and Mary stayed on the same side and about fifty yards behind.

'If he turns to look our way, Mary, I might have to grab you for a quick kiss.'

'I hope he does, then.'

Thanks be to God it wasn't raining, thought Reece.

There was nothing worse than having to follow someone on a cold wet day, it dulled sprit and moral. Tourist One continued to walk towards the Town Hall Square. Passing through the square, he turned left through the main crossroads stopping at the traffic lights to cross. April was still ahead of him on the other side. Reece and Mary stopped to pretend to do a bit of window shopping and when the lights changed, Tourist One crossed and for a moment, Reece lost sight of him, but April still had him.

'Tourist One now static, looking around slowly, don't turn into the street yet, Alpha One, he's looking for us. I can nip into a shop here and watch him through their window,' April said.

'Roger, Alpha Three. We'll wait for your signal.'

So now he was really at his game, thought Reece, what's he up to?

'He's entered a café halfway down the street,' said Grey.

'Roger, Alpha Three, we'll walk past and meet up with you.'

'Roger that.'

Reece and Mary walked past the café where they saw Tourist One standing with his back to the door at the counter. Further down the street, they stopped with Grey.

'He likes his tea and coffee this one,' said Grey.

'I'd like to get in there to see if he's making contact with someone from inside the café, but I've been close to him twice already.'

'I can do it,' said Grey.

'No, I want to keep you fresh for the surveillance later.'

'What if I go in?' offered Mary.

'I can't ask you to do that, it's too dangerous.'

'I won't get too close. I'll just get a quick coffee; God knows I need one. He's less likely to know me, and his sort don't have much respect for women, so already I don't like him.'

Reece looked into her eyes; every time he'd been with this woman her strength had impressed him even more.

'OK, but don't take any risks. Just a coffee, sit down, and observe without being too obvious. If he lingers, don't hang about. Leave when you've finished your drink. If he leaves, wait thirty seconds before you follow. If that happens and we're gone when you come out, make your way back to the Town Hall and go into the café there where I'll catch-up with you. We'll be out here so if you need help scream and we'll come running.'

Mary smiled the broad smile that always made him feel reassured by her. She kissed him on the cheek and walked away and into the café.

'You're going to have to marry that girl,' said Grey with a grin.

'You might be right. Let's split up to each side of the street and take an end each so we have him no matter which way he walks.'

Chapter Fifty

Broad had told Fraser that for the moment they had some sort of control but later the situation might force their hand and they might need to move. If they had to move, they could take Tourist One out of the picture alive or dead. His disappearance from the scene would make the rest panic and most likely call off the operation. But, in the end he couldn't take that chance, these people were fanatics and fanatics are unpredictable.

'Control, this is Alpha Two, over.' It was Joe Cousins who was still covering the Irlam address.

'Come in, Alpha Two.'

'We have another Asian male leaving the target street on foot. Heading up in our direction.'

Broad took over the mike.

'Roger, Alpha Two, stay with him.'

'Roger that. Alpha Four, with him on foot.'

'Control, this is Alpha Four, target went into the local supermarket, will go in and observe.'

'Roger that, let's put him down as Tourist Two,' said Broad.

Imtaz quickly browsed the shop for what he needed: milk, bread, butter, and a bar of chocolate for himself, he paid at the till and was back outside in just a few minutes.

'Following after buying a newspaper,' Harrison said.

'He bought some bread and butter, no chatter, now heading back the way we came. He's youngish with a shortcut beard. Wearing dark blue jeans and a padded black ski jacket, no hat. I can't take a chance following him down Kings Road, returning to the car.'

'Roger that. Did you get a photo of him?'

'No, he was too quick, in and out of the shop, he knew what he wanted, and he may have been there before.'

Cousins, still watching from the car, broke into the transmission.

'I managed to get a few snaps with my mobile and when I zoom in, they aren't bad, not quite David Bailey standard but will do at a pinch. I got a good shot of him when he was crossing the road and had to look right and left. I'll text them over now.'

'Good job, guys. Hold your position but it looks like he's settling in for the night and he may not be alone.'

The Kings Road and Henley Avenue will be getting a closer inspection tonight, thought Broad. Time to bring the troops back for a briefing.

'Tango One, can you return to base, over?'

'Roger, will do,' Geoff Middleton said.

Chapter Fifty-one

Mary had entered the café thirty minutes before Tourist One walked out and turned left heading back towards the Town Hall Square. Mary did as she'd been told she finished her coffee then left the café. When she left, there was no sign of anyone, so she took her time walking back towards the Town Hall and phoned Reece.

'Mary, are you OK?'

'Yes, no problem. Thought you should know when I went in, he was on the phone. He mentioned something about keys and be there before five thirty.'

'Interesting…anything more?'

'Yes, he made two more calls. The first I'm sure he was taking in Arabic, so no help there, I'm afraid, but his last call was in English. All I could pick up was see you there at five. His accent was local I think.'

'You've done great. We'll make an agent of you yet.'

'I thought I already was.'

'You are, Mary, you definitely are. By the look of things, he is heading back into the Conference so you just head for the Town Hall Café and I'll meet you there shortly.'

'OK, Joseph, see you soon.'

Tourist One returned to the Conference Centre the way he'd left and entered back through the security tent.

241

Reece and Grey followed, and he sent April to watch with Jonesy in the security suite. It was now 2.35 p.m. and from what Mary had heard, something would be happening around five.

Not long to wait, another few hours, and the picture should start to clear once more, he thought.

IMTAZ HAD RETURNED to the safe house with the food and made himself and Waheed a lunch of beans on toast with a mug of coffee.

'While you were out, Mohammad phoned. He said all is on schedule. The security is strong in and around the Conference itself but less so the further he walked away from it.'

'If we go to Piccadilly, we'll be far enough away but there might be more security at the station.'

'I'm not worried about security. We can kill them too. We have the guns, the knives, and the bombs. Many infidels will die, and Allah will be   happy   with   us.'

Chapter Fifty-two

They had booked out of the room and left their bags in a locked storeroom behind reception. Lyndsey had gone out for a walk and some fresh air and now he could see her through the glass windows at the front of the hotel speaking on the phone the call only lasting a few minutes before she came back into the building and sat down opposite Costello.

'I just had a call from Mohammad. He says he has booked the handover of the keys at 5 p.m. He has also been inside the Conference this morning and there does not appear to be any increase in the security other than what you would normally expect. I'll collect the keys then leave on my own and go to the apartments, he'll follow ten minutes later. I'll phone you when we're both inside the apartment then we can buzz you in when you arrive.'

'Is there any change for the boys in Irlam?'

'No. As of now they're working on their own. They have their own part to play in this, so we leave them to get on with it.'

Mary had been waiting for Reece sitting in a table near the high windows she'd been reading a leaflet with information about the building when he sat opposite her.

'You know it's called The Sculpture Hall Café and they do fantastic afternoon tea,' said Mary.

'Then let's do afternoon tea I could do with another bite the last couple of sandwiches were rushed and not very tasty to tell the truth.'

'What happened to our friend?' asked Mary.

'He's back inside the Conference Centre. Can you remember anything else he said during his phone conversations?'

'No, not really. He spoke quietly and quickly, and he was facing away from me the whole time looking out onto the street. I tried to be as natural as possible and even though I'm stunningly beautiful, he paid no attention to me.'

'I can't believe that, Mary, you're stunning,' he said with a smile.

She returned the smile and reaching, across the table, took his hand in hers.

'What next, what happens now?'

'I don't know, but he's more than just a tourist or a delegate and it would appear he is the link to the rest of the team we were looking for. We stay close to him and the rest will lift their heads I'm sure of it, we already have at least one more in Irlam and the boys are keeping an eye on him. Either way we should know more tonight, and we can start to make our moves to wrap this up.'

'Do you think Costello is in Irlam?'

'I don't know. But the fact that Tourist One made at least three phone calls would indicate their team is split at the moment, which is something I would do in the same situation if it was me, this gives more options and less chance of the whole team being captured at the same time.'

Mary poured the tea and between bites of food continued the conversation.

'So, the plan is to capture them alive?'

'If we can. But that really up to them, to what they do. Our job is to stop them no matter what and if that means we kill them, then we kill them.'

'Or they kill us.'

'We always used to have a saying when I worked in Northern Ireland, our gang's bigger than your gang. We have to get these people, we have to stop them, and well, they just don't know it yet. For now, let's not think about it too much; let's enjoy this wonderful afternoon tea and the company.'

'I agree, Joseph, but I'll have to do some serious exercise to get rid of all these goodies and cream. You aren't looking as tired now, maybe it's the fresh cream perk up?' She smiled.

'I think the walk about helped but just being in your company helps.'

This time he reached across for her hand and as he did so his mobile buzzed in his pocket. Reece could see from the screen that it was Jim Broad who was calling.

'Yes, boss.'

'Ah, David, I believe Tourist One is still at the Conference Centre, but we now believe he'll be on the move to meet up with someone around five. Do you need any other backup in case you have two or more targets to follow?'

'Good idea, can we get our troop friends to keep an eye in Irlam and send Joe and Steve to me as backup, ask them to park up somewhere in the Deansgate area. The troop should use one of our Range Rovers.'

'I was thinking along those lines myself as long as you're happy with what you'll have there.'

'Yes, that'll be more than enough for now.'

'OK, leave it with me. I'll speak with the troop commander right away. We will also need to move in closer to the house in Irlam tonight to try to find out exactly what we have there. We can wait until well after dark just in case Tourist One goes back there. I'll get back to you later.'

Reece put the phone back in his Barbour jacket and poured some more tea.

'Things are starting to move up, we're getting some reinforcements which will help us keep a closer eye on our friend.'

'I'm glad, I was getting a bit tired there doing everything myself.'

Reece laughed out loud making the people at the nearby tables look round at the two people sitting holding hands across the table once more.

'Mary, you're the calmest untrained person I know in this kind of situation. How do you do it?'

'I've learnt to only worry about this moment, this time, and place. And being with you right here and now, I feel safe and secure and I have to say, happy.'

'Then I'm happy too. But I still worry about you and I like the fact that I can worry as long as you're here with me.'

'You're going to kill Costello aren't you, you're going to kill them all?'

He was slightly taken back by the question. She'd asked as a matter of fact, really knowing the answer herself without hearing his confirmation, but he tried.

'If we have to, yes…we'll kill them. It's really down to them. They are trying to kill innocent people. Our job is to stop them. If they come quietly, we'll arrest them, but if they don't, and it's the only option left to us then yes, we'll kill them. So, no matter what happens you stick close to me, Mary.'

'Oh, don't worry I will.'

April Grey had been watching the screens over Constable Jones's shoulder. Tourist One seemed to be repeating his movements of the morning. First sitting in the café almost at the same chair and table, drinking coffee, and pretending to read a newspaper. Then he'd walked into the main Conference theatre took a seat and watched and clapped in all the right places then back to the same route before returning to the café again.

NOT FAR FROM where Mohammad now sat, in a suite of rooms in the Midland Hotel, the Prime Minister was sitting with a few senior ministers and advisors, putting together his main Conference speech that he would give to the Party faithful the next day.

.

Chapter Fifty-three

Costello had been able to find the van in the giant carpark easily, and that was only because he'd written down the details of the section it was parked in. After picking up Lyndsey and the luggage from the Radisson he took his time driving through the traffic and many road works that lead into the centre of Manchester. The journey had been uneventful, he drove past the Hilton Hotel to park in the nearby Great Northern NCP Multi Story Carpark.

'Mohammad should be starting to make his way to the estate agents. If I move now, I'll be there just before him,' said Lyndsey.

'You stay here. I'll text you and buzz you up when I'm inside the apartment. Will it take you long to get the gear out of the compartment?'

'No, it's easy to remove.'

He checked his mobile phone screen for coverage, which was good.

'Right, I'll wait for your text, see you soon.'

Lyndsey pulled her scarf around her head and face and left the van heading for the lift. The rain was playing its part. *People would be expected to have some sort of head cover in the wet weather, she'd blend in nicely*, she thought.

Costello opened the door at the back of the van and easily gained access to the hidden compartment containing the sports bag with the sniper rifle and ammunition inside. Sitting down again in the driver's seat he placed the bag on the passenger seat next to him. At the same time, he took the Browning pistol out from the belt at his back and keeping it in his left hand rested the weapon on top of the bag beside him, now he sat back and watched what he could see of the carpark.

THE RAIN HAD stopped when Lyndsey crossed the Great Northern Square and turned onto Deansgate pulling the scarf tight across her face as the wind blew cold against her skin. She was glad she was wearing jeans with her short leather boots with a heavy woolen jumper covered by the dark blue ski jacket, all combining to keep her warm despite the wind. Her over the shoulder leather handbag weighing a little heavier with the pistol safely stowed inside. She could see the estate agents one hundred yards ahead on the other side of the street. She continued walking to the next major junction with Lloyds Street two hundred yards further down before crossing at the junction then turning to walk back down towards the estate agents now on the same side of the street, all the time searching Deansgate for the watchers but none were there. She studied the faces of people walking towards her, but they were lost in their own little worlds some of them on their mobile phones or speaking into the hands-free cables hanging from their ears. When she reached the door of the estate agents', she studied the street behind her while looking at the reflections in the large glass window in front of her, pretending to study the laminated copies of properties on display inside the window. She could also see young Jake sitting at a desk just inside the front door reading the documents in front of him. When she entered Jake looked up with what appeared to be a genuine smile on his face when he saw her, a good commission that would come with the signing of this contract would bring a smile to anyone's face, she thought.

'Well Jake have you everything ready for me?'

'Yes, Mrs Webb it's all here. How are you today?'

'Very well thank you, but I'm working to a schedule today so can we get on with it?'

'Of course, I have all the documents here would you like to sit down?'

She sat at the desk as Jake sorted through the papers in front of him, producing them one at a time he asked her to sign in the appropriate places six times in all.

'I need to take a copy of your passport, have you got it with you?'

She produced the passport of Karen Webb giving it to Jake who continued to complete the paperwork. As he was doing this Mohammad entered the office and sat next to Lyndsey.

'Sorry I'm late. Have you been able to sort everything?' he asked Jake.

'Yes, no problem. Mrs Webb has been able to sign everything off and I now have the copy of her passport. I just need the deposit to go through and I'll get you the keys?'

'How much do you need?' asked Lyndsey.

'Including the security bond, three thousand pounds please.'

Lyndsey handed Jake her credit card.

'Thank you. I'll just go to our accounts office for the machine, back in a few seconds.'

When he left, Lyndsey leaned a little closer to Mohammad so that he could hear her without being overheard.

'When I leave, stay and talk to Jake for a few minutes then when you leave take a walk away from the direction of the apartments. Stay out for a couple of hours getting yourself a meal before heading back to the apartments and call me when you're coming towards them.'

'Are you worried about surveillance; I haven't spotted any. Did you?'

'No, but let's just be extra careful now that we're this close to the security perimeter.'

Jake returned with a hand-held card reader and punched in the payment figure then having inserted the credit card, passed it over for Lyndsey to provide her pin number.

'Thank you, that's everything gone through. I'll just get you the keys and you can be on your way. Do you want me to accompany you to check that everything is OK?'

'No, thank you for being so helpful we'll manage I'm sure.'

'Right, back in a second.'

Again, he disappeared into the back office returning with a small set of keys and a document folder.

'Thank you for your business, Mrs Webb,'

He handed over the folder and the keys.

'In the folder you'll find all the information you need and details of how to get in touch should there be any problems.'

'Thank you for all your help, Jake, I'm sure everything will be all right.'

Lyndsey placed all the documents in her bag left the office turning to the right pulling her scarf up around her head once more.

Mohammad made the excuse of speaking with Jake for a few more minutes by asking to see any other brochures he had on similar apartments.

REECE AND GREY had been watching the front door of the estate agents since following Tourist One when he'd left the Conference Centre and took a roundabout route to bring him to the estate agents where he'd entered a few minutes before. They had taken up positions at each end of the street. Mary once more stood and watched the eyes of the man she loved as he looked over her shoulder in the direction of the door recently entered by Tourist One.

'Do you know something, Joseph, you really do have beautiful blue eyes.'

'Do you mind I'm trying to concentrate here?' He smiled.

He'd noticed the woman who had left the offices pulling the red pattern scarf around her head, as she'd walked back in the direction of the Great Northern Square where Grey had been looking at the goods in a window display with some interest while still watching for the appearance of Tourist One, but that didn't surprise him, as the cold wind made it difficult to stand about Deansgate for any length of time if he had a scarf he would pull it round him too.

'What's happening, I'm beginning to freeze here?' Mary still had her back to the estate agents.

'Nothing much, wait a second. Alpha Three, let's swap and keep warm with some movement.'

'Roger that, good idea.'

Both agents carried out the swap with ease. Just as they'd done so Tourist One reappeared onto Deansgate. Reece saw him first and noticed he was walking towards Alpha Three who now had her back to him.

'Alpha Three, keep walking ahead Tourist One has left the building and is now walking to the junction again.'

'Roger, Alpha One. I'll turn left at the junction and find a closed location.'

Closed location meant a safe place from where she could observe without being seen. Reece and Mary moved after Tourist One on the same side of the street as he continued to walk towards the junction ahead.

Grey had turned left into Hardman Street junction and entered a shoe shop with a large window that looked out onto the street giving her a view of Tourist One as he crossed the junction continuing to walk straight ahead on Deansgate. She then left to catch-up as Reece and Mary crossed the same junction about seventy yards behind their target. All three continued to watch and follow Tourist One as he took his time walking through the central Deansgate area of Manchester without, it soon became apparent to Reece, any purpose whatsoever.

He eventually entered a Chinese restaurant in the China Town area of the city. Reece and Mary crossed to a Starbucks Coffee House opposite and waited for Grey to join them.

'OK, April do you fancy a Chinese?' Reece asked.

'Could do, I like Chinese.'

'We need someone in there just in case he is meeting someone. Mary was behind him earlier and I've been near him all day, so it has to be you. We will stay here for a coffee. If he moves on or you need us shout out.'

'Will do.'

She then crossed the street and entered the restaurant leaving Reece and Mary to order a coffee and continue to watch from the window.

'Alpha Control, check out the Deansgate Estate Agent office and see if we have anyone in there who's known,' said Reece.

Chapter Fifty-four

When she'd left the estate agents Lyndsey had turned into the wind coming down Deansgate pulling up her scarf to protect her face. Walking back on the route she'd come she noticed the lovebirds on the other side of the street in a couple's close embrace. It had been a long time she thought, since she'd held her husband so close, before he'd committed himself to Allah, becoming a martyr and leaving her behind to become the White Widow. Now she was back on the same soil with the intent to honour his memory and make the British feel even more pain for their support of a false prophet.

When she entered apartment C12, she noticed how quiet it was, having come up from street level and with all the double-glazed windows closed there was a strange silence. Looking through the rear balcony doors she could see the back door of the Midland Hotel in the distance now lit up by street lighting as the evening darkness began to descend.

THE INSIDE OF the van was lit up as his phone began to buzz in the darkness of the carpark. He could see it was a text from Lyndsey.

I'm in will buzz you up when you get here.

On my way. Costello text back.

Lifting the bag beside him and placing the Browning into his belt at his back Costello locked the van and headed for the lift.

Costello walked straight to the Great Northern Apartment building and pressed the buttons marked C12 and then the call button. Immediately in reply he heard the open lock release the front door. The lift to the twelfth floor seemed to take an age but when the doors opened on the landing, he turned left to find the door to apartment C12 already open. Waiting inside he heard Lyndsey's voice.

'Come in quickly and close that door, there's an awful draft when it's open.'

'Nice to see you too. You want to try to sit in a cold van in a cold carpark.'

'You're here now. Do you want to set up? Jake has kindly left us a welcome basket with tea, coffee, biscuits, and milk.'

'I got bloody soaked just walking a few hundred yards, so a cup of hot tea is first on the agenda.'

MOHAMMAD LOVED CHINESE food and he'd used this restaurant before and knew the quality was excellent. Although it was still early, there were plenty of customers and he always thought that was a good indicator for quality. He was so engrossed with his menu he didn't notice the SG9 operator sit at a table at the back of the room behind him. Grey asked for a menu and spoke quietly into her body mic.

'Tourist One alone, looks like he's only here for the food just eating, no calls, will report.'

'Roger, Alpha Three, we'll stay here and enjoy our coffee or two.'

257

A voice cut across the conversation.

'Alpha One, we're in position parked up on Deansgate if you need us.'

Harrison and Cousins had arrived.

'Great, Alpha Four. Keep position we have Tourist One in a restaurant in Chinatown, but we might need your help if he meets up with anyone.'

'Roger, Alpha One, we're dry, at least for the moment.'

Chapter Fifty-five

Jim Broad was now sitting in the comms section of the hanger listening in to the conversation of his team. Broad knew the final decision when to move, when to act, would be down to him and Fraser would back him all the way whatever he decided.

'Sir, a call from Sir Ian again.' It was one of the communication operators speaking, interrupting his thoughts. Right on que it was the MI6 Chief on the phone.

Calling back so soon, this should be interesting.

'Sir Ian, how can I help you?'

'Jim, I don't know if it's good news or not, but as you know we've been monitoring the airwaves for Costello's phone conversations, but it seems that our friends in GCHQ in Cheltenham can also monitor any text messages.'

Broad knew that the Government Communications Headquarters were good at monitoring things, but he was surprised they could also break into the text messaging facilities of the target's phones.

'Any news will be helpful if it clears the mud from the picture a bit more.'

'Well it appears that our Mister Costello is somewhere close to the Conference Centre as we speak. A text message he received about an hour ago shows him to be near there. But we can't pinpoint exactly where.'

'Do we know the message?'

'Yes, I'm in. Will buzz you up when you get here, Costello replied, On my way. That was all, but we now have the phone the other person is using so we're monitoring that as well. We're starting to link all these people together, so we hopefully will get more which will help you and your team. I've organised the GCHQ for you to get these phone communications in real time through your comms there which will save time. No sense in me getting a breakdown here and then having to contact you. Have you the means to work that?'

'Yes, no problem, that'll be helpful. The team have been following that one guy around the Conference and then the Deansgate area all day as you know. We don't think he's contacted anyone other than by phone earlier. He's currently sitting having a meal in a Chinese restaurant in China Town and we have people covering him. We have the troop on standby in Irlam at what we think is the safe house ready to move in close later tonight, so I believe we've at least two of their people covered.'

'What about Irlam, Jim? Are you thinking of hitting the house?'

'Not for now. We'll try to get close enough to find out who's in there first, but I think we're getting close to the end game. If there's people in there and they're the kind of people we believe they are, then we can't let them leave and get mixed up with the public.'

'Agreed, but if we move too soon and the rest of the terrorist outfit are already gone, we may only get the small fry and the big fish will disappear. It's something we have to think about. Either way, call me back before you make your move. If I get anything more, I'll let you know right away. I'll bring Bryant and the PM up to date. I also think that now we have Costello and at least one other close to the Conference area we should get the Gold Commander and the Prime Minister's security team to beef up their cover. I know we expect Costello to make his move tomorrow, but I don't like him being this close without an actual location or eyes on him.'

'Agreed…but an increase in cover needs to be discreet not the Normandy Landing. I still think Costello is working to a schedule so let's give our teams a little more time.'

'Thanks, Jim, I'll keep in touch.'

The call ended, Broad studied the electronic maps on the wall once more one of China Town and one of Irlam both with a red dot showing exactly where he believed, at least two dangerous terrorists were currently located. Blue dots showed the locations of the SG9 team in Manchester and the SAS team in Irlam.

'Tourist One on the move,' April Grey broke through the silence in the room.

'Roger that, all teams be aware,' replied the comms operator.

The next voice over the network was that of Reece.

'Alpha One, I have him. By the look of things, he's heading back towards the Conference area. Alpha Two can you cover the foot approach to the front of the Midland Hotel, Alpha Four stay mobile in case we need vehicle cover.'

'Roger, Alpha One' replied both agents.

The voice of Broad broke in on the conversation.

'Alpha teams from Control. We have been informed by our friends that there are at least two more, including Costello, in your area. GCHQ have picked up a couple of text messages which indicate they may be holed up somewhere close to the Conference Centre so be aware. If they get anything concrete will let you know.'

Reece acknowledged receipt of the new information and continued to follow Tourist One as he walked straight by the Conference entrance and the front of the Midland Hotel.

Where are you off to now? thought Reece.

'Tourist One continuing on Peter Street past the Midland,' reported Grey, who was ahead of the target on the opposite side of the road.

'He's stopping and taking out his phone.' Reece could see him clearly from where he'd stopped with Mary outside the Midland front entrance.

'Now talking to someone, Alpha Four, can you come in from your end in case we need the help?' asked Reece.

'Roger, on my way,' Harrison replied.

Tourist One finished his call and started walking in the direction of Deansgate at the junction with Watson Street he turned left.

'I have Tourist One,' Harrison's voice spoke clearly over the air.

Now it was the turn of Jim Broad.

'Alpha Team, be aware your target has just spoken to a woman. He told her he was almost there. She replied she'd buzz him in. Looks like he is going to be meeting with his buddies, so stay on him.'

This was the time when the adrenalin would be pumping up in the watcher's systems. Now they were close anything could happen. Mary couldn't hear both sides of the conversation, but she'd been with him long enough to recognise the change in his voice when he spoke.

'On your toes, people, looks like our fox is going to ground.'

Reece kept up a steady pace fifty yards behind the target with April Grey behind Reece and catching up on the opposite side of the street. Harrison gave another update.

'Tourist One using intercom on the front of an apartment building. Now going in and waiting at lift, will try to get closer.'

As Reece and Mary followed, Grey reached the left turn that Tourist One had taken Harrison walked over to meet with them.

'He went into that block of apartments. It's called the Great Northern Tower, after the square in front of it, I guess. He was buzzed in. I can only say the lift definitely went up.'

'Great work, Steve, at least we know he's probably in there with Costello and a woman, so three here, and two in Irlam. Let's lock this down and see if we can zero in on what apartment they're in. Alpha One to control, did you get all that?'

'Roger that, Alpha One. I'm happy that we have this team narrowed down to two locations. Now we need to find out exactly which apartment they're in. I'll do some research here and keep an ear for more phone use and get back to you. Is there somewhere you can lie up in the meantime?'

'I'll keep two at a time in the car parked in Peter Street with a view of the front door. The rest of us will return to the security suite at the Conference so we can speak more securely.'

'Roger, Alpha One, call me when you get there.'

'April, you've been out in the cold for some time so go and get in the car with Joe. Steve, you come with me and Mary back to the suite. Alpha Two, can you park up with Alpha Three in Peter Street with a good view of the front door?'

'Roger, Alpha One, on my way,' replied Cousins.

Less than a minute later the BMW parked in the ideal spot to observe the building's front door. Grey joined Cousins in the car leaving the other three to walk back to the Conference suite.

Chapter Fifty-six

Mohammad had made himself a cup of tea and joined Lyndsey and Costello in the apartment sitting room. Both had been watching *Sky News* concerning the day's activity at the Conference. The pictures also showing the Prime Minister alighting from his car when attending a lunch with businesspeople in Manchester. The news reader then made a comment on what was expected in his speech to the Conference tomorrow.

'He might have to speak through a hole in his head.' Costello laughed.

'Not might, will,' said Lyndsey.

'I'm just glad to be in from the cold for now,' said Mohammad. 'I'm thinking of tomorrow…how are we set up?'

'No change. Sean does his bit and Waheed and Imtaz do theirs. In the panic and inevitable lockdown, we leave by different routes. Sean is going to set up in the morning, you get into the Midland, and if you can give us a heads up when the Prime Minister is heading towards the back door, then Sean has some warning which will help. His conference speech is pencilled in for 11.45 so we can expect him to walk over around eleven so be ready from 10.45 onwards. I'll get the van and we'll drive out of the area which, if we're quick enough, should be easy to do in all the panic.'

As she was speaking, Costello went over to the dining room table where he'd left the sports bag sitting on top. Unzipping the bag, he reached in and removed three large parcels of bubble wrap and began to unwind the wrapping from the objects inside. Mohammad and Lyndsey silently watched him produce the rifle barrel then the shoulder stock then the breech and trigger mechanism. Next, he took a smooth dry cloth and wiped down each of the parts before assembling each part into the whole. Finally, he attached a tripod stand and sniper scope. When he'd finished, he placed the completed weapon back to stand on the table the barrel almost the same length as the rest of the rifle. Pointing to the rifle he turned to speak to the two silent watchers.

'This, ladies and gentlemen, is a TRG 22 Rifle with a match sight mounting set and foldable bipod for stability when using. It's one of the most accurate rifles around and one of the best sniper rifles in the world and in the hands of someone who knows how to use it, such as myself, a deadly killing machine. I've spent time zeroing the rifle in before I came here, so I'm ready to play my part.'

'I know you've had something to eat, Mohammad, but Sean and I could do with something. Could you phone somewhere for a delivery?' asked Lyndsey.

'I'll check Google; what do you fancy?' replied Mohammad.

'I'm in the mood for some Indian food. What about you, Sean?'

'Sounds good but not too spicy.'

'That's great. I know a good Indian down near the station I could go and get a carry out from there, be back in about twenty minutes. I'll

get a bit of a mixture with some rice, that should be OK for both of
you?'

'Suits   me   and   some   chips,'   said   Costello.

Chapter Fifty-seven

In his suite in the Midland the Prime Minister loosened his tie and kicked off his shoes as he pushed himself back further into the leather armchair. The almost finished speech lay on the coffee table between himself and the two other men in the room. Sir Martyn Bryant and Sir Ian Fraser sitting in similar chairs opposite both had a crystal glass of malt whisky in their hand. Peter Brookfield took a long sip from his own glass of the same refreshing spirit. The lighting in the room was low adding to a relaxed atmosphere. Sir Ian had returned after his meal with Jim Broad and had updated both men in the room with the latest movements of Tourist One and the subsequent phone calls.

'So, Sir Ian, you believe you have these people tied down to two locations…one of them quite close to here. What now?' asked the Prime Minister.

'We're happy we have at least two under control at the house in Irlam. We don't know if there's anyone else there, so we're moving in closer later tonight to confirm one way or the other.'

'What then?' interrupted Bryant.

'We don't know what weaponry they have inside the house or how many to use it. Either way we need to keep them confided to that location without giving them the opportunity to blow the whistle on us to the rest of their friends, who we now think are somewhere in the apartment block not far from here.'

'And where are we with that end of things?' asked Brookfield.

'As I've said before there may be at least three in there, Tourist One surveillance observed going in. There is an unknown woman inside, possibly Sharon Lyndsey, who buzzed Tourist One into the building and we now believe from intercepted text messages, Sean Costello as well. We're monitoring all the phones both at Irlam and now the apartment.'

'I think what the Prime Minister needs is some sort of end plan. Do you have one, do you have an idea of how this will end, what about the people out there who know what your team have been doing?'

There it was again, the famous Sir Martyn Bryant ass covering, thought Fraser. What are you going to do never mind what was agreed, I'm not letting you wriggle out this time, thought Fraser?

'As you know, Prime Minister, from the very start, SG9 was set up for such a scenario and at the very start of all this they were given the heads up to track these people down and deal with them, to work ever in the shadows. Now is not the time to second guess us but to be determined in completing what we set out to do, not just for this operation but for the original idea of opposing this very kind of threat to our country and to our people. The SG9 team have completed the first part of their task by tracking these terrorists, for that's what they are, terrorists, down to a location where, with a little more work we can finish the task. I believe we have to send a message. We have to let the people out there know we'll protect them no matter what. The real people out there don't care how we deal with the likes of Costello and Lyndsey as long as we protect them. Fail and they'll crucify us. Fuck the media. A week down the road and it's another story they're chasing.'

He knew by mentioning the people out there that Brookfield would as a politician convert the word people to votes in his head and there was nothing the voters loved more than a strong leader.

'Of course, Sir Ian, I totally agree so let's get this out of the way as soon as possible. As things stand it's going to get more coverage than my speech tomorrow. It's just the timing and how we're going to deal with it.'

Bryant had said nothing, just nodding his head in silent agreement.

'Of course, Prime Minister, so if you don't mind, I'll get it *out of the way* as you put it.' Sir Ian finished his whisky and left the room.

'I want you to keep a close watch on things, Martyn. No mistakes and no comebacks.'

The politician was determined to cover his back.

Chapter Fifty-eight

April Grey had fallen asleep almost as soon as she sat inside the car. Cousins continued to watch the front door of the Great Northern Apartment building, he let her sleep. A few people entered and left the building but not his target. The rain had stopped, and the evening light had faded into darkness, the street lighting lit up the square and its buildings making identification of the people coming and going easier. Grey had been sleeping for an hour and a half when he saw him come out the main apartment door.

'I have Tourist One leaving the building and turning down Watson Street.'

April Grey woke immediately as the reply came over the radio from Reece.

'Roger, Alpha Two can you follow on foot, Alpha Three stay with the vehicle, we'll come to your location.'

'Roger, Alpha One, will do,' replied Cousins, he was out of the car and walking at speed in the direction Tourist One had taken.

Grey watched the door of the apartments to see if anyone else was watching or looking for surveillance, there was no one.

Cousins kept fifty yards behind closing the gap when his target turned a corner out of sight only to reacquire him once more. Target One didn't go far, he passed the front of the Hilton Hotel on

Deansgate and walked towards the train station before turning left and into an Indian Restaurant, The Raj. Cousins kept the team updated with every twist and turn. Cousins passed the restaurant and saw Tourist One standing at the counter with a menu in his hand. He found a safe place across the road where he could see the front door.

'Surely he's not eating again?' said Reece over the radio.

'No, he is still standing at the counter. He may be ordering a carryout,' replied Cousins.

'Feeding his friends in the apartment no doubt. Stay with him Alpha Two we'll meet with Alpha Three in the car.'

Twenty minutes later, Cousins reported Tourist One on his way back to the apartments. Reece, now sitting with Grey and Mary in the BMW watched as Tourist One pressed the door button and the apartment number he wanted to be buzzed into the building. Seconds later Joe Cousins joined the rest of the team in the car sitting in the back seat behind Reece.

'It looks like they might be settling down for the night, so we should try to run a sleep pattern for ourselves. I'm sorry but we're going to have to use the cars, it won't be comfortable, but we need to stay close to the targets. Mary, I'll drop you back at your hotel,' said Reece.

'I can sleep in a car.'

'No, you need to get some sleep we need you fresh in the morning to help us spot Costello if he's about, I'll pick you up at six. Joe and April can stay here, Steve, you come with me. No risks, if you see anything, let everyone know.'

'This might be a long shot, but apartment buildings of that size usually have a warden or security man. Do you think I should go and check at least if there is one, he might be able to tell us where in the building our friends might be?' asked April Grey.

'It's worth a try, April, but that building has 257 apartments, I googled it, so we don't want a panic or a situation getting out of control so tread carefully,' replied Reece.

Reece and Steve Harrison took Mary back to her hotel in the second BMW then returned to park up at the bottom of Watson Street looking back in the direction of the Great Northern Square and in line of sight with April Grey and Joe Cousins.

'All Alpha callsigns, this is Alpha One I'm parked up on Watson Street one hundred yards from target door. Let's take turns, people. I'll start for the first two hours everyone else try to get some sleep. Any luck with the enquiry, Alpha Two?'

'No luck tonight there was a sign on the door that says someone will be available between eight and five tomorrow, so we'll have to wait until he or she turns up.'

'Right, let's speak to them when they do, we could also approach the estate agents where we saw Tourist One, they should be open around nine. Or better still.'

Reece spoke into his body mike.

'Alpha Control. Local police usually hold details of key holders in case of a fire or burglary of businesses. Can you chase it up and see if we can get some information from them on our friend Tourist One and if he got the apartment from them? They might just be able to tie it down to which one they're in. It's a risk as Tourist One might work for them but I don't think so I think it's more likely he is a client.'

'Roger, Alpha One, will get back to you.'

'What's happening with the Irlam address, Alpha Control?' asked Reece.

'The Tango Team are moving forward around 0200 to recce the building and place a mike on the window. Depending on the results, it's the intention to hit the targets when they leave the building and they have them under visual control.' This time it was Jim Broad who had replied.

'Roger that, Control, unless we get more information on which apartment they're using, we'll hold and observe here,' replied Reece.

'OK, Steve, you get some sleep if you can. This whole operation looks like it's going to kick off soon one way or the other, I'll give you two hours.'

'Thanks,' said Harrison as he pressed the recliner button for his seat and tried to get into a comfortable position. Within minutes he was asleep his breathing slow. Reece knew that Grey and Cousins would be able to do the same and would be asleep in the BMW across the square. By now the local police would be told to leave the people in the cars alone. Putting the area of the Conference and the hotel out of bounds to regular patrols wasn't on the cards. There were too many dignitaries attending the Conference. Reece knew that when they moved on Costello and friends, they would have to be sure to wear the armbands provided by ACC Lockwood, even then they would be at risk of being mistaken for the enemy by over hyper police officers with little experience and the adrenalin rush of a gunfight going on around them. The waiting while trying to stay alert was the hardest part of surveillance but Reece knew the waiting would be over soon, so staying alert was the most important part now.

Chapter Fifty-nine

At two in the morning the night was quiet and the darkness deep except when directly under the few street lights illuminating the shadows around the Kings Road and the few streets it serviced in Irlam. The troop team had sent the van back to the Hanger at Barton to pick up a few pieces of equipment. Four SAS soldiers in full assault clothing and equipment left the back of the van and made their way to the front of the target house. Two of them took up positions at the end of the driveway at number two Henley Avenue, with their MP5 H&K rifles with suppressors fitted covering the other two soldiers who moved forward to the front downstairs window. One rifle covered the front door while the other covered the window where the two soldiers in front now approached low down and quiet. All the curtains in the house had been drawn closed and the lights in the downstairs front room were still on. The four-foot-high shrubbery and hedging gave them the cover they needed from the street. One soldier placed two sucker devices, sealing them to the glass while the other covered him with a SIG Sauer pistol. As close as they were to the window, they could hear muffled voices from inside. A dog was barking in the distance. Happy the listening device was securely stuck to the glass, both soldiers returned to the end of the short driveway and all four back to the van. The whole time they were outside and exposed was six minutes, another job well done.

Inside the van a signaller from the regiment sat facing the electronic equipment picking up the short frequency feedback from the sucker mike, now on the terrorist safe house window. He flicked a switch which would boost the signal back to the hanger where Jim Broad could listen in real time to any conversation in the downstairs area of the target house. Surprisingly, at first the voices were still muffled then after the trooper swivelled a few dials on the equipment the voices came through clearly.

'Imtaz, hold the camera steady, that's it. I make this statement because I'm willing to die in the great battle against the enemy of Islam and Allah, blessings be upon him. I accept this task and will fulfil my destiny. The Great Satan America and her little Satan Britain, will be punished for their failure to acknowledge the one true faith and for the murder of the followers of that faith, this is why they must be punished. Allahu akbar, Allahu akbar, Allahu akbar.'

'Allahu akbar,' a new voice said.

The recording equipment in the troop van had picked up the whole conversation. Jim Broad realised he'd been holding his breath throughout the short clip of conversation. What he'd just heard only confirmed everything he already knew about the type of people he'd been dealing with they couldn't let them leave the house, a suicide bomber let loose on a public street didn't bear thinking about.

The voice that had given his statement of preparation for death spoke again.

'Now, brother, let us get some rest, our battle with the infidel begins in the morning.'

'Allah be praised, brother.'

'That's the downstairs lights out and a light coming on in the front upstairs,' reported a trooper who had eyes on the front of the building.

'Tango One, can you come back to control, we need to discuss an assault on the house tonight,' said Broad.

'Roger, Alpha Control, I'm on my way. I've ordered daylight aerial photos of the target house they should be there now can you have them available when we get back?'

'They are here, and we've uploaded them onto the big screen.'

'Roger that, I'm on my way.'

Jim Broad phoned Reece and brought him up to date with the details of the conversation. Reece answered the call on the second buzz of his phone which had been on silent but sitting on the dash the light had lit up the car interior. His Casio watch said it was 0230.

'So, what happens now, boss?'

'What we've heard, means they've forced our hand. We can't let them get out of that house to mingle with the public and we can't have a standoff situation lasting who knows how long before the press gets on to it and help tip off their friends. In that scenario they could also phone the others tipping them off. I intend sending in a troop assault team on the house about 6 a.m. to take them out of the picture, from what we've heard and from what we know this is not going to end well for us unless we take the upper hand now.'

'I agree, boss, when you go in let me know. We will be ready for any movement here; these people need to be stopped whatever it takes. We also need the caretaker here right now. I need to talk to him and find out who we have here, there's at least three in there so we might need backup ourselves when we move on them. I'm sending you the number displayed on the building's door as the emergency contact number so you should be able to track him down.'

'Leave it with me, I'll let you know how I get on. I'll also be getting the police to give us a secure zone to work inside to deal with both locations and take care of civilians.'

When the call finished, Reece noticed that Steve Harrison had brought the seat up from the recline position and had been awake during the phone call.

'Sorry, did I wake you?'

'No, I've been trying to sleep but I never can in these situations, I get some extra energy from somewhere I don't know.'

'By the look of things, the troop are going to hit the house in Irlam before daylight. I hope we can talk to the caretaker here before then and work out where our friends are staying.'

'If we do find them what then?'

'We have some time to prepare an assault but if they get news that we've hit their house in Irlam we might have to move quickly, we can't let them escape. From now we start to prepare. I want everyone in their vests and armbands on and the H and K out of the boot we might just need the heavy firepower before this is over. I'll go over and tell the others. You stay here and keep watch.'

Reece walked across the square and getting into the back seat he found that April was asleep in the front passenger seat, waking when Reece opened the car door.

Reece quickly brought Grey and Cousins up to date, telling them to prepare their equipment just as he'd told Harrison.

'When the caretaker gets here, we need to have a quick chat with him. In the meantime, Steve and I'll pick up Mike as arranged. April, if the caretaker arrives before I get back, have that chat.'

'Are you OK with bringing her into a dangerous situation?' asked Grey.

'She's lived with dangerous situations all her life. Even with his face change I believe she could still identify Costello and if she gives us that advantage, the risk is worth taking. I've talked to her about the risk, now that Costello knows she might be working with us her days are numbered if we don't get him first. Our job now is to keep on the ball and get these people. The boss will be pushing the police to give us a secure zone for us to work inside and to stop civilians getting involved.'

'Will they know we're inside their zone?' asked Cousins.

'That's the plan, but I don't know when they'll take up position, so keep   alert.'

Chapter Sixty

Middleton and his assault team studied the aerial photos identifying all the approaches to the Irlam house and the buildings surrounding the target area. The rear garden was surrounded by a five-foot wooden panel fence, difficult to get past but not impossible.

Middleton was thankful that the setup of the house was similar to the one at the SAS base and training ground that was used for assault drills and training. The fact there didn't appear to be any innocent civilians made the choice easy, a hard assault through the front door and window with two soldiers covering the back door in case of an attempted escape.

Every member of the team, including Middleton, who would go in through the front door were now dressed in their flameproof jumpsuits with full-face respirator masks to protect against smoke. Each trooper carried two stun grenades, a Glock pistol, and the standard Heckler & Koch MP5 machine gun – capable of firing 800 rounds of 9 mm Parabellum rounds per minute. Each machine gun was fitted with a sound suppressor making it easier for the troopers to hear each other in a noisy environment which would already be overwhelmed with flashbang stun grenades and blast charges on the windows and doors.

Anything that can make the assault on a building where hostiles are expected inside was welcome and had come about from years of experience and practice learning what worked and what didn't.

Even then, SAS soldiers had it drilled into them to adapt as the circumstances arose. Put down overcoming firepower, cover each other, shoot to kill. The John Wayne wound in the shoulder or the leg was movie stuff…not real life. A wounded man can still return fire, a wounded man can still kill you, so kill him first.

Geoff Middleton was confident he had the men to do the job. Each one knowing where he fitted in to the assault.

Middleton finished the briefing, and everyone broke away to make the last checks and to prepare in their own way. The practice drills were over. Some of the troopers had already experienced real fire situations, only two would be experiencing it for the first time.

'What do you need from me?' asked Broad who had been sitting quietly at the back of the room watching Middleton brief his men.

'Now that you've handed over to us it's the aftermath where we'll need your help. One of my troopers will be on comms here and you'll be able to hear the whole thing going down. Afterwards, we'll pull out quickly leaving the ground clear for the emergency services to go in and clean up. I'll be first through the front door,' said Middleton.

'I've already spoken to Mister Lockwood and he'll have the locals on standby ready to move in with an ambulance and fire brigade. There will be a senior police officer on the ground who knows they'll have to seal the house and keep the residents tied down. There'll be a door knock, and statements will be taken.

'We'll put out the gas explosion story stating there'll be a press release when the area is declared safe and some idea of what has happened can be explained. This will give us time to find out where the rest of our friends are in Manchester. We will need similar backup there as well. I've informed the powers that be where we are and what we intend to do. We set our watches for 0600 and then with a bit of luck we'll be able to move on the Manchester address before 11 a.m. If they try to leave before then we have the SG9 team in position to intercept. Good luck, Geoff, I'll be here until this is over if you need me.'

'Good, sunrise is 0710 so with any luck it will be all over at the house and if needed I can let your team in Manchester have a few of my men to help there.'

Middleton turned and left to join his men and finish preparing his own   equipment.

Chapter Sixty-one

With five minutes to go before 6 a.m. the police cordon moved in at the top of Kings Road.

The sun was starting to rise but it would be nearly two hours before the light would be strong enough to pick out the SAS team who were now moving in closer to number 2 Henley Avenue. The attending police officers had been told very little. This was an anti-terrorist operation where they were only needed as backup and to stop anyone entering or leaving the road. The officers noticed there was also a fire engine and an ambulance parked up on the main road obviously under the same instructions as they hold back and wait for orders.

A minute before six a.m., a Transit van and two blacked out Range Rovers parked on the main road and eight fully combat dressed, heavily armed soldiers all wearing respirator masks left the vehicles and made their way, in twos, down Kings Road.

The police officers knew not to interfere or ask questions…this operation was way above their pay grade.

There was a fine rain falling and the grass, pavement, road, and windows of the surrounding houses glistened in the reflection of the street lights following the shadows left by the soldiers as thy moved forward in crouching positions. The police officers closer to Kings Road could see some of the soldiers were carrying what looked like small window frames. These soldiers had their MP5s on slings over their shoulders while the others moved quietly with their weapons in the raised position pointing and sweeping to the front.

Middleton spoke into his face mike, constantly reporting to Alpha Control the progress of the mission.

'Alpha Control, Tango Team moving into position, will report when making entry.'

'Roger, Tango One, waiting out your numbers,' replied the SAS trooper in the control room.

Jim Broad had covered many operations like this, and it was the waiting that was the hardest. Waiting and hoping for the best. There was always the silence. The straining to hear every word coming over the radio waves. The communication rooms were always quiet at these times, leaving the professionals to get on with their jobs. It was always as if no one was breathing.

The SAS team on the ground had moved into their pre-planned positions: two troopers moved to the rear fence, two to the front downstairs window, and Middleton and three other men to the front door.

Middleton asked for a situation report from the trooper in the van who was monitoring the sounds in the house and was told that all was quiet. Middleton instructed the two soldiers at the rear of the house to move forward. This was part of the plan where they would quietly lift up one of the fence panels and slide into the garden before moving back door. The team had recognised the danger of being heard or seen from the target house, but it was a risk they had to take.

The silence from the house continued as the troopers moved through the fence panel, let it back down into its original position, and moved up to the rear door. There was still no sound or movement from inside the house as the soldiers at the front window removed the sucker mike and placed one of the framed charges up against the window while Middleton did the same at the front door.

The street was deathly quiet. Even the breathing of the SAS men was quiet and controlled behind the face masks. Middleton gave a thumbs up and the ten second fuses on the shaped frame charges were set and the troopers pulled back to the end of the garden path. The explosives were set in such a way that when the blast came the explosion was forced inwards. The flash, the bang, and the falling debris wouldn't only waken the residents in the street but many people in the surrounding the area but most definitely the people inside the house.

Before the last of the debris had hit the ground, Middleton's voice came over the airwaves, 'Go, Go, Go.' In seconds, the SAS troopers were inside the building, two taking the stairs, two inside the living room, and two into the kitchen after shooting off the back-door hinges. Two more men covered the building from outside. Inside the house, the troopers hit darkness and smoke was hindering their vision, but the respirator masks protected their eyes and breathing. Calling out 'Clear' as they moved through the house. The two troopers who had entered the through the kitchen door took over covering the living room while the two troopers who had entered through the front living room window turned to join Middleton and the second trooper who had headed up the stairs through the blasted front door.

As they reached the main landing, Middleton turned right with a trooper behind him. He moved to the main bedroom and stood with his back to the wall and opening the door, he threw in a flashbang. At almost the same time the two troopers who had entered the house through the front window followed up the stairs, turned left on the landing, and executed the same procedure at the door to a front facing bedroom. Both flashbangs went off at almost the same time, brightly illuminating the bedrooms followed with a loud bang. The final two soldiers were now covering the open bathroom and the third bedroom door which were both at the rear of the house.

As Middleton and his men were to discover, the front bedroom he attacked was empty. It had been Costello's room but was now vacant. The second bedroom contained a very shaken Imtaz who only had time to stand beside his bed and fire blindly with his pistol where he thought the door was, the blast and light from the flashbang had done its job. When the first trooper entered the room, he recognised the Asian man who'd been photographed going for the local shopping trip.

The rounds he fired hit the bedroom wall to the left of the soldier. With his Heckler & Koch already levelled, he fired back with a burst of five rounds hitting the man who, afterwards, reminded him of a rabbit caught in a car's headlights; eyes wide and scared. Three of the rounds hit Imtaz squarely in the chest and the other two hit his face and temple blowing his brains out the back of his head and spreading a halo of blood and gore over the wallpaper behind him.

Middleton's voice came over the airwaves, 'Contact, wait out.' That was the signal to the SAS radio operator and Broad that contact had been made with the enemy and there would be no more communications with them until the operation was complete.

Waheed had been in the rear bedroom of the house. His mind had been spinning about what the morning and daylight would bring. He and Imtaz had slept fully clothed to be prepared for all eventualities. The loud blasts had woken him from his light slumber, and he knew immediately what was happening. The enemy were here, and he was prepared to become the martyr he'd always known he would be one day.

That day was here.

He stood beside the bed facing the door as it opened. He could see for a split second the black gloved hand as the SAS Trooper threw in the flashbang. Waheed knew what to do he'd trained for this in the desert. As the flashbang sailed through the air, he dived behind the bed, closing his eyes and placing his hands over his ears. Even then the noise and flash that came burnt into his eyes and ears. He armed the small bomb he had beside the bed and tossed it towards the bedroom door as the first of the two troopers crept in.

The soldier saw the device flying through the air and instinctively dived to the left of the bedroom door when it exploded but the blast, in the confined space, killed him instantly. His body armour unable to provide protection at such close proximity to the explosion with the nails embedded into the Semtex doing most of the damage shredding his skin and penetrating deep into his body destroying the rear bedroom wall of the house. Waheed, still down beside the bed, had been protected although some of the nails tore through his back arms and legs.

He was still conscious and rose with his pistol in hand to continue his battle with the infidel. As he did so, he called on his God, 'Allahu akkbar, Allahu akkbar.'

SAS soldiers trained for such a situation: don't stop, keep fighting until it's over. The second soldier and Middleton, who had joined him, rushed through the door with rifles raised and they both fired at the rising Waheed hitting him twenty times and throwing him back against the wall before he fell forward onto the shredded bed. The wall behind him covered with blood and mixing with the cement and bone sticking to the bullet holes that peppered the wallpaper.

The SAS men checked their downed comrade confirming the worst.

There is a collapsible Clock Tower which is assembled on special occasions on the Parade Ground at the headquarters base nicknamed the Head-Shed by SAS operators but known the world over as the Hereford base of 22nd SAS Regiment or Stirling Lines after the regiments founder David Sterling. The Clock Tower also bears the names of every SAS soldier killed in action. Soldiers of the regiment who survive such operations call it beating the clock. Unfortunately, on this occasion another name would be added to the Clock Tower list.

Rolling the body of the terrorist over to take a photo of his face as they did with all such enemies, Middleton noticed the dead man was smiling through teeth that had a wide gap.

Middleton's voice came across the airwaves once more. Jim Broad listened with intent. 'Alpha Control, house secure, two enemy and one friendly KIA, bring in a cordon.'

It was Broad who answered. 'Roger, Tango One, will do. Sorry to hear you've lost a friend. Return here as soon as you can for a debrief and reassignment.'

'Roger, Alpha Control, on our way.'

On the command from Broad, via the Gold Command in Manchester, the emergency services moved in to secure the house and the street.

The residents had been wakened by the explosion and the confusion that came from such a rude awakening. The troop Transit and Jeeps moved to the end of the street and Middleton and his men were quickly picked up having lifted two mobile phones and any documents they found they were driven out of the Kings Road and Irlam back to the hanger.

As the police, fire, and ambulance crews moved in to surround the target house and seal of the street, GCHQ, on the instructions from Broad, froze the phone, Internet, and mobile signals within a quarter of a mile of the street.

Gold command would, when asked to, release the agreed press release of a suspected gas explosion and the area would be sealed off until a full check of the area had been made.

Broad sat in on the de-brief of the assault team when they returned then phoned Sir Ian Fraser to brief him.

Chapter Sixty-two

'What happens now, Jim?' asked Sir Ian.

'From the weapons and explosives used by the two at the house in Irlam, we can expect the rest of these people to be similarly armed, so we take no chances. We hit them hard, if they want to come peacefully, they'd better put their hands up quickly. We've been trying to contact the building society people and the building's caretaker without success. There's a company number with offices opening at 9 a.m. we will chase both. The caretaker comes on duty at 8 a.m. so we'll be there to talk to him when he arrives. Reece and his team have the building under close surveillance and the police are moving in a cordon as we speak.'

'Thank you, Jim, I'll update the PM and Martyn Bryant. My feelings are that this won't end well, but we all knew why the Department was set up, so let's get on with it.'

'The next few hours will tell a tale. I'll be letting Reece know after this call to get in there and sort it.'

THE PRIME MINISTER was an early riser even though he'd been awake to past three in the morning working on his Conference speech. Now sitting in his suite with Bryant and Sir Ian he was quickly taking on-board the latest update from C, his head of Her Majesty's Secret

Service. Although he'd been expecting the operation to come to a head, now that it was here, he still felt some unease in his stomach. He'd experienced this feeling many times before when he knew people would be looking at him for the leadership he'd desired all his political life. The decision had been made, the operation had started, and one of the reasons he'd been up so late working on his speech, was that he had to work on a different opening which would encompass the resulting deaths and what it would mean for the war on terrorism, the future of the country, and the type of politics he'd put in motion when agreeing to the formation of the Department SG9.

'All right, let's get on top of this, Sir Ian. When will your people move in?'

'We hope to have the details of which apartment the terrorists are in just after 8 a.m. We'll be moving in shortly after that. Now that the SAS are finished in Irlam, they're back at Barton being debriefed and reassigned to the apartments. In the meantime, SG9 have the building under surveillance and Gold Command are moving a police cordon in to secure the access to the area once our people move in.'

Throughout the briefing, Sir Martyn Bryant had said nothing. Now he spoke, giving both the PM and Sir Ian a chance to drink what was now a cold coffee.

'And you're happy we have the communications in Irlam screwed down so that the terrorists in the apartments have no idea their friends have already gone?'

'As much as we can. The media are only getting a small gas explosion briefing at the moment. Of course, we can't be one hundred per cent, but at the most they'll be confused. Mobile coverage has been closed down with no signals going in our out. If they do try to run, we'll be ready for them.'

The Prime Minister stood and shook the hand of both men.

'Thank you, gentlemen, I hope our next meeting sees the end of this. If you'll excuse me, I have meetings to get to. I'll also be briefing them regarding the operation in Irlam and the upcoming one here, under the strict embargo that they're sworn to secrecy until it's over.'

BRYANT AND FRASER shared the lift down to the foyer.

'You have my mobile number, Sir Ian. Keep me informed every step of the way. I'll be here in the hotel holding meetings with the police, and members of the Intelligence Committee and Cobra to update them on your progress.'

Sir Ian Fraser left by the rear entrance to the hotel. His driver spotted him and pulled up at the door. Sir Ian got into the rear seat behind his bodyguard sitting in the front passenger seat. Sir Ian always thought it less dangerous to him if he got into the car himself instead of someone having to hold the door open for him.

'Take me to the hanger at Irlam please.'

No more needed saying. He phoned Jim Broad and told him he was on his way.

REECE AND STEVE Harrison had arrived at the hotel a few minutes after 6 a.m. Mike was waiting in the reception area and smiled when she saw Reece come through the door.

'Ready?' asked Reece.

'As always,' she replied.

Reece was pleased that she'd dressed sensibly for the day, dark blue jeans, black trainers, and a blue hooded top with a white coloured blouse underneath. Reece thought no matter what she wore, she always looked beautiful.

'Steve is outside in the car. We will have to go near the apartments to keep up a surveillance presence for the minute. Are you OK with that?'

'Yes, no problem, let's go.'

By the time they got back to the Square, the troop assault on the house had started. Reece waited in the car with Mary and Harrison. From the little they could hear over the communications with the hanger, they knew that there had been deaths at the Irlam house. Reece knew not to radio the hanger or phone Jim Broad. There would be no answer while they were busy with the ongoing assault operation.

He waited in silence with the others until his phone buzzed with a call coming in from Broad. Reece listened without comment as Broad brought him up to date with the operation in Irlam.

'Where are you now?' Broad asked when he'd finished.

'We're waiting for the caretaker to arrive with eyes on the building as we speak.'

'Great, I'll try to get Middleton's people there after we've debriefed them.'

'Thanks, let me know when they're on their way. What about the police cordon?'

'I've spoken to our friend Mr Lockwood personally. He's been told from on high to give us any support we ask for. I know they have the equivalent of SO19 uniform police trained in building assaults, but I've told him we have enough people of our own to deal with this, so no mistakes, David.'

'No pressure there then. We have it covered for now and with any troop backup well covered. I just hope you can keep a tight blackout on the Irlam operation until at least 8 a.m. and we get the chance to speak to the caretaker and identify exactly where these people are in the building.'

'That's just over an hour away so I hope we can keep the lid on it until then. GCHQ are keeping all Internet and mobile phone communications closed down in the area until 8 a.m. at least. They will also be doing the same around the apartment once you find out where they are.'

'Any name for the caretaker yet?' Reece asked.

'Oh, yes, I forgot to say, it's Kevin Williams. He lives in Salford but has been out at a party all night not known where he's not answering his phones'

'No problem, we'll keep an eye out for him, will let you know when   he's   here.'

Chapter Sixty-three

Inside apartment C12, in the Great Northern Tower block, all three terrorists had been up for about an hour. Coffee had been made in the pot twice and the conversation had gone over the plans for the day. The clock on the wall said it was 7.45 a.m. There was no TV, but the radio was tuned into Radio Manchester and the usual traffic report stated the usual traffic jams around the approaches to Manchester City Centre on a working weekday morning. Mohammad was dressed in his suit and getting ready to leave for the Conference after the eight o'clock news.

They had gone over the plan for the day a number of times. Mohammad would go to the Conference then, at around 9 a.m. make his way to the Midland Hotel and from inside hopefully give a heads up to Costello that the target was on his way to the rear exit. Lyndsey laid out the plan of attack at the same time as the attack would be going down, she would be sitting in the van in the NCP car park ready to move to the front of the Great Northern Tower to pick up Costello. All would then get out of the area in the confusion when Imtaz and Waheed detonated their bombs.

Costello had looked through the scope of the rifle three times already since the light had improved. He could easily pick out people walking between the hotel and the main Conference building. It was still too early for the delegates, so they had to be Party workers or security. There was little or no wind and as the light became stronger, he had no doubt in his mind that he could hit every target he'd looked at in the head, with a follow up to the main torso, in plenty of time before the target crossed the open ground to safety. He'd kept the sliding glass doors slightly open, so there was no need for movement which might be seen from the ground in daylight. This had made the room cold, so all three were wearing a coat over their clothes, even with the central heating on full blast the room was freezing at this time of the early morning, before any warming winter sun had risen in the sky. This was also why they were on to their third pot of coffee.

'I think I'll leave now and get a full English breakfast in one of the cafés, without bacon' said Mohammad. 'I'll text when I'm through security and into the Conference area.'

Lyndsey looked at her phone and noticed she had no signal. 'My phone signal has dropped out must be a problem.'

Both men checked their phones noting the same problem.

'All right,' said Lyndsey 'Let's not panic, it could be a local problem but let's not take any chances. Mohammad, you go ahead with the plan, go get your breakfast, get yourself a newspaper. If all is OK and you're happy you're not compromised, exit the hotel's rear door. If you think there is a problem, open the paper as if you're going to read it. If you do sense danger, we'll pull out and you do the same. It would be better to live for another chance than to get caught unnecessarily.'

'What about Imtaz and Waheed?' asked Costello.

'They will be martyrs to the cause and the distraction they'll make will help us retire to fight another day. Their deaths wouldn't be in vain, they'll strike a great blow in the name of Allah,' replied Lyndsey.

'Mohammad, walk out of the door at 9 a.m. exactly. I don't want to be bent down looking through the scope for hours.'

'I can do that.'

'We should be able to see you at a stretch from our view here anyway but that would help me.'

The radio brought their attention back to the announcer bringing the eight o'clock news. There was nothing significant and the mention that the Prime Minister Peter Brookfield would   address the Conservative Party Conference at eleven thirty this morning meant to the three people in the room that the operation was still on.

Reece had been listening to the same broadcast in the car and the fact there had been no mention of the house in Irlam meant that Jim Broad had done his job and stopped any news of the suspected gas explosion getting out for the minute. The next broadcast at eight thirty would be different. As the radio station turned to the traffic and weather reports for the day, Reece noticed a man in a long dark coat with its hood up approach the door to the Great Northern Tower and press the buttons on the entry keypad. Reece could see the man through the glass door turn left and using a set of keys from his pocket open a door to the left of the lift and stairs.

'I think our caretaker has arrived. Mary, you come with me. When I question him, it might be good to have a woman with me to keep him calm two unknown men this time of the morning might spook him, and we want his quick support. Steve you stay here and keep your eyes open.'

Reece pressed the radio mike. 'Alpha Team, I'm going to have a chat with our caretaker stay alert.'

April Grey and Joe Cousins replied, 'Roger that,' as did Alpha Control.

Leaving the car Reece and Mary quickly crossed the space to the door of the Tower Block and Reece pressed the button for the reception.

Chapter Sixty-four

When the man answered the door, Reece was surprised. In his mind, caretakers were always old retired men but then he remembered this young-looking man opening the door had been out all night at a party. Kevin Williams looked like a twenty something student wearing blue jeans with trainers and a Pink Floyd T-shirt. He was about six-foot with his black hair tied back in a ponytail. He was thin build with brown eyes on a thin face with a small goatee beard. Reece produce his security services ID and he could see the immediate look of fear on the man's face although Reece thought that was probably to do with the strong smell of the pot he'd obviously been smoking at his all-night party.

'Mister Williams, my name is Joseph. Can we have a few moments of your time?' Reece didn't bother to introduce Mary as he knew Kevin Williams wouldn't ask, his eyes were still fixed on the identity card inches from his face.

'Yes, of course, come in.'

'Is there somewhere we can talk in private?' asked Reece as he returned his ID to his pocket and Mary followed him into the hallway.

'Oh yes, of course. This way.'

They followed him into the small office he'd come out of before answering the door. Reece noticed there was a real nervousness both in

Williams's demeanour and voice, he would have to proceed gently if he was to get the help he wanted.

The office was small. More like a broom cupboard than an office with a desk with a laptop and a CCTV screen showing the front door and what Reece assumed to be the fire escape door at the rear of the building. There was two small swivel chairs and a small four drawer filing cabinet. Williams sat down on the chair at the desk. Reece and Mary continued to stand.

'What's this all about?' asked the nervous caretaker.

'You're not in any trouble, Mr Williams. Your party life is none of our concern,' said Reece.

He could see from the caretaker's face that he knew what Reece meant. His smoking habit was obvious but when he realised he wasn't in trouble, he relaxed.

'I'll help in whatever way I can.'

'We're interested in a new tenant who may have moved in yesterday. Do you have these records?'

'If they moved in yesterday, then the first I might know about it is if they're on my system here.' As he spoke, he pointed at the laptop.

'Can you fire it up please and check now?' said Reece.

He was glad he'd gone in softly softly with this man. He'd seen people in the past who, when being questioned by someone like Reece, automatically start to put barriers. Quoting their rights and asking for legal representation.

'Yes of course.' Williams turned to the laptop and after pressing a few buttons he brought up a screen showing the list of tenants in the building.

'The only new tenant moving in yesterday was a Mister and Mrs Grey in apartment C12.'

'What floor is that and what direction do the windows face?' asked Reece.

Mary was impressed how Reece had worked this man and got him onside without pressure.

'As the number says, it's C12 so on the twelfth floor. It faces to the back of the building with a balcony and patio type glass doors onto the balcony.'

'Did you see or speak to them?' asked Reece.

'No, they could have come in at any time to view it or move in. I didn't see them. I only see people when they have problems or if we cross in the hall. The estate agents that are registered with my system just update it remotely when people move in or out.'

'Does your front door CCTV record people coming in and out?'

'Yes, it's on a twenty-four-hour loop before it wipes itself and starts again at 9 a.m. every day.'

Reece looked at his watch 8.15 a.m. *Something's going our way for a change*, he thought.

'Can you bring the CCTV up from around 4 p.m. yesterday?'

'Yes, no problem.'

Again, the caretaker pressed a few buttons on the keyboard and a grainy picture of the front door entrance came up on the laptop screen.

The clock in the corner of the screen showed the time running down from 4 p.m. As it was nearing the end of the working day and students returning from college, there was a lot of people coming and going.

Looking over the caretaker's shoulder, Reece asked, 'Can you fast forward it until I ask you to stop?'

'Yes, no problem.'

For the next few minutes Reece and Mary watched the screen, Reece asking the caretaker to freeze the frame on two occasions until at 5.23 p.m. he asked him to freeze the screen once more. The pictures were in black and white but even though the picture wasn't very clear, he could see it was a woman wearing a scarf but Reece believed it was Sharon Lyndsey. Reece made the caretaker replay the frame five or six times and took a screenshot with his mobile as the caretaker informed him, he couldn't do it because of confidentiality for clients.

'Breach of confidentiality will be the least of your worries,' said Reece. 'If you obstruct me anymore, you'll be doing twenty years in Strangeways.' The look on the caretaker's face told Reece he got the message.

It was the best that Reece could do, and he didn't have time to argue. Playing the footage again, Reece pressed his hand hard into the caretaker's shoulder and shouted, 'Stop.' A tall man wearing a baseball cap with a clear NY logo had entered the building about twenty minutes after the woman carrying a large bag of some sort over his shoulder. Mary gasped, Reece could see from her expression and the fear in her eyes she knew who it was.

'Are you sure, Mary?' he asked.

She looked closer at the frozen picture. The man was looking straight ahead but had lifted his head slightly to see what floor the lift was on. It wasn't a full-face picture but enough for Mary to see the nose and mouth. This, along with the way the man had walked from the door to the lift, confirmed for her that she was looking at Sean Costello.

'Yes, I'm sure, I wish I wasn't.'

That was good enough for Reece. He stepped outside the office and spoke into his body mike.

'Alpha Control and Alpha Team, be aware that we've confirmed identification of Sean Costello in this building believed at this time to be in apartment C12. I'm going through the last twenty-four hours of CCTV and we have him entering the building fifteen minutes after a woman who may be Lyndsey around 5.30 p.m. yesterday. I'll check the rest of CCTV which isn't great quality.'

Reece went back into the caretaker's office and took another photo of the man and sent both photos out to the team and Jim Broad. He spoke to the caretaker, 'Let's keep going through it until this morning.'

Stopping the CCTV on two more occasions, he watched their target, Tourist One, enter and leave the building returning with the carryout dinner they'd seen him buy the night before. Now he knew for certain it was food for Lyndsey and Costello and that all three were still in the building, most likely in apartment C12.

When the CCTV had caught up with the clock on the wall of the office, it was now 8.30 a.m. Residents were starting to come and go through the front door.

April Grey's voice came over the radio confirming that Tourist One had just left the building and had turned right in the direction of Peter Street and the front of the Midland Hotel.

'Alpha Four, keep with him, everyone else hold your ground,' instructed Reece.

STEVE HARRISON LEFT the warmth of the BMW and followed Mohammad keeping fifty yards between them. April Grey stayed in the BMW parked near the entrance to the NCP car park and Joe Cousins sat in the car on the Peters Street side of the Square. Looking to his right he could see the front door of The Great Northern Tower Apartments and looking straight ahead he could see the disappearing figure of Tourist One followed by Steve Harrison.

Mohammad had stayed in the apartment to have another cup of coffee and listen to the radio. The fact there was still no signal on anyone's mobiles didn't bother him. He'd been living in the north-west of England for far too long to let what was a regular occurrence such as the loss of a mobile signal bother him. When he left and turned right at the front door of the building, he felt the fresh air on his face and realised the temperature had lifted slightly and the sun was breaking through the clouds with a little heat reaching the ground where he walked.

It's going to be a nice day, he thought.

Steve Harrison watched Tourist One cross the street and head towards St Peters Square where he entered the newsagent's and bought a copy of the *Daily Express*. He then walked to the security tents leading into the Conference at the side of the Midland Hotel.

'He's heading back into the Conference, what do you want me to do?' asked Harrison.

It was Broad who spoke first, 'Stay close to him.'

Reece spoke next, 'Stay close, Alpha Four, but if he makes any move that looks suspicious, take him out, for good if necessary.'

'Understood,' replied Harrison.

Steve Harrison closed the gap to around five yards and followed him through the security area. When Mohammed reached the body scanner, Tourist One showed empty hands and raised his arms to allow the metal detector to be swept over his body by the security guard. Harrison moved to the side of the scanner queue and showed his ID to the security officer before moving through to follow Tourist One.

Turning left, Mohammad entered through the rear door into the Midland Hotel. Harrison kept up a running commentary of their progress through security and as he followed Tourist One into the long corridor towards the front reception and lounge area of the hotel which was buzzing with the loud conversation of conference delegates.

Tourist One found a seat on his own and opened his newspaper. Harrison walked past him and sat at a table were two men were already seated and in conversation. They didn't pay any attention to Harrison but continued talking and making notes in their notebooks on the table in front of them. Harrison noticed that even though Tourist One had opened his paper he wasn't reading it. Instead he was looking over the top of the paper his eyes moving around the room. Harrison had seen this ploy used by armatures the world over in his years as an MI5 watcher, to try to identify security forces or enemy surveillance.

Harrison leaned slightly forward as if he was involved in the conversation of the two men sitting with him.

After twice checking the room, Tourist One folded his paper and checked his watch. Harrison could see the large clock above the reception desk it was 8.55 a.m.

'All stations, Tourist One is looking for opposition and checking his watch, still sitting in Midland.'

'Roger, Alpha Four, it looks like he might be on a time schedule,' replied Reece. 'So be ready to move in if needs be, I'm still with the caretaker so now that we only have two in the building, we'll get ready to move here when we get backup but will remain ready to move if we have to.'

'Alpha Control to Alpha Four, I'll let the Gold Command know you're in the area and have them watch our friend on the CCTV system ready to back you up should you need it,' said Jim Broad.

'Roger, Alpha Control, I'll keep you updated,' replied Harrison.

'Alpha Control to all call signs. Local mobile signals are being unblocked at 9 a.m. After that, GCHQ will keep a close ear on anything from our friends.'

'Thanks, boss,' replied Reece. 'Things could start to be interesting now especially when they find they cannot contact the Irlam team.'

IN APARTMENT C12, Lyndsey heard her phone bleep indicating she was getting a signal again. She checked the screen but there were no messages, just a screen showing the network had been cleared and her phone was working again. Almost at the same time Costello noticed his phone light up for a few seconds as he had it on silent, he now knew he was back up as well.

Costello was leaning across the table looking through the scope on top of the rifle. He'd zeroed-in on the rear door of the Midland Hotel. At 9 a.m. on the dot Mohammad walked out of the hotel and stopped on the steps where he stood still for a few moments with a newspaper folded under his arm. He then walked across the square towards the Conference Centre. Costello followed him for a few seconds before swinging the scope back on the doorway.

'Mohammad feels OK, he kept the paper folded,' said Costello.

'Wait a second.' Costello held his left hand in the air as he continued to look through the scope. A man had just walked out of the door and he was looking in Mohammad's direction. There was nothing strange in this but the fact he appeared to be talking to himself at the same time alerted Costello's senses.

'I think he could have a tail. A guy just behind him seems to be having a conversation with someone using a concealed mike. It might just be someone using a mobile phone now that they're up and running but I don't like it.'

'I don't like it either,' said Lyndsey. 'I've text Waheed and Imtaz with no reply, but they could be having the same signal problems we've had.'

'I'm beginning to not like this coincidence. Text Mohammad and let him know he may have company.'

'ALPHA ONE COME in.' It was Jim Broad.

'Go ahead, Alpha Control.'

'Our friends in the apartment have been trying to contact the Irlam crew and now a text to Tourist One telling him he may have company. They must have eyes on Alpha Four.'

'Roger, boss. How quickly can you get the Tango Team here? We need to move on this soon.'

'They're leaving here now. I'll get the security cordon tightened as soon   as   they   get   to   you.'

Chapter Sixty-five

Lyndsey spoke as she looked once more at her mobile screen. Mohammad had replied with a thumbs up emoji when she'd text him to be aware of possible surveillance.

'I'm not happy with this whole thing. No contact from Irlam and now possible watchers on Mohammad, I think we should abort and wait for another day.'

Costello was surprised. She was usually so positive and now she seemed afraid.

'There's always a possibility that they're on to us. But as you said Irlam phones might be having the same problems we were having and the guy behind Mohammad might just be talking into his own mobile hands-free mike or could be general security for the conference. We've come this far, and we're so close. We should hold our nerve just a little longer. At the very least I can do a lot of damage with this little baby.' He stroked the rifle with a look of love as he spoke.

'You're right. I might just be a little paranoid but let's take some precautions. I'll go down and have a look around. Then I'll wait in the van ready to take you away whatever happens. Now our phones are up and running again we can keep in touch. You OK with that?'

'Yeah, but before you go make me a pot of tea and I'll keep an eye on things. We're in the final leg and when Mohammad goes back into the hotel, he'll keep us updated.'

'Tea it is, throw me the keys of the van.'

STEVE HARRISON WAS now in the operations suite in the Conference Centre watching over Constable Jones's shoulder as he zoomed the CCTV camera onto the face of Tourist One. He sat in the café drinking coffee and reading his paper. Harrison noticed that even though he was reading the paper for real, he still stopped to take a look around when sipping his coffee.

'He's looking for me but I'm not there. Let's keep him in view at all times, constable.'

'Will do,' said Jones.

THE SOUND OF the gunfire was loud and close. Reece reacted first. He turned and ran out of the caretaker's office while pulling out his Smith and Wesson. He could hear screaming from outside the building. They had missed Lyndsey on the CCTV as the machine was rebooting for its next twenty-four hours cycle, she'd came out of the lift with two other residents and turned left as she walked towards the NCP car park.

As she'd passed April Grey sitting in the BMW, April had been watching her as she'd walked closer.

There was something familiar, something in the back of April's mind as the woman passed close by. April realised what it was as she neared; the red scarf. The same red scarf she'd seen the night before

311

outside the estate agents. April let Lyndsey pass the car then started to open the door to follow, but it was too late, the woman had turned back towards her and now had a gun in her hand.

Lyndsey knew right away the woman was security forces. She'd seen enough surveillance officers in her life to know the way the woman had discreetly watched her as she'd walked by. As she passed the car, she knew this was it, she'd been spotted.

Turning back towards the car, she pulled her gun out of her shoulder bag, aimed, and fired twice. The woman in the car already had one foot on the pavement. The first shot hit her in the chest throwing her backwards, the second in the neck producing a spray of dark red blood that filled the inside windscreen and window glass of the car in a split second.

Lyndsey turned and ran towards the car park. She dropped the gun back in her bag and took out her mobile and tried to dial Costello. It took her two attempts before he answered.

'Get out, they're on to us.' Was all she said as she ran.

The screaming Reece had heard was from two young girls who looked like students. They were looking into the car, and at April Grey, not knowing what to do other than to scream. Reece, Mary, and Joe Cousins reached the BMW at almost the same time. Reece and Cousins pulled April out of the car and laid her down on the pavement.

'Alpha Control, get an ambulance here fast, agent down. And get the security cordon to move in,' shouted Reece into his mike.

Grey was unconscious but alive. Reece started calling her name and placed his hand down hard on the open wound in her neck, the blood pouring through his fingers onto the ground surrounding her. Her eyes were open, and she was trying to speak.

'April, April, can you hear me? Stay with us!' He started to pull her clothes apart with his free hand to see if she'd been hit anywhere else. He could see the brass bullet head wedged almost dead centre in the chest, but her vest had stopped it penetrating. From what he could see the only wound was to her neck where blood was pumping steadily through a large hole. Reece thought it had hit the artery there was so much blood. He shouted for Cousins to get the first aid kit out of the boot and when he brought the box, he tore the package of the solid bandage and pressed it hard against the wound feeling the warm blood against his fingers.

Mary was kneeling beside him.

'Mary, put pressure on the wound…press down on this bandage and keep talking to her. Help will be here shortly.' Reece could hear the sirens getting closer.

'What happened, Joe?' asked Reece.

'It happened so quick…a woman in a red scarf came out of the apartment block and was passing April's car. April must have recognised her and started to get out when the woman turned and fired.'

'Where's this bitch now?'

'She ran towards the NCP, but I lost her when I was running towards April. I thought her more important.'

Jim Broad broke into the conversation over the radio.

'Alpha Team, be aware that a female called the male in the apartment telling him we're on to them and to get out. The female is probably the one who shot Alpha Three. Backup and an ambulance should be with you shortly. Have you a sit-rep?'

'Roger, Alpha Control, Alpha Three's wound is serious. She's losing blood fast. We need that fucking ambulance here now. Mary will stay with her. We'll go after the woman and close down our friend in the apartment. Make the police aware we'll be wearing armbands for identification. What's the story on the Tango Team?'

'They're on their way to you but will be about thirty minutes.'

'That's too long. We can't wait. We need to move now. Alpha Four, can you have police move in quietly on Tourist One and take him into custody, then join us here at the apartment building? Mary, you stay here with April. Help's on the way. Just keep the pressure on the wound until they get here.'

Reece and Cousins started to move towards the apartment building.

'Be careful, Joseph,' Mary shouted after them.

When they got to the door and pressed the button for the caretaker, there was no response. It was then that Joe Cousins noticed the man's boot on the floor in the corridor to the right of the lift.

COSTELLO HAD MOVED fast when Lyndsey had made the scrambled short call. Leaving the rifle where it was, he'd secured his Browning pistol in the waistband of his trousers then he decided to use the stairs instead of the lift he didn't intend to be cornered either in the lift or the apartment. He was almost out of breath when he got to the bottom of the stairs. He could see people running outside and could hear the approaching sirens. It was then he saw the Emergency Exit sign with the green arrow pointing to the left of the lift. He ran for the door and was pushing the bar cross handle down to open when Kevin Williams walked around the corner and asked him what he was doing. For the sake of silence Costello used his throwing knife. The caretaker's face registered both shock and surprise when he felt the pain – as if someone had punched him in the centre of his chest – before looking down to see a strange piece of metal sticking out from his body and blood starting to pour down his clothes. In those last seconds before the darkness came, he realised it was his blood pouring on his best trainers. He doubled over then fell to the floor the power in his legs and body gone. Death came quickly.

Costello pressed the escape bar and found himself at the rear of the building running towards a door in the fence about fifty yards away.

REECE MOVED FAST when he saw the boots. He knew he only had seconds to react. He pulled his gun and fired two shots into the glass door, he didn't have time to use the buttons for access. The glass shattered, and he cleared the large shards of glass with the gun barrel before using his body to clear the rest and enter the lobby.

Pointing his gun in front, he took a careful look around the corner of the hallway where he saw Williams lying on his back with his eyes open, staring at the ceiling. Reece didn't need a second glance or to check the body for life; he'd seen that death stare too many times, he knew Williams was dead and he could see that his killer had used the emergency door which was lying open to make his escape.

'Follow me, Joe,' said Reece as he moved to the escape door.

Reece left the dead caretaker and ran through the open exit door, arms stretched forward in the standard V-shape, pointing his gun…looking over it ready to squeeze the trigger. As he passed through, he saw a man turning right through the open gate in the surrounding five-foot-high steel fence. As he watched, a hand appeared around the gate and the gun in it fired twice towards Reece and Harrison. Both men hit the ground hard, the bullets shattering the glass door behind them. Reece heard Cousins cry out, 'Fuck, fuck, fuck it!'

Cousins's face now had a stream of blood coming from a gash above his right eye from where a piece of glass had cut through his skin.

'Are you OK?' asked Reece.

'Yeah…that was too close for comfort,' he replied as he wiped the blood from his face with the sleeve of his jacket. 'Where is the bastard?'

'Can you see all right?'

Cousins wiped some more blood from his eye and his face.

'That's better, yes…I'm OK.'

'He fired blindly just to keep us back. We need to close with him before he gets away, com'on,' said Reece.

Reece was glad that Cousins had brought the MP5 from the car boot. They might need the heavier firepower yet. They now moved silently and as fast as they dared.

MARY HAD HEARD the two gunshots as she knelt beside April but with the echo of the sound in the city block, she didn't know where they came from or what direction. She prayed that Joseph was all right.

THE SIRENS WERE getting closer and Costello knew he needed to get away fast. He rounded the corner with his Browning held out. The woman kneeling over the body on the pavement looked familiar…even from behind.

Running forward, Costello grabbed her by the hair and pulled her to her feet. Jabbing the barrel of the gun into her neck he whispered, 'I told you we would meet again, Mary.'

The pain travelled right through her body from her toes to the nerve endings in her scalp. She tried to turn against it then felt the gun against her throat. Mary recognised his voice and tried to keep calm, but the more she tried to pull away from his grip the harder he pulled her hair and pressed the gun into her flesh.

Two young girls backed away: their eyes wide with fear. When they thought they were far back enough, they ran. Costello started to pull Mary towards the car's open door when a voice from behind made him turn.

'Drop your weapon, Costello, and let her go,' shouted Reece.

Costello turned slowly to face the man standing at the exit to the passageway. He could see the gun in his hand pointing directly at him. He could also see another man standing behind with what looked like a rifle pointing in his direction.

'So, Mary. This is your Special Branch friend,' said Costello. Mary struggled again to break free, but Costello pulled even tighter on her hair, the gun still hard against her neck.

'Now, now, there's a good girl, don't hurry me. I'll deal with you soon enough.'

'Let her go, Costello. Put down the gun and we can end this peacefully,' said Reece.

Costello started back towards the car using Mary as his shield.

'I don't think you understand, Mister Special Branch man. I remember you from across the interrogation table in Ireland. You know, like I do, how this is going to end. You're going to let me and Mary here get into this nice car and we're going to drive away, peacefully, as you say or it's not going to end very well. Your choice. Mary and I are going for a little ride and you're going to watch us go or she dies here.'

As he spoke, he moved closer to the car, taking a quick look behind him, he could see the keys in the ignition and April Grey's blood across the dash and the windscreen.

'I'm afraid I'm going to have to speak to your valet service about the mess but never mind, it'll do for now, so we'll be off.'

He used his foot to kick the body on the ground over and further away from the car.

'Stop, Costello. You're not going anywhere,' shouted Reece once more. 'For the last time, drop your weapon.'

Now, as Reece had been taught, he steadied his feet and his breathing and waited for the target to speak once more. Costello taking a breath to speak would be the signal he needed to ensure he didn't miss.

'No, you...' Costello never finished the sentence Reece fired once...the bullet hitting the middle of Costello's temple and blowing off the back of his head and spraying blood, bone, and brain matter out in a straight line behind him. The force of the round spinning him backwards, his grip on Mary lost, and the gun falling from his dead hand. His fall was broken partly by the boot of the BMW and he finally rolled to a stop in the road on his back. His eyes open, staring in surprise at the sky. Reece moved above him and put two more rounds into Costello's chest. Make sure when they are down, they're down for good, so went the training.

It was then that Reece heard Mary screaming above the noise of the arriving emergency service vehicles. She was on her knees looking at her hands with tears streaming down her face. He could see there was blood on her cheek and in her hair. He knelt beside her stroking his hand through her hair, but he couldn't find a wound...the blood belonged to April and Costello. She was still screaming when he pulled her close to him.

'You're all right, it's over,' he said.

Her screaming stopped and she buried her head into his shoulder sobbing. The paramedics quickly hooked April up to a drip and started working on her in the ambulance.

'Can you go to the hospital with April?' Reece asked looking into Mary's tear-filled eyes. 'I need to stay here and chase up the woman and I want you to get looked at as well, can you do that for me?'

Her voice was hoarse with all the screaming and she struggled to whisper, 'OK, but come and find me, I need you.'

'Call it in, Joe, get these two to the hospital, Steve and I will see if we can find Lyndsey. There was only one way it was going to end for this bastard, he knew it and he would have tried to take as many of us as he could before then.'

'No argument from me, David, if you hadn't shot him, I would have.'

Reece walked back to the car. Harrison had arrived at the same time as the ambulance and the armed police response teams. Reece was surprised to see ACC Lockwood.

'Mister Reece, I've taken control of the scene and circulated the description of the woman who shot your friend here. You can get your people off the ground now and leave this to me.'

'That's OK by me, sir. Did we grab the other man at the Conference?'

It was Harrison who replied.

'We have him, David, he came quietly, and the Tango Team are taking him to the hanger as we speak. CCTV showed the woman who shot April go into the NCP down the street but then we lost her.'

'If she's as smart as we think she is, she's long gone but we can make a search through the car park and down to the train station. Lockwood, can you get your people to the station and continue to check the CCTV?'

'You still have priority when it comes to these people, Mister Reece, and to tell you the truth, you're welcome to them, but we'll help you look for her. In the meantime, we'll have SO19 clear the apartment,' said Lockwood.

Reece was pleased that at last he seemed to get the whole idea that the SG9 team were not the bad guys.

The three SG9 agents headed to the NCP car park, Reece in front, followed closely by Harrison and Cousins. The car park was like any other, large and cavernous, and there was no sign of the woman they were looking for. They continued to walk down to the Deansgate rail and tram station, still no sign.

'Alpha One, this is Alpha Control, come in, over.'

It was the voice of Jim Broad.

'Go ahead, Alpha Control,' replied Reece.

'David, we've been checking all the CCTV in your area through our live feed here. We have the woman in the scarf entering the NCP on foot but not leaving on foot. However, we do have a Ford van, similar to the one we were looking for, leaving the car park shortly after the shooting but we lost it heading towards the city centre. We've put out a stop with caution alert to all police in the area, but she may be well gone by now.'

'Understood, Alpha Control, we'll take a final look around the station area then come back to you for a debrief.'

'Roger that, Alpha One. See you soon.'

The further search produced nothing and the three SG9 agents returned to the hanger for the debrief to Jim Broad.

IT SOON BECAME clear that with the two dead terrorists in Irlam and

Costello in Deansgate, Lyndsey was now on the run and keeping her head down. It didn't take them long to interrogate Mohammad and get the full details of what the terror group had been planning. It appeared he was a willing talker and not as brave as he thought he was.

'Any word on April?' asked Reece.

'I'm sorry, David, she didn't make it. She died in the ambulance without saying anything. She lost too much blood. Mary stayed with her all the way, she's at the hospital now,' said Broad.

'Now that we have everything under control here, I'm off to the hospital to pick Mary up.'

Chapter Sixty-six

The Prime Minister and Sir Martyn Bryant had listened quietly when Sir Ian Fraser briefed them concerning the morning's activities.

'On the whole, your team have done a fantastic job, Sir Ian,' said the PM. 'I mean, tracking these people down to completely breaking up their plans, not to say anything about killing three and capturing one. Of course, we must remember the brave SAS soldier who lost his life and your dead agent.'

'It's hard to lose anyone, but she was one of our best and will be sorely missed. Her family will never know the true sacrifice she made. They never knew she was one of our agents, only that she was attached to the police in some capacity. And of course, we must not forget the regrettable loss of the caretaker, Mister Williams.'

'Of course, Sir Ian, and the fact that this woman who you believe to be Lyndsey escaped,' said Sir Martin Bryant.

'Yes, that's the only downside, that, and the sad death of our people and the innocent civilian. We have an all-ports bulletin out with her description and I've instructed our agents and stations around the globe to find out where she is, but she knows all the tricks to keep her head down and has many friends in the Islamic world who will give her protection, but she'll stick her head out of her hiding place again and we'll be ready.'

Peter Brookfield held his hand up to take over the conversation.

'I'll be addressing the Conference shortly. All I'll be saying is that our security services have prevented a terrorist attack in the streets of this city. I won't be specific on what the target was and that'll remain our secret. In the meantime, Sir Ian, I want to thank you and your agents for the great service they've done for our country. They were truly tested by fire and have come through with flying colours. Please pass on the thanks of a grateful nation. I'll see you at the next Intelligence Committee meeting with Sir Martin in London next week and maybe you'll have some more news on this Lyndsey woman.'

Hurghada, Egypt:

Two Weeks Later

Reece and Harrison had arrived at the Egyptian Airport of Hurghada on a tourist flight from London Gatwick. The taxi to the 5-star Hilton Hotel resort in the city took fifteen minutes. The hotel itself overlooked the bay at the southern end of town.

Jim Broad had briefed Reece the day before in the SG9 office in London. As a result of the SG9 operation in Manchester and the follow up, they had sent full-face photos of Sharon Lyndsey to all European, Middle East, and Far East security agencies to look out for and report back to London.

Three days ago, MI6 had received a report from its embassy spook in Cairo that a woman they believed matched the photo and description of Sharon Lyndsey had travelled to the Hilton Hotel Resort in Hurghada after crossing the border from Sudan.

She seemed to like Hilton Hotels, thought Reece when he heard. The photo taken of the her at the border checkpoint had been quickly matched using facial recognition confirming her to be Lyndsey.

Reece and Harrison had been met outside the airport terminal by the resident Cairo spook and given a large buff envelope in a handoff that took a split second.

When they had booked into the hotel, Reece opened the envelope in their room. Inside was a folder containing the up-to-date photos taken by the Egyptian surveillance team of Lyndsey sunning herself by the pool and swimming in the Red Sea of the resort. A short note confirmed she just seemed to be filling the role of a tourist relaxing and using the resort facilities with no sign of bodyguards.

The envelope contained two Berretta Semi-Automatic .22 pistols with fully loaded magazines. The pistol of choice for the assassin teams of the Israeli Mossad Kidon units. Each bullet would contain half the powder, this made the weapon just as deadly up close but with the noise given out of a silenced gun making it easier to conceal and use. The note had also said that in the short time they'd been watching Lyndsey each evening she'd taken a walk to a coffee shop and supermarket in the street behind the hotel. There was a small map with an X showing the café and a photo showing Lyndsey sitting at an outside table.

The spooks could also confirm through a contact that she was staying in the hotel for a week in one of the penthouse rooms and seemed to have plenty of cash. Reece took the note and map into the bathroom and burnt them in the sink; washing the charred pages down the drain. He used his encrypted mobile phone to let Broad know that it was Lyndsey and they would confirm her movements tonight and move at 2000hrs Egypt time the next evening.

REECE AND HARRISON left the hotel at 7.30 p.m. and walked to the café taking seats at the back facing the street. From there they watched

Lyndsey walk out the rear hotel door and cross the street to take up a table at the front, facing back the way she'd travelled.

She ordered from the waiter and lit a cigarette. Even though it was now dark, it was still warm. She wore large wraparound sunglasses, a silk scarf around her neck and pulled up to her mouth, and a white linen dress. She was carrying the same type of shoulder bag she'd carried in Manchester. *No doubt containing a gun*, thought Reece. There was no obvious sign of bodyguards, but they noticed two men of Middle Eastern appearance walk into the café and take up a table to the right of Lyndsey seconds after she'd sat down. To Reece they didn't fit. They were watching the street to the front of the café. Reece recognised the signs they were there because she was there. The Cairo spook had missed them because they didn't walk close to her. That could be a problem, but one they were prepared for. *If they got in the way they were going down with her*, thought Reece.

Reece and Harrison stayed in the café until Lyndsey left and the two men followed her a short distance behind. When Reece returned to the room, he contacted Broad once more and updated him on the two men. They weren't sure if they were bodyguards or Egyptian security, but either way the operation would go down at the café the following night.

As far as the two men were concerned they would work to the rules used by Mossad: if they moved to become combatants then they would be treated as such and dealt with.

Reece and Broad had agreed the escape plan for afterwards. Nothing that would show who they were would be left behind. Lyndsey

327

left the café around 8 p.m. each night so the operation would be aimed for that time.

The following night Reece and Harrison took up the same seats at the café and ordered coffee. As far as both could see there was no CCTV which was to be expected…Lyndsey wouldn't want to be caught on camera either. She arrived and sat at the same table as yesterday, closely followed by the two men. Their table was already taken by a young couple holding hands over a pot of tea, so they chose a different spot.

Reece watched Lyndsey closely. She looked every inch the tourist wearing the same wraparound sunglasses and light clothing similar to that from the night before. She sat facing the street watching the world go by as she took sips from her cup. The two men sat deep in conversation looking around them as they talked.

Reece and Harrison did the same and to anyone watching the scene, it was a normal café filled with everyday customers enjoying their coffee on a warm evening.

Lyndsey searched in her shoulder bag and producing her purse she left a note of money under the saucer on her table and started to rise. This was the moment Reece and Harrison had agreed to move. The two men were also preparing to leave, and one produced his wallet, starting to extract the money to pay their bill. Reece moved behind Lyndsey as she stood while Harrison stood in front of the two men blocking their view.

The two lovers told the police afterwards everything happened in seconds although it seemed to be in slow motion.

Reece got close enough to whisper in Lyndsey's ear, 'This is for April.' He pointed the Beretta at her right temple and as he pulled the trigger he was close enough to see through her sunglasses and the look of surprise as the two bullets, fired in quick succession, blew a hole through her brain. The blood spray was short as it poured over the white linin cloth on the table in front of her. Reece held her as she fell, and he was able to set her back in the chair and rest her head on the table.

Harrison had the two men covered with his gun as they saw what had happened to Lyndsey. Both reached under their jackets but too late. Thanks to being seated, their options were limited. They had become combatants. Harrison shot the one to his right twice in the chest while, as they'd planned, Reece did the same to the one on the left. Both men fell, knocking over the surrounding tables, both dead before they hit the ground.

The young lovers were in shock and looked on, mouths open as the two gunmen turned and walked casually down the street towards the corner of the hotel opposite and disappeared into the night.

THEY WALKED DOWN to the deserted beach and within seconds a Royal Navy dingy with two Special Boat Service operators arrived. They sailed out one mile to where they boarded the Royal Navy Destroyer *HMS Ardross* which had, until two days ago, been on exercise in the Red Sea. The ship sailed to Cyprus, leaving the Egyptian authorities totally baffled that the two men had completely disappeared.

Not knowing who the men were and the discovery that their victims were Islamic terrorists, they believed the assassinations were the work of Mossad. The Egyptian authorities didn't want the world to know Lyndsey and her friends had been enjoying themselves in their country so they decided not to look into the murders too closely, better to   let   sleeping   dogs   lie.

Malta: One Month Later

David Reece sat on the bench at the head of the costal walkway between Qawra and Bugibba watching the waves of St Paul's Bay splash over the rocks below. He always enjoyed the walk along this path first thing in the morning when everything was still fresh, and the sun was just above the headland in front of him. The walk took him about a quarter of a mile from his small piece of heaven on earth the Villa St Joseph. From where he sat, he could see the new motor carriageway as it passed around the headland heading towards the capital Valletta.

Mary sat down next to him. Even though it was the middle of November, the sun still radiated heat warm enough to allow them to wear light jackets over their T-shirts. When she sat down, she asked, 'What are you thinking, Joseph?'

He looked at her beautiful brown eyes as if for the first time. He loved how this woman could see into his soul and take away all the fears of life.

'You asked me that once before and I think I told you I loved you and we'd be together after the work was over. Well, the work is over for now but there'll be other times when I'll have to work, maybe be away from you and I don't know if I want to do that anymore.'

'Let's not worry about the future, let's just have today, now, right here.'

'You're right. The work is done'

'So, as I said, there's nothing for us to do now except drink our coffee and then head back to the villa where we can make warm passionate love all day.'

He loved her smile and the love they made together.

'Answer me a question. Why do you still call me Joseph even though the job is over? You're no longer my agent, you're the woman I love?'

'I know, and I love you too. I first knew you as Joseph, and you saved me from a life that was destroying me inside when you were called Joseph. So you'll always be Joseph to me. The one man who kept his promise.'

'All right, Joseph it is, but only for you, now let's go get that coffee.'

She took his hand and looking into his eyes she smiled.

'Let's   skip   the   coffee.'

About the Author

The author has twenty-six years of experience working in anti-terrorist operations throughout the world and has used that knowledge throughout this book. Because of this background David Costa is of course a Pseudonym.

This book introduces David Reece, a terrorist hunter with a Black Ops Group SG9 attached to the British Secret Service MI6. His remit: to find the terrorists and eliminate them. In the first of three novels, we follow Reece and his team in their hunt for a terrorist cell who are determined to carry out a spectacular attack on British soil by killing the Prime   Minister.

A Note from the Author

I hope you enjoy this story and if you would like to hear more or send me your thoughts, please feel free to do so.

www.https://DavidCostaWriter.com/home

Email. David.costa.writer@outlook.com

Twitter. @Davidcostawrite

Facebook. David Costa

Printed in Poland
by Amazon Fulfillment
Poland Sp. z o.o., Wrocław